A WYATT BOOK *for*

W

— ST. —
MARTIN'S
PRESS

Also by Robert Drewe in Picador (Australia)

# *The*
# DROWNER

## ROBERT DREWE

A WYATT BOOK *for* ST. MARTIN'S PRESS

New York

I want to express my gratitude for the Australian Artists Creative
Fellowship which enabled this novel to be written.

THE DROWNER. Copyright 1996 by Robert Drewe. All rights reserved.
Printed in the United States of America. No part of this book may be
used or reproduced in any manner whatsoever without written
permission except in the case of brief quotations embodied in critical
articles or reviews. For information, address A Wyatt Book *for* St.
Martin's Press, 175 Fifth Avenue, New York, N.Y. 10010.

Library of Congress Cataloging-in-Publication Data

Drewe, Robert
    The drowner / Robert Drewe.
       p.  cm.
    ISBN 0-312-16821-7
    I. Title.
    PR9619.3.D77D76   1997
    823—dc21                      97-14671
                                     CIP

First published in Australia by Pan Macmillan Australia Pty Limited

First U.S. Edition: October 1997

10 9 8 7 6 5 4 3 2 1

*For my mother and father*

*and for C,*
*of course*

*If I were called in*
*to construct a religion*
*I should make use of water.*
PHILIP LARKIN


*The man must not drink of the running streams,*
*the living waters, who is not prepared to have all*
*nature reborn in him—to suckle monsters.*
HENRY DAVID THOREAU


*Life*
*a little water*
*a few words on the tongue.*
BERNARD NOËL

*The*
# DROWNER

# Contents

The Art of Floating Land   7

Spa Water   33

Woman Kissing Cockatoo   89

Blackwater   141

Entropy   167

Studio Portrait with Bicycles   227

The Lunatics' Douche   255

Marionette Joyeuse   277

The Reservoir   305

T hey met first in the bath.
This is the feeling, the smell, the sound, of their bodies colliding in the bathwater.

The water is ten degrees over blood temperature. Mysterious, flattering light falls from above. Their heads swim in alkaline gurgle and babble. Then her yelp and his spluttering apology echo off the pillars and ceiling while billowing bodies titter and flirt around them.

Experience it again, this portentous warm accident. His innocent blind lunge, only half-swimming stroke, half-stretch, but too vigorous and vulgar for these languid, ghostly wits.

Plat!, he strikes female flesh, soft yet resilient, jumps up too fast, hair streaming in his eyes, and overbalances against her, the second, inexcusable, slithery bump causing her indignant gasp.

Relive the humid confusion. She shoots upright in the bath, an emphatic statement of wet bathing smock, breasts and thighs. Then, amazingly, answers his embarrassment with an action of her own: a brisk performance of recovered poise. She sinks backwards under water, spears up through the surface, forehead elegantly tilting back, eyelids closed, hair dropping in that effortless dark sheen. Now strokes herself upwards from the chin, elegantly wiping the moisture from her flushed cheeks and forehead, smoothing her impossibly sleek head. Wet linen pasting to her body.

*And now they're eye to eye in the bathwater, like characters from one of history's sensual asides. Their own awesome and intimate atmosphere—lavender, alkali and sweat, all trapped and activated by the steam—envelops them.*

*This is in the bath, in Bath. Early July. Hot yellow lilies grow along the river between Bath and Bradford-on-Avon. A strange summer of hot flowers and foreign, hot-climate birds. A small green fortune-telling parrot, a swan black instead of white. A season of hot theatrical declarations . . .*

N ow he turns his mouth away from something thin and slippery on a spoon. Someone dabs his forehead. *Memory fevers easily erase the arrowroot or sago taste, the hessian wall against his cheek, the pub hubbub, the thick red air. But the camels' bubbling roars, the incessant jangling of their harness bells, their endlessly shifting, rising, dropping silhouettes are harder to dislodge.*

*And the heat, of course. Sweating on his stretcher, he half-consciously claims the temperature and transforms it again into that Roman bathwater just warmer than their bodies, into the sharp pink ovals of her cheekbones, her lip-beads of moisture. Comforting, and strangely slippery, too, like mercury on his fingertips.*

*Heat's bearable, but cold's for schizophrenics and would-be suicides. During the cold sweats once (last night? last century?) he'd heard her arranging the Lunatics' Douche for him.*

*At the time he was shouting Christmas carols and Afghan cameleers' orders to scare the insects off him. He couldn't believe his ears when her Portia voice interrupted.*

*A clear and ringing enunciation, as if she were playing to the gallery of the Royal.*

*'A column of cold water two storeys high must fall on his head. Cold water the weight of ice. Stupefaction should last at least one hour.'*

*That crystal voice of love. And dulcet shards of—what—the other?*

*Delirious, he still knew the douche as treatment for the worst delusions. One pulse beat, two, and then the column hit him like a stalactite, a sword of water. At the impact his red-nippered bull ants scattered, the needling march flies took off mid-bite. Those glassy tones and noisy pictures in his head splintered and fell away.*

*He surfaced from tinkling depths of polar-green. Shaking his head and shivering, he looked around the tent for her. Of course she wasn't there. Only the pale, exhausted nurse, red dust in the down of her cheeks and forearms, who flicked his imaginary insects off him and sponged away his mess.*

*Now the nurse trickles real water, though condensed—tepid and brackish—into the corner of his mouth.*

*'What month is it, Mr Dance?' she asks. 'What year?'*

*He's fumbling at a vest button, peeping inside. 'You know,' he whispers evasively. What a strange accomplishment, these rosy blossoms on his chest. More today, or less?*

*'What place is this?' she perseveres.*

*He edges his mouth towards the water cup again, but she withholds it until he answers. A few pieces of the crystal voice tinkle in his ears, his temples still flicker from the douche.*

*'Whatsaname.'*

*'What are you doing here?'*

*She gives him the water anyway.*

# THE ART OF
# FLOATING LAND

HE IS A TINY BOY being carried down to feed bread crusts to the ducks in the Avon when his father shows him what drowning is.

Only nettle high, thistle high, riding in his father's arms in a burst of sun warmth across the squire's field and down to the river. Swinging over the stings and prickles fringing the bank, high above the squire's strange horned, coughing sheep and their loose droppings. Feet drumming against his father's stomach, his father's nose in his hair, his cheek, and both of them babbling sweet rhymes of tickles and nonsense.

'Look,' says his father, and suddenly squats and points at dirt.

A loamy line meanders across the grass. A mole tunnels in the river bank. Already it has dug so close to the water that a fine stream turns away from the river, trickles through the molehill, and down the gently sloping field. This waterprill spreads thinly, a pace wide, about twenty paces long. The earth is parched from the dry winter, but wherever the waterprill runs everything is green and fresh.

So he was told anyway. So many times he's sure he remembers it. The story of the mole. How the first drowner discovered how to govern water. This was the four-hundred-year-old secret of Wiltshire and its clear streams.

Warmish water streaming through light chalky soil lying

over fine flint and gravel. This is a heaven for drowners. This is his father's life. But what he remembers vividly from that day is the nettle-eating sheep. Their pale, dead goats' eyes, mad, skewed horns and old men's hawking coughs. In his memory the sunburst fades. A veil of thick white rain falls on the dark sheep and greying fields. It patters on the elms as they whip and sway their branches to the fall. Blackbirds sing sharply in the wet trees. Everything looms and shivers above his head.

His father brings water on to the land at will, and takes it off again. Arthur Brabazon Charles ('Alphabetical') Dance floats water meadows. Alphabetical Dance loves swift water the way some men love horses. To hear his proud murmurings about his floating lands you would think he was referring to his feathery-haired son and babbling daughter. He calls his work 'my little drownings'.

People are respectful of these other creations of his. He's an artist, a craftsman, a personage. Everyone—the squire and the parson, even the most authoritarian miller—defers to the drowner's judgement. Alphabetical Dance knows the soil, the subsoil and whatever lies beneath. Just as he knows the contours of the land, the slightest deviation from level and the location of each deviation. He knows the streams and the sounds they make, and the river water, too—its colours, speeds, temperatures and consistencies, and all the different regions it passes through. He understands a river all the way back to its source—the spring, the rain, the dew, the darkening nimbus. He knows the relationship of earth and water.

Drowning is complicated. Alphabetical Dance disciplines his water meadows into an intricate system of trenches, ridges and drains. They draw water from the river and transform it into a shallow, continuously moving film. This sheet of water has to nourish and protect the tender grass shoots without swamping them. Even when his 'little drownings' are complete, he stays vigilant. He looks out for frost. He studies the gradient of the land for minute shifts in level and angle. He watches for cloudiness, alert for scum. He must gauge the precise force behind the flow. Too fast means the grass roots will be washed away, too slow means stagnation. He depends on his eye.

Before the first drowner, before the mole and its waterprill, Wiltshire farmers shared a quandary—winter hay was gone by March, and ewes and spring lambs needed food. Then the early drowners learned to control water, to divert it lightly onto the meadows to protect the roots from the cold and encourage growth. When the ground was wet enough, they sluiced the river back on course. From autumn through winter, they drowned the meadows, then dried them. When the first grass tips showed they drowned them again. Then in March they shut off the water for a month before the ewes and lambs fed on the new grass. When their normal pasture was ready, the sheep went to it. And the water meadows were drowned yet again, and left to produce an extra crop of hay.

In the broad valleys between the downs this drowning and reviving has formed the rhythm of Wiltshire's agriculture for four centuries. These intricate skills, passed from father to son, from master to apprentice, make up the ebb and flow of Alphabetical Dance's days.

These days early in his son's third year are windy mornings of sudden bursts of birdsong, of sparrows flying with bent straws in the wind and rooks blowing in the sky. These mornings chilblains and wet feet don't worry Alphabetical Dance. The wind rushes over the river and whips the thin hazels on the bank but in the breeze his cheeks stay warm.

Everything is occurring as expected. The hedges are thick with tight buds, the fields show tender green under the yellow bents and fibres of last year's grass. Dog-mercury carpets the woods. The river runs full and clear as a trout's eye. The same force in his blood makes it sing.

The happy hay of a toddler's hair is in his nostrils as he sets him down. Optimistic lifetimes lie ahead as the little Dance boy, the drowner's son, suddenly bold, runs up from the river through the new grass with his short skirt blowing before him, shrieking, laughing and scattering the sheep.

In March all the frogs mate in Bullslease pond. On the spinach-green surface of the water float hundreds of frogs' foreheads, eyes goggling, stern and seemingly disembodied, although the submarine part of each frog grimly grips his mate below.

On the Sunday morning of the ceremony the boy starts awake, thinking of mating frogs. Mucousy occurrences below the surface. In his sleep he'd heard the cold chiming of underwater bells. In reality the bells are ringing at St Laurence's across the river. The urgent bells, and the keen smell of ironing and boot polish wafting up from the kitchen, drive him from his bed to the window.

He looks out along the valley of the Avon and across the downs. Small villages about a mile apart edging the banks of the river. The houses mostly of the sixteenth century, built in squares of flint and stone. Their thatched roofs, partly golden with yellow stonecrop, seem to quiver with wakefulness and anticipation.

He sees smoke, or thinks he does. A cloud of gnats is rising in such a dense column over the river that people in the village, also mistaking it for smoke, are sounding the four church bells as a fire alarm. *I'll tell John Brown, I'll tell John Brown,* the bells seem to say, then *Tom-my Lincoln, Tom-my Lincoln.* (Wryer Baptists will later appreciate the irony of the bell alarm and the established Church so stridently heralding the biggest nonconformist gathering Wiltshire has seen in twenty years.)

From the window the river fizzes like a fuse. The plume of gnats spirals up and down the Avon, a tornado of smoke. The bells keep ringing. Swallows dart and wheel into the cloud and people begin to line the banks.

Will dresses slowly, watching the smoke, watching for the fire cart. White shirt and new black gabardine trousers, the damp scorched smell of the iron still on them. He has been told he should fasten the trouser legs with his bicycle clips to hold them down. The year before last his mother sewed stones into the hem of Sarah's dress so it wouldn't ride up in the water. And in the seconds during which he glances around the room for a mislaid bicycle clip—briefly recalling Sarah's glowing face and rattling hem of pebbles—and turns back to the window again, the smoke has gone. Nothing to be seen but the small scattered villages and the grey-green wiothe-beds and the shoulders of the downs rising above them.

The bells stop. Their reverberations fade. Sunday floods back and fills the silence. In the resumed buzz and twitter of a spring morning he slowly finishes dressing. No hope now that events might be postponed, that this Sunday of all Sundays might be thwarted by the burning river. He doesn't share Sarah's or their mother's enthusiasm for religion. Sarah's fervour amazes him—even zealously collecting picture postcards of her favourite ministers. Pinning over the bathtub a hand-tinted postcard depicting *Mr Harold Thring Smiling While Preaching* to remind her of being baptised. The preacher's lips and hair gleaming orange. On bath nights Will flicks water at smiling, preaching Mr Harold Thring.

His mother is Chapel (and so are he and his sister), his father is Church. 'Like the squire,' says Alphabetical Dance, half-seriously. Religious conflict is expressed chiefly in their Sunday competitions of humility and goodness. Deep female sighs and eye-rollings versus frowning male worthiness, with her bottle of sacred Jordan water sitting in the centre of the mantel like a referee. But his father's hunger usually means his withdrawal from the battle by lunchtime, leaving the other side to martyrdom and marmalade toast.

He's winking at the children. Provocatively slicing himself a slab of mutton. 'Grace, I've been hearing about those Christians from the New Jerusalem Church and I'd welcome your opinion on earth-bathing.' Eating pink meat off the knife like a ploughman, knowing she hates that. His juicy mastications roaring in the silent room.

'Baptism by soil, certainly makes a change. That Dr Pugh and Miss Arundell in Urchfont got themselves buried naked up to their heads for six hours a day. Stuck it out for nine days, I hear. Beautifully powdered and dressed, the heads. Appeared not unlike two fine cauliflowers.'

In the Sunday suspense she almost rises to the bait. He's having trouble keeping a straight face.

'Mind you, even out of the ground Dr Pugh liked to dress in cut turfs. Massaging himself with nervous balsam of his own making. Turned his skin green as moss and his last fortnight on earth he ate no food at all.'

But he doesn't tease for long. Where's the fun in a response of silence? Tight lips that stay pursed well into Monday? Anyway, his strong feelings about religion are only to do with drainage and seepage. His passion is roused by the churches' proud and foolish habit of building on rising ground. He says rain from the churchyards drains down into the local wells and poisons the water.

'Graves and gravity!' he snorts. 'Show me an outbreak of fever and I'll show you corpse-spoiled drinking water.'

It is interesting therefore that his annual drowning cycle takes place with the regularity and solemnity of religious festivals. It begins each year at Michaelmas when the river, in his opinion, is 'thick and good'. The true faith of Alphabetical Dance is water.

The mood of Sundays weighs heavily on the eleven-year-old boy. The air has a different look, smell and sound to him. A humble grey light casting asphalty shadows over and far beyond the Ebenezer Baptist Chapel. A threadbare day holding a scurfy sadness, as if someone aged and pious were hunched inside his body.

Waking to the subdued kitchen murmurings of the Sabbath, the prim odours of soap, starch and scorch, his soul feels old and tired. His spirits plummet, stifled in a second by the idea of Sunday best, prayers, the worthy, dull routines of chapel and Sunday school. All the passive, insipid, bygone nature of the day.

Inside the bare, square chapel he looks up from their own bald and waxy Pastor Gerard to the hermetically sealed windows of opaque green glass set high in its walls and imagines he's in some underwater prison. On Sundays he feels submerged, a hypocritical prisoner of the past. And when he finally emerges into the air, swifts wheel and scream around the grey church roof.

Long before he and his mother and sister reached the river, the water carried the people's voices singing 'Shall We Gather' up over the meadow and along the road. The bank on one side was steep and densely wooded, the sun had not yet risen over the rim and the water looked deep and still, penetrated by night.

Shadows on water are more sinister than shadows on land. The mobile black surface recalled his father's old bogey-myths: river phantoms, night-eels who savoured men's entrails, goblins who gorged at night and withdrew like fogs at dawn. And nymphs posing as beautiful washerwomen to lure men to the riverbank. Only sleeping when the morning mists steamed from their victims' drowned mouths. Will buttoned his shirt collar against them and tried to steer his mind to Jesus.

There were clumps of horses and donkeys and hay carts and farm traps tied to trees at the top of the bank. All the way around and down the sides of this natural amphitheatre crowded tiers of men, women and children. Boys were climbing trees, and some had crawled way out on rocky outcrops for a better view. There were people upriver as far as he could see. In the distance where the sun shone they were singing 'Shall We Gather'. He could hear the words rolling downstream, jumbled up with the burbling of the water and the breeze in the treetops until, as the sound swept nearer, the massed voices drowned the sounds of the river.

The candidates for baptism were huddled in a black and white flock on the bank. Their friends and families stood back a little, in recognition of their status. Most of the women looked pale and drawn, but several girls were skittish and pinkly vivacious, like bold, veil-less brides. Some of the males trembled with emotion. Most of them fidgeted self-consciously with their tight collars or their bicycle clips. They weren't men and youths he looked up to. Spotty municipal clerks, shiny drapery assistants, damp-fingered librarians, most of them. Young men with the neutral patina of religiosity.

Damp patches of tension in their armpits. He was the youngest of them, and his delighted mother, who had been smoothing and dabbing at his hair, now patted the back of his neck and pushed him towards them.

There was a sudden hush and a short black figure stepped into the water and waded out into the river pool until he was waist-deep. While he secured a firm footing on the river bed, three helpers, one of them fat Mr Freeth the haberdasher, came and stood between him and the waiting group on the bank and made a human chain. They faced downstream, and the running water banked up in ripples behind Mr Freeth's buttocks. There was another burst of song and then silence as, one at a time, the awestruck candidates came down to the brink, paused a moment, and with a small splash plopped in and waded to the outstretched hands of the pastor's helpers.

And too soon there was no one ahead of Will. Hands plucked at him and pushed him forward. The edges of his vision clouded and narrowed so tightly he could barely make out the ranks of watery smiles, the polite tiers of blurry angels hovering under a sky as white and clotted as paste.

*The beautiful, the beautiful riverrr . . .*

In a trance he stepped into the river. The shock, the clamminess of his trousers, just registered before Mr Freeth hauled him up and pushed him against the current to another man, who did the same. Then looming before him was the legendary Mr Harold Thring. Before Will could snatch a breath or gather a single Christian thought, little Mr Thring, surprisingly strong, grabbed his shoulders and dunked him like a biscuit in a tea cup.

Cold water flooded into his ears and eyes and engulfed him.

Above him Mr Thring's voice said something religious, but all he heard was babble. Mr Thring's hands heaved him up into the air again and passed him back along the line to Mr Freeth, who led him, dazed, to the bank. He scrambled up and stood dripping while his mother brought him a towel and hot tea. The cold water had made him want to piss. She looked on him fondly as she dried his hair. Her eyes were glistening and she kept saying, 'Oh, William. How reverent! How impressive!' Even Sarah smiled on him.

There were others still being baptised and as he sipped his tea he watched their dunkings with a growing detachment. The sun was on the water now and he was trying to concentrate on Jesus, but his bladder and the ritual in the river below somehow drove Him away. The efficiency of the immersions, the bedraggled flock, made him think more of shepherds at a sheep-dipping. Under his towel, in his wet trousers, he trickled secretly down his legs.

Now his mind drifted around the way the women's dresses alternately clung and billowed in the current, and the feeling of the sun on his head, and the sugary dregs in his tea cup. His mother was still humming 'Shall We Gather' and the tune was embedding in his brain. In the sunlight a kingfisher suddenly pierced the skin of the river—a quick sapphire needle spearing his vision, too—and flared away.

His Sabbath mood was on him one November when he and Sarah diverted home from Sunday school along the river bank. Neither of them was up to speaking. Sarah carried their Bibles and prayer books and her tongue kept making smug clicks on the roof of her mouth. This week's illustrated religious text was rammed in his pocket. Holding a shepherd's crook like a boat hook, Jesus tended gambolling lambs on a field of soggy paper.

The way the noon light struck their familiar haunt gave it a similar watery Christian look. The river was older and greyer than he'd seen it, the rest of the day was leached and hazy. In the breadth of his sight no waterbirds swam, no fish rippled the surface, no boys fished. A weak sun bled into a sky as pale as birdlime. Flighty breezes caught the raw willows on the banks, then left to huff in the tops of elms. An over-respectful dove cooed in an elder tree. In a danker reach of the river the Sunday feeling burned the back of his throat and he had to speak.

'What if I was to throw myself in the water?' he said. 'And drown?'

Sarah stopped clicking and blinked. 'You wouldn't!'

'I might.'

This feeling was new: the satisfaction of her wide-eyed anxiety and sudden loss of authority. He felt older, taller. When they came to a boat landing spattered with duck droppings he walked briskly to the end of the little wharf, peered over the edge and teetered thoughtfully on the brink. Specks of scum streaked past in the layered current. Algaes and fish-mucus, upriver flotsam, a dead rat and a branch like a clawing hand.

He saw his own body and luxuriated in images of parental grief. He said, 'A good place to jump from.'

'You can swim anyway.'

'People can stop themselves from swimming and just sink.'

'It's not deep enough.'

'You can drown in a bathtub. Old Piddle Quirk drowned in a ditch at Market Lavington.'

'Go on then.'

'All right, I'll do it.'

'I'd like to see you.'

He lurched forward.

'No, Will, don't! I'll tell.'

Fortuitously then a neat triangle of ducks swam round the bend and past the landing. The drake was the apex, the aloof spearhead. The flanking females quacked pugnaciously behind. Will was losing interest anyway. Some child had left a jar of bullfrog tadpoles on the bank; to change the subject he tipped it over and scooped up the tadpoles. Thick black bodies wriggling softer than decay in his hands.

One by one, he threw the tadpoles to the ducks. Still warmed by her panic, strangely exhilarated by the shift in the world's ways, he watched the triangle disintegrate into chaos.

Another example of his father's artistry with water: he creates ponds to entice the mist and clouds. He traps water vapour in his dewponds. One April Saturday he announces casually that a new dewpond is wanted near Martinwood. Lately he has become bulkier, grizzled as a boar. His ears and nose are sprouting. He's all spiky eyebrows, too, and his thick body rolls as if to test the floor. He looks edgier these days, stiffer and closer to the ground, and his voice is lower and muttery.

'Only time I can spare,' he says.

'It's Palm Sunday tomorrow,' she says.

'But not today, Grace, and I can't help the seasons,' says Alphabetical Dance steadily, not looking at his wife. 'The old dewpond got iced up and crumpled in winter. Anyhow, it's looking, not working. It's only our eyes'll be doing it.'

'*Our* eyes?'

'I need Will for this.'

Amazing that a cloud can form so quickly above and around her. Dewponds unsettle her. There's the pagan element, and the problem that siting a dewpond requires nighttime observation. One of Nature's drawbacks is that it doesn't rest at midnight; it's irritatingly illogical and drawn-out and too readily seeps into the Sabbath. Nature creates freaks, like the white otter her husband has recently trapped, stuffed and provocatively installed in a glass case on the mantel. So crockery is noisily adjusted, jugs and cups shunted into important new alignments on the dresser. Meanwhile her dish displacements create a vacuum that sucks all the air from the kitchen. A dark mood of nimbus, she bustles eventually into the sitting room, towards the sanctity of the Jordan water. And is mocked by the adjacent albino otter.

How to bustle without losing ground? How to separate Nature and Almighty God?

'It's not Easter yet, Grace,' says his father, heading for the door.

The trap is already loaded with tarpaulins and sacking, and a bottle hidden under them for the chill. At the door he turns and for the first time faces his wife's stormy eyes. For a long moment he looks about to say something more. But he says, 'Don't you worry if we're late for once.'

She turns away.

His father calls over his shoulder to him, 'Put on your dew-beaters. And a coat for the hilltop.'

And they leave. He has never before noticed the act of leaving the house, the significance of departure.

They drive the pony and trap up as high as they can go. Up the perversely named downs, which are most definitely *ups*, the whole patchwork of the land's weathers and whorls and striations unrolling before them. There, rainy river valley, and there, magenta dusk, and there, sunny meadow, and over there, looking south across the misty sweep of Salisbury Plain, he believes he can see the Channel.

The escarpment steepens sharply and they unharness the pony, pile it with tarpaulins, and lead it up the narrow sheep track. Following the oblique trail of droppings and high smell of ammonia to the top. Sheep urine and the vegetable combustion of the hillside defying the sharp wind. Snagged in the brambles, scraggy, waving wool-ends as big as lambs taunting a soaring falcon.

*She turned away from me!*

It's the custom of dewpond makers to wait on the highest peaks for the night fogs, which fall on the high downs even in summer. People sleeping at normal hours are unaware of these fogs, so wet that a man riding on the downs before dawn finds his clothes sticking to him and every tree dripping water. Dewpond makers squat on the foggiest hills and wait for the sun to burn through the mist banks and tell them where to site the ponds. As they wait, huddled under tarpaulins, too cold and damp with haze to sleep, they drink a dewcap to keep warm, and they tell stories.

He was digging a dewpond above Devizes once, his father tells him, and brought up a pelvis on his mattock. It was a mass grave, countless pressed and layered skulls and femurs calcified together into a rich stratum. The thing was, it looked as much a part of the earth's structure as any seam of slate or quartz. He and his labourers withdrew their picks and shovels and stepped back to consider this geological formation. They had already carted clay and limestone and straw up to the hole, put in a fortnight's time and labour, but they filled it in.

'Who were they? Where did they come from?'

Under the tarpaulin his father could be a Druid. Beyond his hooded figure nothing happens but the swirling of the void. The clouds have dropped so low they now envelop them. The pony has been swallowed by clouds. There is cloud on his own fingertips and cloud blurring his boots, and when he breathes he takes cold damp into his lungs and tastes clouds.

His father's muffled voice says, 'These hills were Bronze and Iron Age hill-forts, and henge tombs before that. Human sacrifices and plague and wars from Day One.'

The soft bitterness of evaporated people is on his tongue. The cold sourness of bodies unearthed in the mist.

*She didn't say goodbye.*

His father sips from the bottle, clears his throat and pats the chalk and sandstone ground. Pinches up some wet dirt in his fingers. 'Cavaliers defending Devizes drove a company of Cromwell's men over this escarpment.'

Will leans against him, peering into the murk.

'You know Mary Beamish hears the screams of men and horses on still nights.' He sips again. 'But those old Roundheads and Cavaliers are busy most nights somewhere or other. Re-fighting their most ferocious battles in the sky.'

All he hears is their thick breathing and the soft patter of fog on their waterproofs. The smeary, moonless sky is unflamboyant. Nothing vibrates on the hill but the wind on the dewy grass. Nonetheless he feels weighed down by ancient sarsen stones and clouds of history. Barely suffered by the rituals of the knowing earth.

'Reminded me of a chunk of French nougat, that seam of skulls was pressed so tight in the chalk,' his father says. 'Shame you Baptists don't drink whisky.' He takes a swig himself, pulls his tarpaulin around Will's shoulders and sits close.

Flickering skin on his scalp, skin unrolling cold down his neck and back.

*Oh, my dad.*

At first light Alphabetical Dance nudges his son and stands and shakes the stiffness and moisture from his shoulders. He steps out from under the tarpaulins surprisingly chirpy, clears his throat, stretches, squats again, scoops his hands into the grass and splashes dew up in his face.

'Might learn things today,' he says.

A miniature spiderweb holds a kaleidoscope of dewdrops. Sheeny tracks of snails and slugs crisscross through the dew. Kestrels already cry over the hill. Will brushes dew from the pony's coat and warms his hands on its flanks. His father turns away politely and pisses a green path down the silvery hillside, and when Will mentions food he nods.

'Hold your horses, unless you want to boil up some nice snail broth.'

When most of the mist has burned away, small clouds stay in the hollows. To site the dewpond they search out these dips which have kept the haze. There a pond might last. Then his father tramps the dewy ground looking for that special misty pocket with the qualities he wants. Ground wide enough and free of rocks to allow the digging, puddling and ramming of a pond twenty yards or so across. 'No bloody sarsen stones in the middle, but not too chalky either or the worms'll burrow up and hole it.' And on a gradual slope ('to give the winter ice room to expand and not cut into the sides') and also ('m' yown preference') abutting a tree or bush.

All the silver is tramped off the grass by the time he spots a suitable hazy hollow. A wind-curled tree leans into the depression. The sun is well up. Will's legs are wobbly from fatigue and hunger. Dew sprays off his father's boots as he circles the tree, pensively breaks off a twig, circles it again. The boy wills it to be the special spot.

Squinting into the sun, his father says, 'The mist will condense on these leaves, you see, and fall into my pond.' Will is doubtful but feels like cheering. His father winks. 'And a bit of rain as well.'

To mark it as Alphabetical Dance's site, he heaps small rocks into a cairn. His mark. Then looks shrewdly at Will. 'No Sunday work involved, just a little decoration of stones.'

Surprisingly, this ruffled badger then brushes himself carefully down, rubs his boots with sacking and brings out a comb to part his hair. 'You might want to smarten yourself,' he says.

By the time they lead the pony down to the trap and harness it up, the sun is on the downs. His father whistles something through his teeth. Still in no hurry but with the air of someone heading somewhere. His stubble glints ginger. He's as blithe and twinkly as a pirate in a book. Dew still puddles the sheep track and smothers the dandelions and wild geraniums.

'Warming up,' says Alphabetical Dance, peeking at his watch. 'But it's not true spring till you can put your foot on three daisies.'

Will's mood, however, is bleak and wintry. Missing chapel on Palm Sunday! Descending the slope, it seems a fast drop to damnation and his unhappy mother. Then suddenly they are facing east, and below them the roads from the plain are dotted with people from neighbouring villages, on foot, in carts and on horseback, all heading in their direction, towards the hill. Children's squeals and laughter float up. People are setting up stalls along the road, lighting cooking fires, tapping barrels of ale and tuning up musical instruments. The squeak of a fiddle and the aroma of frying bacon slice the air.

Alphabetical Dance inhales deeply of the present and the long ago. 'Palm Sunday fair,' he says, noncommittally, and without looking at Will he allows the pony to slow and stop by the spring at the foot of the hill.

They breakfast on bacon and flat gingerbread cakes, on walnuts and Lenten figs. They drink hot tea and warm elderberry wine and the traditional drink of sugar dissolved in water from the spring. Crunching gingerbread, Will watches a boy blowing a tin whistle pass by on a painted donkey. It's Saul Bodkin, his age. Saul's insouciant manner, the clever way his donkey's ears poke through a cardboard witch's hat excite Will's deepest envy. Not knowing such shrewd jollity—and scarcely knowing entertainment—he can hardly comprehend this bold and tasty morning.

At noon Alphabetical Dance accepts a nip of gin, then moves on to mugs of ale. Church services are over and crowds of people dressed in their best clothes join the drinking and eating. Bitter ale and gin and cider and country wine, ham and beef and viggety puddings a yard long and broad beans boiled in spring water—as many as can be stabbed by a three-pronged fork—for a penny a serve. An old woman gives Will a wooden cup of cider, and stands by nudging him until he drinks it.

By one o'clock people are singing. Will wanders through the rowdy crowd in the meadow. Oddly, he now has a mug of ale in his hand. Grinning faces from his village loom and vanish. Viola Brownbill, Maude Grundy, 'Old' New, Mr Ramage the miller, the blacksmithing Woosett brothers—

Shadrach, Meshach and Frank. But no one from the Ebenezer Chapel.

By two o'clock people are smirking and bantering and, soon after, kissing. Maude Grundy pats away men's prods and squeezes. Some men and women join hands and begin to dance Threading the Needle across the meadow. Shad Woosett and Viola Brownbill form an arch with their linked arms. Other couples scamper through it, threading the needle, some stumbling and giggling, until the last couple reaches the head of the line. Sometimes they circle Will, their mouths and eyes wide and riotous, sometimes the procession crumples and skitters off, shrieking, across the meadow.

He roams among them, looking for his father. A lot of the men resemble him in his new ruddiness and thickness, but he isn't there.

Loose-headed and toothy, sweat and spittle flying, the dancers are stomping by, chanting over and over: 'The tailor's blind and he can't see, so we will thread the needle.' As they frolic back across the meadow, 'Old' New falls on his back and the others are laughing too much to help him up. When the procession reaches the spring, however, it judders to a halt, and the hot-faced dancers snap upright, dig into their pockets and purses and, their expressions suddenly sober, throw money, votive tokens, into the water.


Will lies in the greener, softer grass by the spring, at the bottom of the hill where he'd spent the night learning his father's skills. The meadow is blurred white with daisies. A stirring is everywhere. Nothing is dead or still. His head throbs with the chirruping of the earth, the buzzing stones, the ringing water.

Merrymakers are a slurry of shapes and sounds around him. Fleshy blows and grunts and harsh laughs slap the air. The Woosetts are punching and wrestling, now striking each other with wooden staffs. They accept the blows like rewards—the taking of the blow more important than the giving. Blood runs into their dull, accepting eyes and leering mouths. A shrieking woman lifts her dress and shows her bush, then slumps to her knees and vomits into the dandelions. The sun is not yet behind the downs. He still can't see his father. He's struck by an urgency to find the cairn of stones. He strains to see the dewpond site, but the glare is still too sharp and he closes his eyes against it.

Strange that it's here, by the juicy brink of the spring, in the sheep pellets and glinting grass of the meadow, that he faces his mother's worst demons. The pagans of history's, and the future's, mists. The big woman who wakes him by clambering onto him. Laughing and rubbing her arse up and around his narrow thighs. Pressing her strong body. A smeary face with skin like hail damage. Swampy body, cider breath. Her foxy familiar manner.

'Well, at least you've got one another's noses,' she says.

His own astonished breath jolting from him as she rides his skinny belly, pelvis, legs. Hooting at his squirming fright and the wit of her own fat jiggety antics.

A moment later she rolls off him and reels away muttering through the grass. Shrieks and cheers shake him further. Raising his head to the dazzle, he's forgotten his whereabouts, the time, even the cause of his giddiness. His absence from chapel strikes him first. Then he has reason to sit up abruptly. Sliding from the sun, speeding down the steep, almost perpendicular hill towards him, comes a horde of screaming tobogganers, their faces twisted by bravado and mockery and beer, and the fierce novelty of using as sleds the skulls and jawbones of horses.

# SPA WATER

THEY SIP GLASSES of spa water. Their hair is still damp and their cheeks flushed from the bath and its excitements. After a bath in the King's Bath it's the done thing to liaise in the Pump Room and drink a pint or two of the *aqua sulis* which fell as rain ten thousand years ago.

'So,' he says, for want of anything better.

'I am an actress,' she says, raising her chin a little, and looks it.

'I'm a drowner.'

A white lie. Used to be a drowner. Or could be a drowner. But he'd thought *she's an artiste* and he was so impressed it just burst out. And it was easier to put a poetic slant on what a drowner did.

'A drowner?' She seems a little uneasy at that.

The water smells peculiar. It contains forty-three minerals and is supposed to be good for you, but it tastes like warm flat-irons. She has a habit of raising her eyebrows and as she sips again she does so.

'What do you *drown*?'

'A drowner controls water. He makes land float, and meadows of water and ponds of clouds.'

Laying it on like his father, who had taught him the drowner's skills so he could take over. But he won't be, having three weeks before, on his twenty-second birthday, completed his articles with the noted Bristol civil engineer David Faulkner Oates. Although for a moment his own voice, his performance, sounds to him disconcertingly like Alphabetical Dance at full steam, the look of her, the intensity of her gaze encourage him. His hands ripple in the air as he describes the mole tunnelling on the river bank.

The old mole story seems to please her. Now he's struck by the defiant yet delicate angle of her cheekbones. This hint of vulnerability and the optimistic sunlight falling across their table makes him adjust his particulars.

'My profession though is engineering.' He swallows a self-conscious sulphate belch. 'My father's the Hartbridge drowner and I learned drowning from him. He drowns the land'—his airy gesture takes in the Pump Room and its suave customers, so pink from their baths that their cheeks and ears look buffed and glazed—'and then he revives it.'

Handel trickles from a piano in the gallery. Two pumpers do brisk business dispensing the waters from an elaborate fountain. Her eyes are the grey-blue of lakes at first light. Cool, high, Lake District tarns with both shadow and a speck of sunrise in them.

'I love the outdoors. You could call me a pantheist.'

So to this young woman, this *actress*—her name is Angelica Lloyd—Will gushes the family's yarns. He babbles anything that comes to mind. His grandfather being the drowner before his father, and his great-grandfather before him, and so on. His grandfather having once pulled the skull of a prehistoric ox from the deep pool in the Avon. The skull was from the Palaeolithic era, one-third bigger than an ox's today, and Will's father, then a boy of nine or ten, looked on, awestruck. Bad luck the museum wanted it.

'Even fossilised the horns were five feet, tip to tip.'

'Fancy.'

'Grandpop also found a hippopotamus in Surrey. In a river. Well, the bones.'

'What next?' She has another habit of dipping her head toward his shoulder when a remark pleases her. Of urging him on by patting his arm. He's astonished that a strand of hair momentarily brushing his shoulder, such a random touch, could leave such glowing imprints.

'You've heard of Moonrakers?' he asks, and he swells with wit and folklore. Extraordinary how a fragrant stray hair-tickle could make you feel like the last man on the face of the century! 'Well, my old man venerates the moon and is steeped in the magic of water.'

'Do go on. I love otherworldly stuff.'

He puts on a village accent. '*It be bad luck to spy the crescent moon through glass, or to sleep where moonlight strikes your face.*' Then he laughs, to show he's had experiences away from the countryside.

The way these old fancies intrigue her shows she's not a village girl (who would be bored witless by such blather). Well, he's happy to paint his father as rustic seer. Never mind that the pragmatic Alphabetical Dance is hardly more wizardly than Ramage the miller, whom he outranks in the local hierarchy. And much less fey than Mr Vinnicome the vicar, who just outranks him. She laughs too, and touches his arm again. Two modern people.

Did she know that the moon and water were both female, whereas the sun was male?

'Yes.' But the idea pleases her.

'Or that if the new moon lies on its back, or holds the old moon in its arms this scandal will cause rain?

'Scandal?'

'The, *ah,* wanton attitudes.'

'Only nature, surely, the phases of the moon.'

'Just an old wives' tale.' He hurries on. 'Plants must grow with the waxing moon, and with the changing of the moon the weather will change.' Now he's running out of enchantments and sounds like any old turnip farmer.

But she's helpful to this keen boy. 'A *drowner* sounds so tragically Shakespearian. I've played Ophelia in Plymouth and understudied Ellen Terry in Bristol.'

He searches his mind. 'And Portia?' A little too breezily.

'Brighton, Salisbury and Bristol—at the Hippodrome again.'

'Acting,' he says. He blows air through his lips as if he's overwhelmed by the vivacity and mystery of the prospect. 'You must be very imaginative. To act.'

She modestly sips her *aqua sulis.*

'I did enjoy *East Lynne.*' With appropriate eye-rolling, he recites, '*Dead, dead, and never called me mother!*'

'An old crowd pleaser, that's for sure.'

Suddenly out of his depth, he grabs at straws. 'I suppose drowning and acting both depend on a mixture of art and observation.'

'How so?'

He's off again, buoyant and expansive, elaborating on how bringing water on to the land at will and taking it off again was really a high art. And knowing the right time to do it came only from the keenest observation.

'The drowner's motto is *On at a trot and off at a gallop.*'

She's gazing off towards the fountain. 'I wonder what the

*actor's* motto would be.' Her laugh has a crystal edge. '*My own performance over all.*' She turns back to him. 'My father is Hammond Lloyd.'


'What decided you against *drowning?*'

By the time she asks, each knows from the other's rapt attention that a more important parallel dialogue is taking place.

What he's silently appreciating are those devil-may-care eyes. The lascivious eyelashes, moist lips, shrewd teeth. All overlaid with his body's recall of that second's tensile softness in the bath. The beauty of her form and movement.

Above all, her great novelty.

Similarly, she's not voicing the attraction of his amusing eyes and mouth, and the outdoor forearms protruding from the slightly too-short sleeves with the missing button. The memory of their bodies touching in the water. The surprising effect now of his damp combed hair and tang of freshly washed animal.

But her spoken question was crisp enough to turn Pump Room socialites from their gossip. Her looks, dulcet tones and theatrical emphases already drawing surreptitious glances and whispers. People trying to place her.

The water music dribbles to a stop. In the hiatus he says: 'A matter of sheep shit.'

Her brows shoot up. She's not unaware of her surroundings, the eavesdroppers, appropriate social behaviour, relations with the theatregoing public. Like that man with the important-looking nose and chin disapprovingly clearing his throat and shooting his cuffs. Or the swollen woman stopped in mid-sip and making a sour face.

He'd managed to surprise her.

'It's true,' he says. The local crops depended on well-manured soil. Sheep manure was best and the manure of the Wiltshire Horn best of all.

He's in his stride again. 'The Wiltshire Horn had the strange ability to hold its dung all day.' Ewes and lambs walked to the water meadows, fed on the new grass and returned home to the grain fields at dusk. 'Then they dropped it just where it was needed.'

Her heart is sinking under these smelly facts.

'Another advantage of the Wiltshire Horn,' he goes on. It wasn't overladen with flesh or fleece. Light enough not to flatten the water meadows, heavy enough to prepare the soil to the right consistency for sowing.

A medium-sized, house-trained sort of sheep. Some murmur of polite interest is unavoidable. 'And?'

He talks of development, mechanisation. His hands are waving. Progress. The Wiltshire Horn being crossed and re-crossed out of all recognition. The resulting breed, the Hampshire Down, a big improvement in both wool and carcass. He says loudly: 'So it doesn't matter that it's a less dependable shitter.'

She can't believe she's discussing dung in the Pump Room, or anywhere. *There must be more to him than this!*

Of course, he says, the delicate intricacy of a water meadow responded ungratefully to machine-driven hay making. And so forth. Progress again. *Blah-blah.* A drowner needed workers, and manual labour these days was prohibitively expensive. So his father was one of the last. Probably *the* last drowner.

Her look is suitably sympathetic. But he shakes his head.

'No, no. I'm a progressive myself.'

'Then I'm glad you got all that off your chest.'

He smiles at her condescension. Oh, he fancies her.
'And you? Have you always acted?'




Ever since she was Moth, a fairy in *Midsummer Night's Dream*.
She and Kate—Peablossom—both twelve-year-old gossamer
girls on the edge of excitement. Fluttering about with
Cobweb, Mustardseed and company in their first appearance
at the Royal, or any theatre.

Peablossom making the biggest impact. Of all the fairies
flapping around Oberon and Titania none had fluttered more
prettily than the shadow-dancing Peablossom.

The *Bath Register's* review had pointed this out. So, hurt-
fully, had he.

'My darlings!' he'd said in the dressing room, sweeping them
both into his arms. *Sweet.* He could have been their suitor.
Attentive. 'Sit your little elfy-selves down! Let me rub those
tired feet.'

Much more taken with Peablossom than Moth.

Did she remember a brown coat? Mother beetle pottering
quietly, smoothing costumes, patting wings proudly in the
background.

'Oh, oh, so delicate, so vulnerable,' he'd repeated for the past
ten years, in the endless post mortems of their performances.
Moisture regularly rimmed his eyes at the memory. 'She
could break into pieces in your hands.'

As an actor Hammond Lloyd's main concern was his own performance and the projection of his personality. He readily admitted this failing, although of course he wouldn't have called it that. He was proud to be one of the most popular dramatic players of his time. That he invariably converted Shakespeare's characters into projections of his own stage personality, as both Wilde and Shaw had so caustically insisted, could hardly be denied. Nor could his relish of the most extreme melodrama—*A Poor Girl's Temptation, The Spectre Bridegroom, Sixteen String Jack, The Bells* and, of course, *East Lynne*—which had made his name.

He accepted the theatre's adaptation of his childhood nickname to his performances. So what? These days whenever a play's words contradicted his portrayal, Ham Lloyd simply ignored them. Playing Shylock as a mad King he could lop a good fifteen minutes off *The Merchant of Venice*. Playing him as a put-upon Danish prince he could add ten.

Alternating his many mangled versions of Shakespeare with teary melodrama had brought him prosperity and fame. It was hard to ignore *him*. He was still a handsome devil. His popularity and stage presence were enhanced by his stockiness, the cascading red hair, the pugnacious chest and stomach, the piercing blue-eyed gaze locking on Will's the second they met. And, on this over-strung day, a stomachy metallic breath sharp enough to make Will's eyes sting.

Their first meeting, and when Will arrives for Sunday lunch at Hammond Lloyd's rooms at the Grand Hotel, Ham, countrified in paisley cravat, hacking jacket and moon-coloured moleskins, is already on his second bottle of claret. They haven't scoffed their first oyster before Ham, in the middle of a scandalous anecdote about a famous actress, scrapes back his chair, rises from the table and, unbuttoning his flies as he goes, and still loudly addressing them, saunters out to the balcony and urinates into the street below.

Buttoning his pants as he returns to the table. 'I'm a bloody bad boy of course,' he says to Will.

Oysters slide down gullets.

She sips champagne. She says, 'Oh, Father.'

As Hammond Lloyd's snores shake the suite, Will restlessly wanders the rooms. Photographs in silver frames sit on the sideboard, the tables, on every surface: Ham and pretty actresses in and out of costume, adoring each other. The younger actor is fuller-lipped, willowy, rakishly gaunt, somehow taller. He looks as if he could be the current Ham's son.

But there are no children other than Angelica, who now seems to be humming some tune high in her head while uttering no sound. This is unknown country to Will. Every look of hers is cryptic, her conversation is convivial but clipped. It's as if they share some secret, but he has no idea what it is. He needs more clues to her mood than her perching on the edge of the sofa riffling through *Punch* and nipping at the occasional strawberry.

He swallows a champagne belch. 'He knows all these famous beauties?'

'He doesn't miss a leading lady.'

'Ah, your mother?'

'She is away.'

She doesn't elaborate. Shortly, in a thin voice, she sits forward and says, 'One of my jobs as a child was to make soda water.' She had to charge and fill the gasogene on the sideboard at home. One day she went to fill the big silver, wire-covered gasogene and was surprised to find it flat and almost full.

'I squirted some into a glass and discovered it was gin.'

She tipped in the powders, anyway: the bicarbonate of soda and tartaric acid from their blue and white folders. And some extra. 'Maybe I thought I was turning it back into water.' Her voice is still without emotion. 'It charged and charged.' It was fortunate that in returning to this hiding place, her mother cut only her hands in the explosion.

Telling the story seems to agitate her, for she gets up suddenly and purposefully from the sofa. As she does so he reaches out and spontaneously clasps her hands—as if *they* were the ones injured, and recently—in his.

His gesture makes her smile, an enigmatic smile that he will remember as a defining moment. As the first stage.

The wine fumes, the background cacophony of phlegmy snores. Ham's offstage presence further defines the moment for Will as Angelica takes his hands in turn and cups them firmly on her breasts.

At dusk when Hammond Lloyd reappears, sluiced and crisp and smelling of cologne, he brings Angelica a red rose in a champagne flute. It's a little ceremony for everyone's benefit. He gives a contrite bow and shows his teeth.

'For you, dearest.'

'Sweet!' she says.

He gives Will a sidelong glance. 'Sit down, dear boy. You're meandering round and round like a turd in a jerry.'

And then she is perching on her father's knee, ruffling his hair, splattering his cheeks with giggly kisses. Within seconds they are singing and dancing some music-hall routine together.

He applauds dutifully, and gives them an uncertain smile. All this is new to him.

His hairless legs hung over the front of the bath. His calf muscles were like fists. After a strenuous performance, or to ward off a chill, he liked to put his feet over the rim into a bowl of hot mustard water. For a prolonged wallow, he kept an extra jug of hot water alongside.

White as snow, pinkening only as he extended northwards. He lay back, soaking luxuriously. ' "The Oxford hipbath." ' He recited the advertiser's slogan, as always, putting on the northern High Street shopkeeper's voice he found amusing, and rewarded her with, ' "Mankind's special choice for saddle stiffness after hunting." '

She laughed. Her job to draw his bath, bring him the bowl of mustard water, the extra jug. Hear his lines. Laugh at his clever accents.

The water just reached his waist. 'Pour it in there, Little Root. And a little there, too.'

Just like his dresser.


The time, furious with him, she kept the filled hipbath outside all night. It was a heavy frost, mid-winter. Hungover next morning, he plonked down on a sheet of thick ice which broke in the middle under his wide arse. Showed no reaction. Sharp points and jagged edges sticking all round the sides of the tub like *chevaux-de-frise*. Even the sponge a mass of spikes which he had to thaw in his hands.

Not allowing himself the smallest gasp or teeth-chatter as he rinsed and sluiced and soaped, his control as icy as the floating pieces he scooped from between his thighs and passed to her.

Acting the stoic. Cold and noble and already purpling on lips and nose and fingertips.

She broke first, laughed, brought him a warm towel.

'Of course I will need a massage,' he said.

Standing up like Jack Frost, all mottled blue and ice in his orange hairs.

That warm grassy day of her particular question.

Kate's blouse slipping off her shoulder when it was her turn to carry the picnic basket. The boater sliding back on her head, and her hair fluffing forward as they climbed the hill from Bath.

The question burning in her mind all the way. She, above all, had to know. Finally asking it when they stopped for a breather and a sip of cider in a field near Batheaston.

Kate's hair fluffing out more as she shook her head. Kate Cowan of her childhood, friend for ever, yet her demeanour suddenly a stranger's. Affecting an indignant Ophelia-like disarray.

'No, of course not,' she said.

Her cheeks pinkening from heat or embarrassment. Her eyes and the line of her jaw evasive. 'How on earth could you think it?' And then the hot-air balloon scudding over their heads and changing the subject.

About twenty feet off the ground, and dropping fast, hitting a hedge, bouncing up again, and then coming down in the next field. Bucking and flipping in the wind, inflating and contracting like a giant jellyfish, a Portuguese man-o'war. Kate reaching it first. Sworls of colour twisting around its surface. The basket ploughing into the soil as it was pulled and jolted along. Both of them holding it with great difficulty, because it resisted like a heavy, fighting fish. Tying it to a tree. Panting and tense about what they would find. And there being no one. An open clasp-knife lying there, apparently used to sever the guy-ropes—one cut through and another gashed in several places. Half an inch of rapidly melting snow in the basket. Imagining the balloon having risen to high altitudes before coming down. And being dragged across rocks—it was grazed and one or two ropes had sheared off. A strong marine smell hung over it. Shingles and shells were trapped in the wickerwork. The balloon had been swept along the seashore and dipped into the ocean. It had been everywhere.

A woman's silk scarf tied to a guy-rope, and a visiting card for one L. GOUBERT, MEMBRE D'ACADEMIE D'AEROSTATION MÉTÉOROLOGIE, ET FABRICANT DE VANNERIE EN TOUS GENRE.'

'The scarf—like a knight's favour,' Kate said.

The picnic now seeming inappropriate. The balloon bobbing and straining to be free, a live thing again. But neither of them turning around. Eyes straight ahead so as not to chance spotting the crumpled body of a dead balloonist on tree-crown or rooftop. Neither of them speaking.

Kate leaving her the picnic basket to carry back. Kate weeping silently all the way.

Kate was understudying Ophelia. Although she hadn't been called on so far during the season. But Ophelia.

The thing was, she still saw Kate as Peablossom. So did he.

Another thing he'd said of fragility: 'Oh, isn't that an attractive quality?'

She had envied fragility ever since. Even in her pubescent Moth days she had never been fragile herself. But she doesn't feel generous. He was getting too long in the tooth for Hamlet.

And then, parting at the bridge, Kate's eyes fierce, her voice rising from some deep place suddenly crying, 'Yes.'

Waves of strange air roared between them. A barrier of meaty, intestinal air forming for ever. Black rain in the eyes. Taste of blood in the mouth.

'Yes, yes!'

Whenever she thinks of the asylum she sees a white owl and a game of cricket.

A white owl nests in a tree by the asylum gates. The path from the gates, running through an avenue of beech and oak and across a dark lawn to the buildings, is called Owl Walk. Lichened stone walls loom at its far end, then barred lunatic wards, ventilation towers, high iron railings. Behind the buildings lie the asylum's mortuary and cemetery and a neo-Gothic chapel rising from scraggy firs. Rooks rake the cemetery lawn for twigs.

The cricket oval for asylum officers is next to the graveyard. A cricket match always seems to be ending. As the last batsmen walk off the field to polite handclaps, a low hum sounds across the wicket. Male patients have been standing listlessly along the boundary, and now, humming, they drift together across the field like the tributaries of a river until they converge at the officers' wicker tea basket. Owls' horns of stiff hair poking out. Crooning, they hoist the big basket on their shoulders and carry it up the avenue of oaks like bearers in a safari.

You can tell the inmates by their smell and jagged haircuts. The smell permeating their clothing. Sweet and stuffy but not unpleasant. Men going slipslop over the linoleum. Women in one-piece serge crying like babies, *Unh, unh, unh.*

Her mother is above all this. She pats her hair, pulls her top lip over her teeth and talks of moving to new quarters. A section called The Annexe for the Less Lunatic. She is looking forward to it.

'Villas, really,' she says.

Some of the less lunatic work in the officers' houses and gardens and cook and help with the officers' children. If they refrain from venting emotions in letters to the Queen, the Prime Minister, the Commissioners in Lunacy and the Home Secretary, they are also allowed to attend the annual amateur dramatic evening in the recreation hall. Nothing too dramatically extreme. J.M. Barrie's *Quality Street* and Arthur Wing Pinero's *The Second Mrs Tanqueray* have been successfully staged, and a lecture entitled *Land of the Midnight Sun,* featuring a lavish diorama of dissolving views of Lapland.

Another twilight world: the four circles of lunacy.

The slightly more lunatic work on the asylum's farm, in the laundry and cookhouses: simple country folk with their flyaway hair, stutters and shabby clothes. The majority, the generally lunatic—the cinder-eaters and Virgin Marys and Princes of Wales—shuffle through the wards and exercise yards, under one delusion or another.

Then there is the outer circle, the violent insane. Unvisited, half-starved for safety reasons. Bony arms honed down by a diet of thin soup. Reaching out between the bars of padded cells as she goes past.

The smell of boiled cabbage. The sound of a fit. The mortuary rooks flopping down from their nests.

But an asylum has its art as well. No madhouse daubings—

subdued shades and muffling textures representing frankness and reason. In the administration wing, huge curved curtains of cream unbleached calico waft her down a corridor into the superintendent's office. On his walls, severe but charming engraved ovals of a man and a woman in disordered dress, twigs in their hair and arms yearning diagonally. The same be-twigged couple featuring in a dozen coloured presentations and certificates for meritorious nursing conduct for those Attendant Upon the Insane. As well, photographs of some of the more fashionably dressed and better composed lunatics on visiting days.

Dr Curthoys allows relatives of the less lunatic to bring fruit or cake.

Neolithic skulls and a mounted cricket ball sit on his desk. The superintendent is an amateur archaeologist and phrenologist with an enthusiasm for digging into the local bell-barrows.

'Are we staying at the Red Lion?' he inquires. Asylum visitors customarily stay at the Red Lion, in the quaint Georgian marketplace beyond the walls. He gives a chuckle. 'You know a local martyr was publicly burned to death outside the inn in the sixteenth century for denying the doctrine of transubstantiation?'

He can keep his historic tidbits. 'I suppose they thought he was mad,' she says.


Dr Curthoys is also a great believer in hydrotherapy. Her mother's treatment regularly includes the Lunatics' Douche. Dr Curthoys explains to Angelica that the douche relieves congestion of the brain, firstly by causing a shock to the whole nervous system, and secondly by causing a reaction and increased supply of blood to the vessels of the skin of the scalp and face, 'by which the brain inside is relieved'.

He hoists a skull in his hand to demonstrate. Taps it with a pencil. Pokes it through a Neolithic eye socket to where her congested brain would be.

Depending on her mother's delusional state, he explains, the treatment is intensified by putting her feet into hot water, 'and sometimes the lower half of the body'.

'We are also experimenting with galvanic baths and the latest electrical treatments.'

The calico curtains are quite calming.

'I see.'

But then their very colour and texture turns up in a straitjacket.



Two mongoloid girls squat on the floor holding hands, and an old deaf woman with a white beard calls a bedstead *Mama*. In her mother's new ward the air feels used and hot.

'You must excuse my appearance,' her mother whispers. 'Ham and I had a reception to attend at the Garrick. Irving was in great form and the champagne flowed interminably.'

A new attendant, ajangle with whistles and keys, is on duty. When he moves between her and the windowsill her mother begins to tremble. He sets his feet firmly in position, rocks back and forth, watching for batsman's error, anticipating a catch. He is a dark, long-armed Yorkshireman employed for his skills as a fast bowler. He knows her weakness. She is compelled to brush invisible crumbs off any flat surface and carry them to the windowsill. It is important that her room have unimpeded access to a windowsill or equivalent for the disposal of crumbs. But the fieldsman is a rock. Nothing can get past him. Standing patiently with a small cupped hand of air-crumbs. Standing alone, small half-stranger. One side of her face has begun to droop and she smells damp and coppery.

On her way there from the Red Lion one Saturday afternoon Angelica passed two distraught women, smartly turned out, London-looking. 'We have seen a body!' they cried. 'A face staring up!'

Out for a country ramble, the women had seen a face in Watson's Pond. Both burbling about open eyes, yawning mouth, an escaped lunatic.

'A woman?' she shouted at them. 'In the pond? Tell me!'

She felt tousled, hot and frightening. White owls were a presage of death.

They stared at her, quivered, moved away. *Not another one.*

'A man!'

She took a deep breath and actually felt her roaring blood lurch and slow in her skull, her temperature fall. She strode through the asylum gates, down Owl Walk. Things sharply registered: acorns plopping down, lichen fading on stone, ivy inching up walls, weeds pushing through paving cracks, rust blossoming on bars, cinders anticipating their excruciating crunch underfoot. Rooks flopped like blacksmiths' aprons.

Willow stolidly cracked leather and sane hands clapped softly. Lunatics stood sighing around the boundary.

*I will not allow myself to feel like that again.*

And, later:

*The second she doesn't know me any more, I am going.*

At first Will sees her as the sum of her components and mannerisms. Her suffusing sexual elements. Touching him, then flicking out of reach. She is the hand on his naked wrist, the head dipping on his shoulder, the flyaway glance. The light, cool fingers on his burning neck.

The contrast of her solemn physical poise and careless sense of dress: thrown-on garments, bits of miscellaneous costume. Pale skin pinkening when she's flustered. Sometimes her stature and demeanour awe him: as heroic as Joan of Arc. So at night, alone, he squirms like any amphibian, driven by stark glands and instinct. He could grab this high-breasted paragon to him, suck her skin, bite her nape, grip like a bullfrog.

Never mind the predatory eels noting his distraction and striking from below.

And then she blinks, changes gear, a shadow passes across her face and she becomes various idiosyncrasies jammed together. A sudden sullen angle to her lips. Something to do with reckless self. Some secret nearly sly simmers in the eyes more green than grey.

He has two relevant dreams of her. In one they are out walking with a vicar and a prostitute. The vicar is egg-headed, whey-faced. The prostitute wears stained shirtsleeves like a butcher; blood runs from her split lips. This motley hackneyed pair walk arm-in-arm.

'Will the dog ever eat again?' the vicar asks them.

'The flag is at half-mast,' he answers, pleased with his religious insight.

But the vicar slaps on a pith helmet and runs off into the meadow. Horses peer thoughtfully at them over the hedge from the corpses' field. Angelica tiptoes through this disorder with a queenly, I-told-you-so angle to her eyebrows. Her skin shines like a lamp is behind it. Pearl rings drop from her fingers to the boiling ground, sizzle through the surface crust. The sea booms nearby. Ochre waves frothing like sewage on the shore smell, however, of crushed citrus leaves.

Nothing fancy about the second dream, just standard lust. Her hair falling on his face as she leans over him. Soft hairs, too, under her arms. Her breath like clover is over his mouth. The cushion of her lips. He slips his hand over and around and under and between her. The warm vertical slide of his fingers.

In the dream she is both wanton and shy, her eyes under him wide then tightly closed.

A strange coloured bird sings a tremulous melody like a cascade of pure water.

'Do you want to know my feelings?'

He looks at her cautiously. 'Yes.'

'We have known each other before.'

'When?'

'In another life.'

'Really?' He's amused and flattered. It's hard to either argue the point or talk sense. Looks and smiles are unlikely to shake that confidence.

'Were we . . . infamous?'

'I just know we were together.'

On a Thursday evening rattling with insects they walk along the river from Bath to Bradford. The mood is funny, eccentric. A second crazy river—the Bath-to-Bradford canal—accompanies them. One moment it runs at their elbows, the next far above their heads; boats float both above and below them. Warm smells fill the air: hay, roses, sweet william. From the hills, the sound of sheep bells. Hot yellow lilies tip into the water and at their approaching laughter creatures rustle away in the crisp bushes.

Both of them are bold and shy. Allowing their hips to bump as they walk. The path is white in summer dust. Round-headed children with sunburnt faces stare expressionlessly from cottage doorways. They, too, seem on tenterhooks.

She leans happily into him. The late sun shoots from a prism on her breast, a crystal brooch. Her eyes, too, are twinkling.

'Aren't we . . . sympathetic?' she says.

Along the intimate spectrum between melancholy and hilarity they already share lovers' moods. Everything seems to be tiptoeing urgently to this ardent moment. Without discussion, distractedly arm-in-arm, they are searching for a spot they have noticed before and never mentioned. A hideaway, a soft vegetal bed.

They see it simultaneously and draw each other, each the leader and the led, knee-deep in reeds, under this willow on the river bank.

The fronds part like an Oriental curtain into their veiled cave. Some bird flaps away as she places her bathing shawl over a mound of leaves.

Suddenly he feels as whispery as a child, thrilled at this mischievous hide-and-seek. In a fluid movement she eases him onto the shawl and kneels beside him. Under them, dry leaves explode like fireworks. She touches a vein on the back of his hand, moves along it, and sighs, maybe with relief.

But she isn't one for whispering, and the sudden defensive clarity of her voice surprises him. Her words cut through the leaf rustle and insect hum.

'What with the theatre life and so forth, I'm far from a virgin.'

A sudden pulse in his neck gets in the way of speech. He coughs self-consciously and reaches out to her, but her hand on his wrist tightens and holds him off. The blue in her eyes greens toward the pupils; her gaze is steady but a little moist. She seems to be waiting for him to say something, some signal.

Through the leaves behind her, a shimmer of river. Willow fronds frame a black swan swimming obliquely against the pull of the water. Charcoal black, red beak, neck thin as a riding whip; it leaves a drifting wake. A curious thing, he thinks: swans are supposed to be white, plumper, more feminine and domestic-looking. Mantelpiece birds, emblems for bedroom dressers.

He ponders the oddity of the black swan as she unloads her unrequired information. This swan is no ornament: rather a too-bold brushstroke, oil paint on a watercolour canvas. In its dark clarity it could be an elongated figure two. Or a comma, a breathing space in the river's flowing narrative.

When this question mark swims out of frame he tells her to hush, and touches her.


It was different from his erotic dreams. In its moist heat and resilience, far better. Room within room of increasingly fluid heat folding back, and then the warmest subterranean wave sweeping up and breaking over them.

Afterwards he's unable to speak anything useful. But lying in the rushes in their new intimacy, she murmurs to him, 'Now we can tell each other all our secrets.'

'No, thank you.'

'Why won't you tell me?'

'It's yours I don't want to hear.'

'Well, what's the worst thing you ever did?'

He's beginning to notice insects and itches. 'I'm not going to tell you.'

'Neither am I.'


In the night he wakes in her bed to soft, steady weeping and lies a moment pretending sleep, barely breathing, his heart hammering.

'What is it?' he says eventually.

'Let me tell you just one secret. Please.'

'Yes.'

'My mother is certified insane.'

He lies still, dealing gently with her while she talks on through the night. From time to time he kisses her wet face. Now and then one of them gets up, and returns to the bed and the other's embrace. Now they are close. As for the dreaded moment of the chamber pot, neither are stealthy tricklers—but neither his gurgling jet nor her farmyard gush embarrasses them.

In the dark pre-dawn he begins to confide in her, too. He says he wishes to drastically change his life and situation. He warms to the subject: how frustrated he is with this cobwebby century! Now his knees jab and twitch under the bedclothes, his voice rises defiantly from the pillow. He's tired of reacting to long-existing conditions. He wants to experience different surfaces, risks, landscapes.

For that reason, he confides—his voice drops dramatically—he's wary of ever falling in love.

'Is that your secret then?'

'Near enough.'

'How humdrum. To love *is* to change. They say.'

'I would need to be convinced.'

Only a very young, half-educated man could sound like such a pompous, Gilbert and Sullivan-loving fifty-year-old. 'What happened to Mister Adventure?'

By now a beam of sunlight is glistening on the white marble slab of the washstand and firing in all directions off the basin and ewer. He has never before seen a bedroom jug and basin made of cut-glass; in his house they are serviceable enamel. In the light's icy brilliance he reaches for her again.

'I talk rubbish,' he says.

'Another dark secret,' she says. 'I'm never going to marry.'

'I was going to say that.'

'I have a present for you.'
The act of giving has made her shy and self-conscious. She shows him a bright wooden cage. Inside is a little Australian grass parrot, boldly fluffing up emerald and gold. She clears her throat.

'I hope you like him.'

'He's very handsome.'

'He used to be an oracle, but he's happier being a parrot.'


A barrel organ had announced the oracle's presence. A blowy February afternoon. She was returning from the Phonetic Institute in Lower Bristol Road and the organ and cage were in her path. She was hurrying along, head down, and looked against her will, preparing herself for the inevitable monkey, the darting, pained eyes in a corner.

Instead a small bunch of green feathers fluffed the wrong way by the wind. The reversed feathers passively resisting the gusts. The harassing wind revealing the bird's downy centre. As a little girl she used to blow the pile on her sealskin muff.

*Ladies and Gentlemen! A unique opportunity! These foreign birds will consult the FATES for you! For only ONE PENNY they will predict your FORTUNE!* So the sign said. In a far corner of the cage cowered the bunch of reversed feathers. She couldn't avoid it. The Fates would be consulted.

'Eh, signora!' The organ-grinder took a stick and began to torment the parrot. Poking it, scraping the stick across the bars. Eventually it darted across the cage, eyes bright with fury. Scraps of paper had been tied to the stick and its beak fought the stick until it caught in one of these messages.

The organ-grinder withdrew the stick and removed the paper. The parrot returned to sulk in the corner. Her fortune lay before her.

The significance of the plural. These foreign *birds*.

'How much for the parrot?' she said.

She has a small tale of revenge to go with Will's present. She'd needed a perch for the parrot's new cage, and at the bottom of the old cage lay the stick the organ-grinder had used to tease it into consulting the Fates. When it saw the stick the bird was furious. Longing to explain herself, she'd put the stick in the cage anyway.

'He avoided the perch for a week,' she tells Will. 'Now he sits on it all day. I like to watch him dozing. It's nice that his enemy is now his footstool.'

'Very nice. Now he shits on him.'

Her visiting card is attached to the cage. On the front, printed, *Miss Angelica Lloyd*. On the back in ink are some scratchy hieroglyphics, a small *v* hanging in the air, an upward-then-downward curved line like a shark's fin, and a small upside-down *u*. She's too embarrassed to point them out.

He looks quizzically at her. 'But what did the Fates say?'

'I can't tell you that.'

'It's possible to direct your own fate,' he says.

'I don't believe that.'

'I know a fellow on the Somerset Levels, Henry Porteous, who has stood in the one position for four years.'

'What good is that?' She frowns, wants him to notice the card, ask a question. Wants him not to.

'Henry has his own posture, settled as an oak. He leans on a partition wall between his living room and bedroom. At first his head rested against the wall, but bit by bit it bumped a way through. So did his shoulders, and his chest came to rest on an inter-joist.'

She's rolling her eyes.

'Of course after standing so long his legs are atrophied and beginning to rot, but he still eats and shits like a horse where he stands. No one but his old sister Josephine will come to the cottage to feed him. People have tried to move him, but he shouts and threshes and risks collapsing the roof beams on everyone. "What's the law against standing up in my own home," Henry says. "Where does the Lord say we must sit on chairs?" So there he stands, rooted to the spot.'

'*Phew,* imagine!'

'He's in complete control,' he says.

'Except he's not going anywhere.'

'That's fine with him. He has acted. It drove him mad that his house was moving away from him and he could do nothing to stop it. The houses there sink down into the peat. Wetness is a fact of life that tips everything on the diagonal. Horses on the Levels need feet like frying pans just to walk across a field. And men like to test things. There's this engineering term—Angle of Repose. The maximum angle at which something can exist without sliding.'

'Anyone can fall beyond the angle if there's a woman to hold him up.'

'Better a joist or two. I like the idea of a man being the foundation of his own house.'

'What religion are you?'

'Baptist. No, atheist.'

'I've tried both of those and found them lacking,' she says.

The new lovers enjoy following the rituals of the bath. There are a dozen ways of taking the waters. When they are used as a simple bath the bather is advised to let the vapour that has collected during the preparation of the bath escape, then descend gradually into the water.

Will and Angelica like to approach the bath from opposite sides, down separate stairs, like strangers. They enter the water slowly, the momentum of each making a gentle disturbance which soon strikes the similar disturbance of the other. Only the lack of breeze prevents this clashing of currents from throwing up a minute plume of spindrift. Their tides lap back and forth and ripple against their thighs.

Hip-deep, they face each other boldly, as if for the first time. The teasing warmth, the skidding smoothness of wet bodies.

When they step from the bath, attendants envelop them in warm sheets and press them softly. The gentle friction helps the sheets absorb the moisture. Then the sheets are allowed to slip down, the attendants press blankets around them and they move to a dressing room for a vigorous rubbing with warm towels.

'When I'm bathing alone,' Angelica says breezily, 'I sometimes ask for a bucketing.'

What happens is she lies prostrate on a wooden mat while two of the tallest and strongest attendants stand over her with large buckets and pour cold water on her with great force.

Will says nothing.

She looks surprised and defensive. 'It's most stimulating.'

Eventually he shakes his head disbelievingly. 'What must it remind you of?'


She won't allow the effect of the bath to be spoiled by a bad mood. In a moment she smiles at him. 'You see, I'm named after a root that grows in streams. *Angelica archangelica.*'

'I eat it like celery,' he says.

'It was growing by the bank where I was conceived.'

He considers this image, of red-faced Ham thrashing about in the reeds, then reaches out and strokes her upper arm. 'Be thankful they weren't lying in a mugwort hedge. Or a field of stinking-hellebore.'

'Or toothwort,' she says. 'Henbane. Broomrape. Dogwood.' She collapses against his side. 'Miss Dogwood Lloyd!'

All these riverside plants he knows like the growths of his own body. Acrid stinking-hellebore, its green petals dyed crimson at the rims. Fleshy toothwort, the colour of a muddy white pig. Broomrape, wrinkled and brown. Henbane, whose veins run blood. In winter stinking-hellebore appearing before any other plants were in bloom and the only colour in the visible world was the orange and red of willow and dogwood at the water's edge.

For some reason he also thinks of herb paris, a pretty flower but no flower, opening on a black berry with a green-legged spider at its heart. An old country cure for madness.

She darts one of her glances at him. 'Anyway, I've noticed you find bathing quite stimulating, too.'

'Tell me where the angel comes into it,' he says.


'I'll show you where the angel comes into it.'

He blinks.

'We'll need to remove our clothes.'

'Oh.'

'Just lie there.'

After the bath his body is awake and sensitive. She begins by slowly covering his head with her hair. This silent gesture closes his eyes. Then her hair flows down his body. A human waterfall.

Hair flowing is like a dance. She moves her body smoothly as she descends, so that her hair brushes down his body in a single long uninterrupted motion.

Her slightest touch is a statement, a language. A flowing blue line drawn with a fine-nibbed pen on sensitive paper. When she reaches his feet, she turns slowly, without breaking contact, and returns to his head.

'Now I will massage you.'


She nestles his feet into her pelvic warmth. 'The feet and calves are too often neglected,' she says.

'Criminally neglected.'

'Don't laugh. Anyway, yours are flat.'

Her thumbs are digging and pressing into his tender arches, her fingers gripping his toes, rolling his ankle and heel bones. Invading the virgin spaces between his toes. He has never felt these sensations before.

But he says gruffly, 'They're just feet.'

'Wrong. I'm encouraging the movement of congested fluids towards the heart. I'm stimulating the kidney and bladder meridians. They're associated with the element of water and help to regulate fear.'

'Fear of what?'

'Sexuality and change.'

'What else is there?'


The calves, the thighs. He lies on his back. She's on her knees, rocking as she strokes. Their silhouettes bob on the wall. At times her cool skin—a brush of abdomen, a tip of breast—flicks against his leg or side, softer than touch. At no stage does she break contact. Her sensual presence is subdued but suffuses everything. She is like a drop of dye in a glass of water. And when occasionally she catches a spiky whiff of his body she seems to quiver slightly before continuing.

She kneels by his thigh, massaging it with her whole hand. Using her body's weight, she directs her energy into the heel of her hand. She works the inner thigh with her right hand, and the centre and outer muscles with her left. She works deeply and evenly along the length of the quadricep, from the knee to the thigh joint, staying in line with the muscle.

His muscles are young and limber. She keeps just below the level of pain. And of arousal.

With her thumbs she finds his points of tension. She takes a deep breath and starts the movement, breathes out and leans into him so he feels heat deep in his tissues.

She says: 'The thighs are held tight by repressed anger and sexual tension. This can bring a powerful emotional release. You shouldn't worry about sudden sweating or a change in breathing. Maybe you will cry.'

'I doubt it.'

A deep thumb jab brings a sharp twinge. At his yelp she says, 'You know we are ninety per cent water and should move and change our lives as fluidly as possible.'


She loves her skill. To massage a body releases something in her. She likes to add musk drops to her massaging oil, or sometimes concentrated clove oil, almond, cinnamon or lemon oils.

She tells him, 'I know someone who can't stand the feeling of oil on his skin.'

He grunts, face-down. 'So?'

'I use talcum powder instead.'


An old back was slicker, whiter, more liquid under her hands. Softer muscles, jellied flesh, pores stretching to the horizontal. But muscles and flesh nevertheless. A slippery expanse of experience, a moled and dimpled plateau of knowledge, a whole country of human perseverance at her fingertips. And, deliciously, a back strangely vulnerable, too; her pats setting off little puffs of talcum as its power ebbed from spine and shoulder blades and flowed into her.

Filling her up. She was strong and in charge. Knuckling each vertebra. Pressing harder, squeezing and kneading until it registered. It took a while. Her hands and shoulders were stiff; her own back ached with the effort. Even then it was hardly a moan of surrender.

His voice rose rich and yeasty from the mat. 'I'm just dough in your hands.'

She brought her hands lower, found the hollow to the side of the centre of his right buttock, pressed her knuckle in it and twisted it, two, three, four, five times each way. Imagined she was bolting him to the floor.

At the fifth twist she heard a faint mutter and, without breaking contact, moved the point of her right elbow into the hollow and leaned with her weight, pressing and twisting so intensely she imagined for an instant she was blacking out.


She had massaged an even older back. Aged eighty-three: Mr Pitman's. She had met him at the New Church of Emanuel Swedenborg in Bath. Mr Pitman was hurrying home to the other love of his life besides the New Church, an obsession since he was a young schoolmaster at Wotton-under-Edge. Phonetic writing. She was trying on Swedenborg's philosophies for size, seeing if they fitted better than any of the others. She came down the steps of the New Church behind him and noticed him holding his neck crookedly, his fingers gingerly plucking the stringy tendons.

'I could relieve that crick,' she said.

Mr Pitman was actually Sir Isaac, knighted for services to stenographers, but she didn't know this until after she had seen him in his saggy lemon drawers, bending to touch his toes, pressing his palms flat on the floor. He was in good condition, relatively speaking, owing to a lifetime abstinence from meat, alcohol, tobacco and cowpox vaccinations. Only the knotted muscles in his shoulders, from sixty years of being at his desk by half past six, six days a week, hinted at his age.

Mounds of phonetic literature, heaps of paper covered with little wavy scratchings, lay over his tables and floor. Clearing space to lay her mat, she asked, 'Is this your study?'

'No, it is my office,' he answered, hitching up his drawers with inky fingers and lowering himself to the mat. 'I do not study, I work.'

Sighing under her hands half an hour later, he said, 'I know what your clients must find satisfying, but where is the intellectual stimulation for an actress in kneading flesh?'

'Oh, I get pleasure from it,' she said, and immediately cleared her throat. Waves of his musty odour rose from the mat. His breath smelled like pen nibs, and his skin like old first editions. Sir Isaac, face down, was unaware of her blush. 'I want to travel. Most places have no need of actresses but a terrible shortage of masseuses and stenographers.'

He agreed. 'Men always want someone to rub their necks and dictate to.'

They reached an arrangement: an hour's massage a week for an hour's instruction in stenographic sound-hand. He reasoned he could afford one hour off a week; he would more than make it up in increased flexibility. So at his Phonetic Institute she learned his radical system of phonetic symbols and abbreviations. At his home in Royal Crescent, after she had played his neck and spine like a piano, he gave her dietary tips and herbal nostrums.

Will finally noticed her notebooks, the strings of marks like choppy waves—some blowing back on themselves like spindrift—and asked, 'What are those hieroglyphics, anyway?'

She said, 'Old Mister Pitman is teaching me his method of shorthand writing.'

' "Old *Mister* Pitman?" Isn't he famous and knighted for it?'

'Well, I soothe his vertebrae and he teaches me gramma-logues.'

'You massage Sir Isaac?'

'Just a little rub.'

*A little rub.* More like entering a special room until now locked away: a room whose existence and secrets were known only to a few. And, God knows, this few were too many.

'I'm looking to the future. I'm not the world's best actress.'

'Don't think like that.'

He told her these shorthand signs reminded him of the individual signs and messages the gypsies made from river rushes. Each family had its own symbol. A rush twisted lightly with a sprig of heather, a certain bird's feather or a head of wheat would say who the maker was, where he had been, what he had done.

Non-gypsies could not decipher these silent, surreptitious messages. A simple river rush, faded and fallen beside the dry road, would be noticed only by a searcher looking for it. Then its position—right or left and pointing up or down—could tell a gypsy where his friends were camping, or on which side of the river the police were in wait.

She shook her head. 'There is no subterfuge about short-hand. It's not a secret.'

He gave her soothing strokes, his own personal movements. His touch was becoming much more thoughtful.

'One day I'll show you another of their symbols,' he said.

He talked to her of male and female country. To do with hardness and subsidence, dryness and wetness. Pagan ideas. He didn't mention the vulgar terms engineers used, but he gave personal examples.

As a boy lying on the downs above Hartbridge with the solid chalk under his back, and the water in the dewponds and water meadows, even in the tea kettle, thickened by the chalk and limestone that had dissolved in them, he would feel himself almost forced up and out of the earth by the rising chalk, pushed vertical and prominent by its straining solidity.

'Like a horse was under me.'

But the low wet moors of the Somerset Levels where he had spent much of his apprenticeship were the feminine, the negative, of Wiltshire's downs. He talked of lying dozing after a pub ploughman's lunch on Southland Moor and dreaming of absorption. Of viscous jelly lolling beneath him, moving in all its moody ambiguities. Curling its thighs and arms around him in a soft, sucking embrace.

'I had to pull myself out of it.'

'Of course an engineer would prefer a nice dry clod of gravelly male dirt?'

'Not if he enjoyed a challenge.'

This water-ground made a noise, he said, like a gossip of flesh. Like eels in a drum. Wetland fishermen left a length of drainpipe in a sack in an eel pond so the eels made their job easy for them, crowding into the pipe, slipping in as neat and tight as intestines coiling inside a stomach. A tactile, black, slick mass.

'The eels cling together so . . . *readily* that when you tip up the pipe they slide out in one single eel-clot.'

He'd almost said *lovingly.* He cleared his throat. He didn't say he recognised this sensual sound, the friction of liquid kissing, as the moist slide of their bodies on a warm afternoon.

It was the Somerset Levels, where men and eels defied the laws of physics, holding up their houses with their chests, or finding no resistance when one body encountered another in moving over it, that had taught Will his occupation, sharpened his skills.

When he'd arrived in Bristol aged seventeen to begin his articles, flickering with nervous energy and fingering a shadowy beard, he had been lucky to find an amiable and encouraging master anxious to recognise ability when he found it. David Faulkner Oates, resident engineer to the Wiltshire and Somerset Railway, had just entered into partnership with John Brindle, an ironmaster, to build railways in Wessex and waterworks in Wales. Helping carry out these contracts from his first year had tested his skills in surveying, in coping with the problems of drainage and ballast, in planning, draughtsmanship and costing, in directing construction and in the management of men.

The wetland was his constant torment, and maybe the making of him. He was just days out of his articles when Ivan Sidebottom, the engineer-in-charge of building the section of railway between Langport and North Curry, fell victim to the wetness with double pneumonia. (Half the local people seemed to suffer from tuberculosis or ague, or rheumatism at least.) Oates was building a suspension bridge in Cornwall and the task of completing the section fell to Will.

He finished the job according to contract and to Oates's satisfaction. He was aware, however, that the chief contracts of Oates, Brindle and Company would be coming to an end within a year. Even if his job were secure, his horizons stretched far beyond the situations on offer. He felt uncomfortable, too, working under the eye of unknown overseers. Lately he felt watched, under steady professional surveillance.

Other things had changed as well. The economic, agricultural and industrial upheaval, the new modes of travel and communication. His imagination had been captured by engineering (in its hydraulic potential maybe just an extension of drowning!), but for him the Levels had exhausted the possibilities of landscape.

The Levels were an engineer's bad dream: of slovenly wandering rivers forever seeping and shifting in the confusion of no gradient. A black joke of perfectly level ground covered with un-level constructions lurching sideways into the ooze. Everything broke the laws and threw out the angles. Entering any cottage, you stepped down a foot or two. Lines of wet on the wallpaper were grubby graphs of the seasons—dampness climbing towards the ceiling throughout the spring and early summer, rising above the mantelpiece at Easter, reaching the window tops by June. Along the cottage walls sloped the ghosts of old doorways that had tipped on the diagonal, been cemented in and replaced with verticals. Pencils and apples rolled off the table.

A farmer building a house would jam wagonloads of tree trunks into the ground, pressing them down ten yards at a time with a horse-driven pile-driver. But ordinary cottages had no proper foundations. When they had to knock down a derelict and oblique shanty to build the railway, they found layers of triangular sections fanning up from the twelfth century. Matted with ancient fishbones, charcoal and oyster shells. Each floor had slipped back into the limitless wet, and been built up again with rubble back to the horizontal.

For three months Will's lodgings were in Bow Street, the main street of Langport, where the buildings ran along each side of a twelfth-century causeway across the valley of the Parrett. The street was built with a solemn market-town solidity, its Lloyds and Bank of England branches jostling sturdy municipal chambers and libraries and institutes.

Strolling home down Bow Street after a hard day of stresses and angles, he would shudder at those rows of buildings leaning drunkenly away from the street. Their lines akimbo. Buildings yawning and stretching and widening their eaves to the sky. Their foundations settling languidly into the comfort of the moor.

Out of true. And always the eyes on him.

The soft terrain meant constant displacement of the rails—and constant work to correct their shape. The rails were laid longitudinally on single balks and packed up with wooden planks. There was a six-man gang positioned every two and a half miles along the line. The gangers carried heavy wooden and iron levers to raise the balk and rail. Four men prised it up and held it while the others packed it with ballast.

Every day he watched this operation. Even though it was standard practice in these parts, every day it seemed more haphazard, defeatist and old-fashioned. It made him feel a failure.

For ballast they used pebbles from the seaside: pebbles so perfectly ground and rounded by the tides the local children began to use them for marbles. Attracted by the marbles, reckless boys soon began playing games of Dare where they lay down on the tracks between the rails while the express trains flew over them.

He had expected professional satisfaction but not sour fear, the daily anticipation of tragedy. He found it hard to travel to and from Bristol knowing the engine, that very carriage, was speeding over children. Young boys squirming between his undulating rails on the constantly shifting ground.

His nightmares were filled with buckled tracks, screaming brakes, flying pieces of children.

David Faulkner Oates wouldn't stand in his way. When he heard of his plans he said, 'You'll need introductions,' and wrote off letters of recommendation to colleagues, commissioners of public works building railways in New World places—Buenos Aires, Ottawa, Auckland, Cape Town.

He could also, it occurred to him, introduce him to an engineer friend of his visiting England from the colony of Western Australia.

'Thank you,' Will said. 'Now my position is clearer, can you tell me who has been overseeing me for the past month?'

'No one,' said Oates.

'No one following me? I put it down to the regular procedure for new engineers. A professional check on my work standards and behaviour.'

'Don't be daft. This is engineering, not espionage.'

*Marion Hubble, wardrobe mistress at the Theatre Royal, Beaufort Square, states she had known Kate Cowan for several years and had seen her every night for the five weeks of the Royal's season of* Hamlet *just ended. She states Miss Cowan had understudied the part of Ophelia, but had not been required to take over the role.*

*On Saturday night last after the cast party Miss Cowan was sitting alone in the dressing room at the Royal and invited her to drink with her. Miss Cowan drank two glasses of champagne and two glasses of port and said certain things.*

*Miss Cowan then asked her to walk home with her. It was the time of the annual visit of Wombwell's Menagerie to the open space by the Old Bridge, and lions and tigers held great novelty there. A man from the menagerie was rumoured to stalk the alleyways at night with a sack, looking for stray cats and dogs to feed Wombwell's big cats, and Miss Cowan said she was scared of meeting him. She laughed bitterly and said, 'He might put me in his sack.'*

*As they were walking along the Quay, Miss Cowan complained that an old friend had behaved badly to her. As they passed over the Old Bridge, at the main entrance to the city, she had pointed out Suicide Row, the spot where the desperate took their leave of the city and life.*

*They went to Miss Cowan's room at the White Hart, where Miss Cowan sat on the bed crying and drinking port. She was attempting to leave when Miss Cowan said that if she didn't stay she would do away with herself. She had stayed another half hour but had to return home to her mother who was a chronic invalid. She went downstairs and Miss Cowan followed her. She was very much in liquor. They went down the street together, and at the bottom of Avon Street as she reached her home at the Ship and Nelson, she wished her goodnight and they parted. It was about 1 o'clock. She heard next day that Miss Cowan had drowned in the River Avon.*

Hammond Lloyd spoke at the funeral, addressing the small group of mourners, mostly theatre folk, in the alcove behind the altar at the small church of St Martin's.

His family had a long and deep affection for Kate Cowan, he began. Layer by layer, stroke by stroke, his voice painted a lyrical picture of her. First as a sprite, then a gamin, a sensitive flower and, finally, the eternal feminine.

His voice thickening, he said he could not avoid mentioning the sad psychological connection, given the effect of the Bard on beautiful, talented, impressionable young souls, of Kate understudying Ophelia.

'Oh, my friends,' he said. 'Water is the element of young and beautiful death, of flowery death, the element of death without pride or revenge, of tender, masochistic suicide. Water is the profound organic symbol of Woman, of Ophelia who can only weep about her pain.'

He cleared his throat. She was willing him not to quote from *Hamlet*. At the same time she knew it was as inevitable as night. After all, how often did he get to play Gertrude? '*An envious sliver broke . . .*' he began, and a tremor went through the mourners. She heard a clogged sound come from the back of her own throat.

> '*When down her weedy trophies and herself*
> *Fell in the weeping brook. Her clothes spread wide;*
> *And, mermaid-like, awhile they bore her up . . .*
> *Till that her garments, heavy with their drink,*
> *Pull'd the poor wretch from her melodious lay*
> *To muddy death.*'

A wave of emotion swept up from the rear of the alcove and lapped at the narrow front pew. As Ham paused and ran his fingers through his hair, it slowly ebbed away. When the sobbing had quietened, he looked searchingly down at the mourners, flung open his arms and began quoting now from *Richard III* : '*O Lord! methought what pain it was to drown! What dreadful noise of water in mine ears! What ugly sights of death within mine eyes!*'

Men gasped, women began to moan and a jobbing actor named Ambrose Menzies cried out, 'Oh, I say!' By then Ham was lowering his hands, placating them, patting the musty, disapproving air, soothing the choppy currents. He could have been a famous preacher the way they hung on the words now trickling down on them like syrup.

'A life with its twists and turns of fortune is very like the River Avon we see glimmering out that window,' he told them.

More deep breaths at the mention of the very source and site of death.

'Of course water is the spring of being, of motherhood,' he went on. 'Water flows like a life, its constant movement responding to its surroundings and to possibility. But, alas, death is also in water. Earth dissolves into dust, fire into smoke. And water dissolves even more completely. It's not for us to judge that for some beloved but tortured souls, water is also the matter of despair, a substantial nothingness, the desired end.'

His voice snagged and caught on *end*. But then swelled again. As he surged on, Angelica noticed how pink and controlled his hands were on the lectern. Blood flowed to his cheeks, filled the capillaries in his nose, swelled his body. She could smell his familiar smell even in the second row, feel the warmth of his breath. In his sombre lapel a tiny ruby stickpin caught the sunlight.

It occurred to her that of course Queen Gertrude's version of Ophelia's death was not, after all, true.

Maybe he would do the gravediggers as well.

'It was in water that Kate perished, yes. But, dear friends, let us not forget that it was *water*, that same silver stream, that with God's help transported our beloved Peablossom, our gossamer darling, to heaven.'

He gave so much of himself, his words, his presence. It was his day, everyone agreed. They sobbed, they clapped, there were even several choked *bravos* (this was a theatrical congregation) as he raised his moist eyes to the roof.

Now seemed the time to ask him. As they left the wake she did so. The emotion, the whisky, might bear fruit.

His eyes were bloodshot, but he looked steadily at her.

'No, no. How could you, above all, think it?' Then he ran his fingers through his hair. 'I'm so tired, Little Root. What I dearly need is a massage.'

'I'm too overwrought,' she said. 'This is my second funeral this week.' The other had been Sir Isaac's or, as she still thought of him, old Mr Pitman. But at least he had died old and accomplished his ambitions. 'I want to be still.'

At the wake she turned aside when a couple of catty actresses inevitably hissed pregnancy.

'You have a budgerigar, I see.'

'The grass parrot?' said Will.

'That is a bloody budgerigar,' declared C.Y. O'Connor, the Engineer-in-Chief and General Manager of the Government Railways of Western Australia. 'From my line of country.'

O'Connor was in hearty spirits if still a little hungover. Two days before, at St James Palace, the Prince of Wales (acting for the Queen who was busy with her Jubilee) had invested him with the insignia of Companion of the Order of St Michael and St George in recognition of his work in the colony.

'Everywhere I go in England,' he said, 'I see our black swans, budgerigars and cockatoos. Forrest is apt to shower Uncle Tom Cobleigh and all with anything strange and feathery.'

After the investiture Premier Forrest had hosted a dinner at the Savoy. Swans were again the motif, twenty of them carved from ice that melted slowly through the seven long courses into numerous little waterfalls, trickling into a central ice pond filled with live—if sluggish—goldfish. Ice fountains played over ornate fern arrangements among whose dripping fronds two hundred London brokers, jobbers, investors and members of parliament celebrated the gold boom that in the past twelve months alone had launched eighty-one new London-based mining companies in the Western Australian goldfields.

The ice swans, the waterfalls, the tinkling fountains were there to attune this City crowd to a particular challenge. As they all knew, gold had already transformed the former Swan River Colony into the Golden West. The next stage had now been reached. If they wanted vastly increased profits they must tackle the water shortage that was holding back gold production and, indeed, infinite wealth.

After dinner O'Connor had outlined his bold scheme to build the world's longest pipeline to pump water three hundred and fifty miles from the coast to the goldfields. A special independent commission of British engineers had already examined the feasibility of the scheme and declared it sound. Sir John Forrest was negotiating the first instalment of a London loan to finance its construction.

'But I'm not here to butter up people with swans,' O'Connor told Will. 'I'm here to appraise the best materials and methods and pumping equipment in England and the Continent.' He turned to his friend Oates. 'And to employ the most imaginative young engineers to join me on the project.'

Will glanced self-consciously across at the dozing budgerigar, one of his bedsitter's only two pieces of decoration (the other being a photograph of Angelica in costume for *A Poor Girl's Temptation*). In its reverie the bird was attempting, in a disoriented, semi-human whistle, 'God Save the Queen'. He turned back to O'Connor and Oates, both nursing teacups on their knees. Apart from Angelica, they were the only visitors he'd had here in Bristol, arriving unannounced and obviously well-dined at 11 p.m.

'I thought we should strike while the iron is hot,' Oates had announced on the doorstep. 'Mr O'Connor returns to London in the morning.'

'Over a section of your railway track. I trust I'll make it safely,' O'Connor said, shaking Will's hand and giving his nightshirt the once-over. 'I hope you can stand the heat. Up to a hundred and seventy in the sun, a hundred and fifteen in the shade.'

Now this lanky, bearded man was lounging back in his digs,

tapping his pipe and talking aqueducts at him loud enough to wake the whole boarding house: 'You'll recall that the longest pipelines previously built were Anio Vetus, begun in 272 BC, which carried water forty-three miles from the hills near Tivoli down to the coastal valley of Rome. And the Aqua Marcia at Subiaco took water sixty-two miles to Rome. Not until twenty years ago did modern engineers match those Roman projects with the aqueduct carrying water ninety-six miles from Thirlmere to Manchester.'

'What about Drake's *leet*?' Will ventured. With its catchment high up in the Dartmoor bogs and its levels winding cunningly for miles across the moors, Francis Drake's *leet*, built to carry fresh water to his ships at Plymouth, was a textbook favourite.

'A sailor's effort, an aqueduct in name only. Anyway, in all those clever-dick schemes the water flowed downhill, which it prefers to do. I'm going to push water uphill. Fourteen hundred feet above sea level.'

'You can do that?'

'For four and sixpence per thousand gallons.'

In his excitement he called the next night at the Royal. The confident anticipation he felt striding through the amiable groups of departing theatre-goers in Beaufort Square fell away when he went backstage. She was in a state, shiny-faced and shivering as if in a fever, clutching a satin robe about her chest and glancing at him distractedly from under two sets of eyebrows.

'I was dreadful,' she said. 'Hideous. I can't get in the mood for a stupid farce. This is my fourth *Charley's Aunt*, and that's three too many for someone my age.'

He always felt awkward backstage. An overawed and clumsy stage-door johnny. It seemed every soubrette, spear-carrier and scene-shifter shared some secret. There was no everyday shyness and decorum between the genders. Bare limbs and insouciant breasts bobbed by in the dressing room. He never knew where to look. He was romantic enough not to want to spoil the stage illusion of mystery and beauty with coarse reality. He could never get over how different actors were from the people they pretended to be.

Her lips were a crimson M above a U. He reached out and touched her powdery forehead, her strange high eyebrows.

'Something very interesting has cropped up,' he said.

She was still shivering. 'They must give me another dressing room. It's the height of summer and number eight dressing room is intensely cold, even when the rest of the theatre is warm. Cold to the bone.'

'Show me.'

She had never been as neutral to him as this.

'It suddenly got cold at curtain call, then I heard footsteps and the swishing of a silk dress. Later a butterfly flew around the footlights.'

He laughed. 'So you have a ghost.'

She led him into number eight dressing room and pushed him inside. It was definitely cooler. His skin and scalp prickled, but it was not unbearably cold and he was amused at how easily the power of suggestion worked on his imagination. Nothing mysteriously trod or swished. Discarded costumes lay everywhere, wigs stood haughtily on their stands, jars of creams and powders yawned open: the humdrum theatrical reality that spoiled the illusion. She had him by both arms in her tense grip, and something occurred to him as she urged him through the room like a shield held in front of her.

'Listen, this is Bath,' he said. 'Under us are ancient cities of water, sandstone caverns and springs and drains and rivers lost in time. It's my business to know about these things.'

He sat her down by a glowing mirror which lit up their pores and highlighted the ginger in his stubble. 'I could tell you about Carboniferous limestone cave systems and the pressure from the high water table in the Mendip hills. There's water running two miles deep under us. This is ancient rain forcing up through faults and fissures in the clay. The King's Spring alone spurts up two hundred and fifty thousand gallons a day.'

She was busily creaming her face to remove the extra eyebrows.

'All this causes acoustic disturbances and changes of temperature. Believe me, your ghost is subterranean water.'

'That's all very well,' she said. Her face was calmer now, shiny and determined. 'I see things, too.'

# WOMAN KISSING
# COCKATOO

WHEN HE FIRST came into the Great Victoria Desert, Felix Locke was struck by the absence of noise and the prevalence of death.

The country was riverless of course. So, because streams and rivers provide the sound for mute landscapes—and if you discounted the calls of crows passing harsh messages about territory and death—it was largely a landscape without noise. There had been no undertaker in the goldfields before him. The hazardous nature of existence would soon be made clear: seven bodies waiting under tarpaulins in the hospital tent and another three lying in salt behind Ellers' store.

The equation was clear enough: no water equalled quick death. Of course water governed every aspect of life. The arid plains and scrubby eucalypt plateaus of the goldfields were made up of rock and isolated hills separated by wide sand-plains. Any depression in the earth's surface existed only to hold pungent salt-marshes, clay flats, brine lakes and snowy deposits which resembled the crumbled marble chips on the graves of the genteel poor.

If any rare rain did fall the lakes quickly drained the sur-rounding land and soon returned to shimmering salt.

But Locke prided himself on seeing abstracts as well as tangibles. Of course he saw the distant clouds of red dust marking the goldfields, the dust rising into the cobalt sky from the general mining method of dryblowing, which separated the light grains of worthless dirt from the heavier grains of gold. But, on the cracked skin of a salt flat beneath his camel's feet, mired in the pink mud and preserved by sun and salt, he also saw the iconic outline of a scorpion and the dotted tracery of a dragonfly.

These delicate dead things on their way to becoming fossil records of the desert, he recorded in a notebook. He liked to underline the character of places. He was from New Milford, Connecticut and as well as laying out bodies and burying them he wrote poetry.

To see the country properly he'd come by train from the pale coastal sandplain up into the gravelly ranges and undulating country to York, then, when the railway gave out, by horse and buggy into the yellow sandplain of the plateau to Merredin, where the bush-fly swarms began in force, and finally by Afghan camel train into the red soil of the goldfields. On the track he'd passed a camel carrying a 500-gallon water tank; his own camel easily managed his cases of preservative fluids, his cosmetics and disinfectants, his razors and needles and combs, unguents and shrouds. What he called his 'corks and chemistries'.

At first he jotted in his notebook: 'Bold timber alternates with thick scrub. Wildflowers make blurred pools of red and mauve in the grey-green scrublands. Golden bushes blaze on the sandplain.' He had lyrical nature poems on his mind.

But soon he found the spiky-sour whiff of wildflowers too redolent of tomcat spray. He was sore from the camel. It was becoming monotonous to record all that sand. More sand.

More scrub. Dryer trees. Redder ground. The Afghans ate only canned fish and damper until Mahomet Mahomet killed a kangaroo and bled it Muslim-style. Felix thought it tasted like venison. Flies drunk on his sweat swarmed over his back and face. The sky was sharp as sapphires. At night the Southern Cross blazed above and he strolled the camp encouraging the shooting stars to perform with swigs of whisky.

He was still one for first impressions: 'The thing about camels is their constant spit and mucus. It's hard to get over the snot in your face or down your sleeve.' After considering camels' slopes and angles and tempo: 'It would be impossible to make love on camelback.'

As for the abstracts, he noted the elliptical way the desert's surface expressed the fundamentals. Sand, wind, sun. On its crust, living things sketched their lives. Sinuous snake trails, traceries of spinifex bush, windblown grass stems drawing geometry theorems in the sand. And scratchers of unknown origin, their claw marks crisply shaped in the dampness risen overnight to the surface of the sand.

He wrote: 'Slithering mysteries of the night drawn by the glancing angles of first light.'


When he first saw the scattered clumps of tents and hessian huts and bough-roofed sheds anchored down against the dirty wind with lumps of quartz and volcanic rock, he took it for the camp of some tribe of mad outcasts. Between him and its ragged outline lay a stringy moat of white salt lakes as dazzling as sunstroke.

In the absence of water most of the prospectors were dry-blowers. A simple procedure: shovel the gold-bearing dirt into the wind and let the barren dust blow away. The miners were of many nationalities and ages but everyone's face and clothes was stained red-brown, obliterating individuality. Filth was no indication of lack of wealth or status. Some of these men were already rich, some destitute.

He stood on the salt lakes' glaring shore. Boiling among the heat mirages, primitive machines cooked water. Wood-stove condensers producing smoky, brackish water from salt. There were ten bodies waiting in the heat for him to process. A charred boy. A legless old dynamite enthusiast.

He was, perversely, almost cheerful.

He thought: *It can't get worse than this.*

Two years later Felix Locke, Dr Jean-Pierre Malebranche and Axel Boehm the photographer are taking the evening breeze on deckchairs on the verandah of the Prince of Wales Hotel, eating tinned Canadian salmon on sourdough rolls and drinking whisky and condensed water—the salty bread and fish making the water's smoky salinity almost unnoticeable—and discussing business.

'You must agree, once you've seen one suicide you'd never consider it yourself,' Locke says to his friend Malebranche.

Beyond the hotel verandah, lights glimmer into the far distance.

Hundreds of campfires burn in the dark, spirit lamps glow from buildings and tents. After the silence and blackness of the bush track, the bright contrast leads a young, well-dressed woman named Inez Gosper to high expectations when her Cobb and Co coach sets her down in the main street.

These presumptions had been teased on her journey by the other passengers, five flirty commercial travellers from Perth with their hampers of samples. One of them, a fortyish pharmaceutical salesman full of dimpling smiles, had given her a packet of Condy's Crystals and copy of the *Miner's Right* announcing the discovery of the richest gold reef yet, the Londonderry. She read:

5000 OUNCES
are already on view in the strongroom.
The escort is bringing in more gold today, including
ONE BOULDER MORE THAN ONE MAN CAN LIFT.
The reef is 4ft. 6in. wide and is one
MASS OF GOLD.
It is pronounced by all the experts
as being considerably richer than Bayley's Find.
NO ALLUVIAL.
GREAT EXCITEMENT PREVAILS HERE.
Londonderry is undoubtedly
THE FINEST FIND THE WORLD HAS EVER SEEN.

And the packet of Condy's Crystals? 'You can't go past it for fever relief,' enthused the beaming salesman.

Fever?

His manner made it clear he thought the women of Australia

found him interesting. By the time they had travelled a hundred miles, with three stops for refreshments, the salesman was patting his crotch soothingly and correctingly as if it contained something nervy and precious—perhaps a prize pigeon.

'The throat must be painted,' he said, 'and a solution of Condy's mixed with quinine and water must be taken twice a day, just before—excuse me—voiding the bowels.'

'I'm a nurse,' she said, crushingly. Fever? She was thinking of gold.

But any expectations of wealth and elegance are soon dashed in the short walk to her hotel. Two blocks is far enough to reveal the dusty rawness of the town, its noisy hotels and grog shops, the billiard halls and brothels, all their swaggering hubbub pouring into the street, clashing and swelling with the blaring brass of a Salvation Army street corner meeting and the reedy rhythmic droning of prayers from the Afghans' camp.

'It would depend on the circumstances,' says Malebranche, licking shreds of salmon from his fingers. 'And the method.'

Locke says, 'Did I mention that customer of mine, the young Welshman who fell for Ruby Nattrice, the singing barmaid at the Windsor Castle? She kept rejecting his overtures. While she was out with another fellow he broke into her room, lay on her bed, big toe on the trigger, and shot himself between the eyes with his Winchester.'

'Yes,' says Malebranche. 'Evans. I signed his death certificate.'

'So Ruby came home and found him. The trouble was young Taffy didn't look romantic and tragic, he looked plain silly. Split his head in two neat halves. Peeled sideways like a banana, an eye on each side. To tell the truth, it was hard not to laugh.'

'Suicides are increasing,' says Malebranche.

'Well,' says Locke, pouring the brine from the salmon tin over a lump of bread. 'I don't see as many drownings as I did in Connecticut.'

Malebranche smiles. 'But every other method, yes? The other side of a gold rush—the failure of unreasonably high hopes. They'll try anything. Shooting, poison, the rope, the razor. Even phosphorous poisoning.' He recalled the prostitute Edie Brooker who had swallowed a solution of wax matches, dissolving the heads of five boxes of matches in a cup of Ceylon tea.

'Better not let on it's possible to drown in a tablespoon of water,' says Locke. 'Just inhale that first little drop of liquid and the larynx can go into violent spasm. Back home in Connecticut I've processed bodies with no water in the lungs that died of lack of oxygen. Businessmen choking on their morning coffee. Babies in the bath.'

'Laryngoplasm,' says Malebranche.

'Dry drowning,' says Locke, between mouthfuls. 'You know what Pliny the Elder said? "The corpses of drowned men float upwards and those of women face down. As if nature wants to respect the modesty of dead women." He's wrong. I've seen them both ways.'

'That was a woman just passed by,' says Axel Boehm.

Inez sits on the iron bed in her tin-walled hotel room bombarded by unfamiliar sounds. She feels hollow and giddy. After the coach and the ship before it, the room's angles surge and slide.

The drunken rowdiness, while not unexpected in a mining town (she has experienced it even in Melbourne), seems threatening and, in her present state, even personally directed. The unsympathetic mix is unnerving: the malign roar of drinking men, the growling of camels, donkeys braying, and all around sheets of roof-iron flapping and screeching in the wind. Having finally reached her destination the realisation suddenly overwhelms her.

Weeping brings surprisingly quick relief. Shortly she dries her eyes, opens her travelling-bag, takes out a pile of banknotes and pushes them inside her underwear. Then, still fully dressed, she beds down uncomfortably and anxiously for the night, too conscious of the flimsy walls to fall properly asleep.

When Inez steps into the street next morning a tall, sharp-angled man is barring her way. He wears a solar topee and a three-piece cream tussock-silk suit that suits the temperature but not the conditions (his trouser cuffs are stained red-brown), and when he removes his hat she sees pomade and dust have turned his ginger hair a rich red.

'I am Axel Boehm,' he announces, 'and I would be honoured to take your photograph.'

He has a reedy German accent, and a camera, tripod and square black case of glass plates standing by.

She doesn't trust his smooth, freckled skin. 'Have you been waiting for me?' she asks. 'This is most untoward. I have no love of the press.'

'Not at all,' he says vaguely, frowning at the sky. 'The light, the light. You will need to stand over there.'

'I am merely a nurse.' She clears her throat. 'Probationary nurse.'

He briskly motions her. 'I have marked the spot.'

In the early morning light he poses her standing with her back to the wide, roughly cleared main street. Her body bisects the street. The dusty canvas and brush offices and iron-roofed hessian stores fan back in a ragged row each side of her. A scattering of coral gums, left standing for their thin shade rather than their blossoms, still grows in the middle of the road. Under the trees two grubby men transact business. A thin kangaroo dog scratches itself at their feet. Three or four other men looking dirtier than by lamplight bash the dust out of their clothes. Camels and horses and coaches and carts of all types and sizes raise more dust as they manoeuvre around the night's bottle heaps and the tree stumps left behind in the haste of clearing. Higher dust clouds hovering over the entire scene show that mining operations have already begun for the day. There is a sting in the sun.

She's surprised to find herself standing on an X in the sand obeying this skinny foreign dandy. Staring obediently at the camera eye, the black hood, feeling men's stray eyes landing on her from all directions.

It's because I'm exhausted from too much travel and emotion, she thinks. This strange passivity.


In the photograph, as is the fashionable pose, her almost-expressionless face hints at boredom and crossness. It accurately mirrors her feelings. The photographer has timed the shot so a Cobb and Co stagecoach behind her appears to have just set her down. In her dress from London, and shoes and hat from Collins Street, with her hint of a frown, and clutching her bag in front of her pelvis, she doesn't look like a nurse, more like a socialite in vastly changed circumstances.

She can't guess he will spend whole evenings holding the finished print up to the lamplight. Staring at the clear eyes, the insolent tilt to the mouth and the point of the chin jutting at the unknown desert. Slender fingers like a bird's foot holding her bag before her. Imagining touching them, rolling each finger between his own. Sniffing the photograph, as if he had captured her light, moist scent in the viscous techniques of his process.

But priding himself on being an objective professional, he can also consider the picture as cultural history. Both in the studio and out of doors, he regards himself not only as a person of experiment—an artistic adventurer adept at capturing unusual natural phenomena: dust storms, flash floods, the indigenous people—but as a sensitive portrayer of sociology.

Sometimes his sociological and experimental sides converge. Because of the climate his gelatine-coated photographic plates are set in what often becomes hot water, and without care the gelatine runs and distorts the image. His experimental nature goads him into sending some of these ghostly distortions off to the papers with wry captions. A distorted image of the same spot where Inez posed had gained wide newspaper exposure when entitled *Street Scene in Hell*.

But he doesn't want to distort Inez's image, or even— although he's an expert at this—to enhance it. Just to . . . yes, inhale it, absorb it, touch the long-missed essence of her gender and class. Forget for a moment the lives of men. Working men with breath like camels. Men with their crusty lashes, nicotined moustaches, disgusting dried red spittle on their lips and stubble, the ingrained beer-sweat-dust stink of unwashed clothes.

In the eternal war between the Nominalists and the Realists, he counts himself, like his countryman August Sander, an avid follower of Realism. Like Sander he believes the great universals are effective and real, and when he takes a 'proper' photograph (or even a commercial studio portrait), the picture isn't necessarily a likeness of old Fred Smith or young Dominic O'Hara that their friends back home would recognise. What can be recognised, he hopes, is a cultural history, a sociology of time and place.

But he can't escape the European aesthetic tradition. The goldfields' landscape is still as stark and strange to him as Mars. When he first arrived the frankness and irony of the place-names made him shiver with pleasure: Dead Finish, Siberia, Island of Gold, White Feather, Day Dawn, Mount Magnet, Poverty Flat, Black Flag, Broad Arrow, Niagara.

On a waterless plateau above Dead Finish he once heard odd noises, like boars truffling in the Black Forest. He peered around a granite ledge and saw two glowering people rutting in the dirt like animals. Dusty beyond sex and age and race, almost beyond species. Eyes closed and fiercely frowning, boots threshing, faces snuffling up the soil. Oblivious to him, the hot, high sun and the whole present world. Snorting and kicking up clouds of dust as if imagining themselves other creatures in other lives.

He is no longer surprised by things chanced upon. He simply takes the photograph. In the same way he's a photographer of the dead. Occasionally they are posed and dignified and casketed, their presentation courtesy of Felix Locke the undertaker. And sometimes they are unposed and natural, just happened upon like any sunset or lightning strike.

Unlike Inez, the lucky, the dead and the fornicating are not self-conscious. A man holding a gold nugget shaped like an angel will give you plenty of time to set up the tripod.

Strangely, what he noticed in each case was the emphasis of the hands, what they were doing.


He emerges from his hood, packs up his equipment, straightens his long limbs and replaces his pith helmet on his gleaming hair. He says to Inez: 'May I welcome you with a champagne breakfast?'

And the photograph? Axel Boehm will later caption it *Miss Gosper Arrives in the Goldfields.*

When, on hearing of the mutual collapse of the Southern Cross Land and Pastoral Company and the Colonial Bank of Victoria, Inez's father had stumbled down St George's Road to the loamy bank of the Yarra at Toorak and, seeing an alternative fate across the river in the narrow terraces and grim chimneys of Richmond, hanged himself from a willow, his dazed widow reacted strangely. 'The trouble with Bernard is I don't know what music to play at his funeral,' she complained. 'He doesn't trust music.'

Music was about all Inez trusted now. Mozart. Vivaldi. The voice of Melba. No longer did she trust her schooling at The Hermitage, or society, or money. Clearly she would have to work at something. It was also evident that work—even ordinary living—couldn't be undertaken in Melbourne. Leaving her mother in the care of her suddenly smug shipping-clerk of an uncle in Bentleigh, she filled a bag with banknotes from the wall safe behind the cue rack in the billiard room and, with hundreds of other emigrants from the land and bank crashes, sailed west on the steamship *Waroonga* for the goldfields.

The steerage passengers were mostly desperate jobless men from across the spectrum of working life, from bank clerks to blacksmiths. But there were young women aboard, too, keeping up appearances as saloon passengers, society girls whose family fortunes had foundered in the crashes and who were too proud to work in Melbourne. Like her they were heading for the goldfields, to the acceptable occupation of the three available there to young women. Nursing.

The lower orders might be off to make their bundle as barmaids and prostitutes but, in the tent hospitals, attending sick or maimed miners for three guineas a week, running errands on horseback, brushing off the flies and dust, emptying bedpans, cooking in the heat or standing over a campfire in the winter desert wind, a socialite turned novice nurse could find, so the girls taking the air on deck had heard—how to put it? *Satisfaction*. Truly. Also men, in the favourable ratio of a hundred to one. Some of them, in the scheme of things, suddenly filthy rich. And even Englishmen from good families. Lords and whatnot.

'I have a question,' Inez said to the gangly German over breakfast. 'Where can I sell some money?'

Despite their friendly banter, the barmaids wouldn't go out with Felix Locke. And the miners didn't offer to fight him. Locke suspected that the barmaids and miners believed he had some irregular attachment to the dead.

Many times he wanted to announce to the bar: 'Relax, I'm no more attracted to the dead than Dr Malebranche is to your Barcoo ulcers, or the nightcart man is to your shit. Believe me, I've got no more stomach for sadness than the butcher or the baker or the gold assayer.' But he kept smiling and bought drinks all round.

He blamed himself for this sorry situation. As he left the Prince of Wales or the Windsor Castle or the Duke of Norfolk of an evening he would call out in farewell, 'I'll get you all in the end!' It always got a laugh. The pub crowd had come to expect him parodying himself and the undertaker's life. He was a character. They laughed, but they shuddered inside. These gold seekers had been printers, blacksmiths, sailors, peers of the realm, lawyers, violinists, teamsters, speculators, doctors, journalists, criminals, clerks and farmers; they were presently rich or poor, yet he reminded them of the uniform hopelessness of their situation. Their momentary existence.

Even, dare they think it, the transient nature of wealth. The final uselessness of gold.

Felix Locke was a gregarious man, short and fair and muscular and full of American quips, quite unlike their image of a mortician. Everyone was polite, shouted him drinks, brayed brittle laughter. But he was an *undertaker*—he *took them under*—and they could never forget it. No man disagreed with him, much less offered to fight him. No woman would go out with him, much less make love.

They were loath even to shake hands. And, he bitterly reminded himself, these were people at the rawest end of existence, international adventurers at the end of the earth. He would catch pugilistic prospectors sneaking wary glances at his pink, callous-free hands, his clean nails, his scabless knuckles. He knew the barmaids winced at the thought of those embalmer's hands on their living flesh. He knew the barmaids assumed—many of them with good reason—that he wanted their bodies.

When men did shake hands—with a hasty bravado—he detected a blink of surprise at his dry palms and firm grip. Ever since becoming an undertaker in New Milford he had concentrated on having dry palms and a firm grip. There was a calming mental exercise he did: by concentrating hard and repeating 'warm hands' to himself ten times he could think his palms dry. And, by so doing, think his nerves away. Slow down his pulse. He could imagine he was bursting with warm and sturdy life.

And he was. It was just that he was a chronic hypochondriac. For whatever reason—his professional preoccupation with death, his frustration at his role as outsider—he imagined himself succumbing to every illness. His lower-back twinges from lifting coffins he feared were spinal cancer. A bad whisky hangover was an imminent stroke, canned-food heartburn was a coronary attack. Venereal disease and its treatments (the dreaded mercury, the legendary scouring umbrella!) were simply too appalling to consider. It was the reason he wouldn't visit the prostitutes, even though Malebranche had suggested they might put an end to his vicious cycle of frustration and hypochondria.

'Look,' he told the doctor. 'Some of your clients pull through. Mine don't. Is it surprising I'm in no hurry to die, too?'

'Visit the French girls,' said Malebranche. 'They're a cut above the rest. I promise you will survive the experience.'

'Have you ever seen terminal syphilis?'

Malebranche didn't deign to answer. He looked at him over his spectacles. 'I can recommend the latest *gutta-percha* Continental protectors. Or sheep intestine, very sensitive. You hardly feel the stitches.'

He shook his head. It was the barmaids he hankered after. He didn't disagree with those pretentious local newspapermen who had taken to referring to the barmaids in their columns as 'Hebes', after Hebe, the beautiful cup bearer of Olympus, the girl who served the Greek gods with nectar. He was already romanticising their standoffishness to him.

But there was one group of people who didn't regard him apprehensively or hide a shudder at the brush of his skin: the Afghans. They smiled down on him from their jangling camels and saluted him. Muslims, with no fear of death, quite the reverse, they saw his role as that of honourable and patient helpmeet to God. Their curiosity was lively. They didn't shiver and turn their minds from his preparations with veins and chemicals.

Mostly it was they who helped him bring in Europeans' baked and juiceless bodies from the desert.

It wasn't that the town was ungrateful at having a proper undertaker at last. Before Locke's arrival the job had belonged to Tom Tully, the odd-job man, who stalked the streets with his vegetable cart on Mondays and Thursdays, like a visitor from the Black Death, shouting, 'Bring out the meat!'

Tully was a wiry ignoramus with scars all along his nose and forehead from walking through panes of glass as a party trick. He buried the dead as they came, in graves scraped out of the sand or, for an extra pound, in coffins knocked up out of packing cases, still with the painted instructions: THIS SIDE UP and STOW AWAY FROM BOILERS. Either way, they lay so shallow that the native animals and the town dogs easily dug them up.

The unsatisfactory situation was brought to a head by the behaviour of Mrs O'Connell, the wife of the publican at the Limerick Castle, whose young son had died of fever. The case had raised the spectre of an epidemic and with Malebranche treating a patient out of town, Tully had gathered the body from the pub, hastily prepared a coffin and packed the boy inside.

On the morning of the funeral the grieving mother wanted a last glimpse of her son. When the coffin lid was opened it was found that the small corpse had turned over on its stomach. In that second Mrs O'Connell's mind became unhinged. She became a recluse, heavily veiled and always clad in deep mourning. By day she stayed shut in her quarters upstairs, but at night she wandered the town, frightening drunken miners with her mysterious and melancholy aspect. Then her heavy tread would be heard on the hotel stairs, the few remaining bar-room customers sobering as they waited for the squeak of her piano stool and the first dark chords to crash above them.

The mining warden, Joseph Finnucane, asked the Mines Department in Perth to find the goldfields a professional undertaker. Felix Locke, who had landed in Western Australia just three days before, answered the advertisement in the *West Australian*.

Perhaps, he wondered, the townspeople were unsettled at the result. They were expecting him to be philosophically different from Scarface Tully, the man with the vegetable cart. More remote, somehow dirgeful and sepulchral. It was a paradox: these boisterous people required more of the very trait that made them uneasy—more damp-palmed melancholy—in their undertaker.

But Tully knew the dead didn't care. In this way the dead that he, Felix Locke, buried were like all the dead before them, for whom time and space had become mortally unimportant. In fact, as he said to Malebranche, 'This loss of interest is the first sure sign that something serious is about to happen.'

Of course the living cared, which was why he was in business. When drinkers accosted him, pathetically intent on telling him what it was they wanted done with them when they were dead (did they think it would stave off the moment?), he would grin resignedly and pass the whisky bottle.

'Have a drink. Remember, once you're dead it's not your problem. You can give it a rest. Call it a day. Put your feet up.'

Some bravo was always breasting the bar and grunting in front of cronies, 'When I'm dead, just put me in a box and throw me in a hole.'

And he would smile and say, 'Yep, that's what I do with everyone.' Then the daredevil would grow sullen and turn away, muttering.

'Some questions,' said Boehm. He had shown no surprise at Inez's query. 'How much money? Which bank?' And, 'Defunct, I presume?'

She toyed with a whiskery bacon rind, but didn't look at him. A pallid egg congealed untouched on her plate. 'Ten thousand pounds. The Colonial Bank of Victoria. Large denominations. Only quite recently defunct. Very recently.'

As if that made it better. He looked at her carefully. 'How long do you plan to stay?'

'Indefinitely.' She gave him an ironic glance. 'I'm seeking my fortune, too.'

The proprietress, a woman with a face like grinning wood, sidled up to their table and exposed her pearlshell dentures in an opaque grimace. She thrust an open bottle at them. 'Here you go. Get into it.'

Boehm poured the champagne. 'There's not a complete barrier to outside information here, you know. Shrewdness is not in short supply. And you're talking about passing off a large sum of useless paper.'

His voice was light but his accent was too harsh for her liking. She fumbled in her bag for a handkerchief, wiped away any hint of breakfast, then turned and looked up coolly.

'I've come to some decisions about money. Money addles people's heads and I've no feeling for it any longer. Money won't cause me any more sleepless nights. I don't care about it, or for those tangled up with it.'

He gave a long and heartfelt sigh. 'It's not like a bad habit you just give up.'

She couldn't be bothered talking. She was feeling more aloof by the second. She looked away, wiped her lips and gazed around this poor excuse for a restaurant. At the next table a young man sat alone. His wig caught her attention first—a rusty windblown affair with a low hairline, like a lop-sided fox-fur muff on his head. It needed adjusting and, as if she were telepathic, the woman with the pearlshell teeth just then straightened it as she passed. The man meanwhile sat straight-backed and motionless in his long-sleeved cotton shirt. His loose empty sleeves hung down his sides and a draught from the door caught them and gently stirred them.

Inez looked quickly away.

Boehm said, 'There's a going rate for most things, but this place is highly sensitive to wealth and fraud. Forget gold, the two real powers here are death and human society. They are the levellers.'

Inez said nothing, but for several seconds in which the plywood door of the cafe snapped open in the gritty easterly wind, tousling her hair, and then slammed back again, her face lost the fullness of confidence.

Her cheekbones, her forehead, her eyes, appeared suddenly prominent to him. The smallest broken vein, unpowdered, glowed under one nostril. Another tiny blood-string shone in the clear white of an eye. Above her full lips was a mole as pale as a pearl. Boehm thought of the levelling of the human face by death and he thought of the wasteful rush of time.

Inez was watching the next table out of the corner of her eye. The proprietress was cutting up the armless man's food. She began to feed him like a child with forkfuls of egg and bacon. She had also brought him a long glass tumbler with a drinking straw, and he turned and frowned back at Inez for a second before leaning his face over the glass and steering his open mouth over the end of the straw.

Boehm poured more warm champagne. '*Explosives*,' he whispered.

Inez took a deep breath. 'I will take what I can get,' she said.

He stretched out his legs and said, 'I will give you a hundred pounds and photograph you from time to time.'

Not being able to bring herself to say yes or no, she said nothing.

Inch by inch, the water draws back and exposes the claypan to the billowing heat. Locke considers a simile. Yes, the clay is as moist and vulnerable as membrane, damp and shiny as human tissue. Sliced, spread and laid glistening. And as its moisture evaporates further the surface contracts like a drying scab.

Flesh equals clay. But the similarity ends when the hairline cracks appear, widening and joining in a jigsaw of interlocking pieces. When it finally dries, the surface gleams like . . . ceramics.

He muses on the pleasant words *ochre* and *umber*. *Sepia*. Cosy poets' words, rolling italicised in his mind. *Burnt sienna*. But these mosaics last only a moment. Soon the glossy tiles curl up at the edges, their glaze dries and fades. The elements crush them into powder and blow them away.

*And no-bullshit brown.*

Locke the hungover poet is still meditating on the shirred skin of claypans when the Afghan finds the dried man sunk face-down in one.

Locke the undertaker drives a buckboard now, a two-seater, just big enough for a clergyman to accompany him on the front seat, with three mourners squashed together on the back seat with their feet up on the coffin. Things have improved since his arrival. In those days he drove a small rented cart and the minister had to sit on the coffin. But the coffin is still carried the same melancholy route through the town and a mile west, past a stand of spindly eucalypts, to the cemetery, where mounds of fresh red sand and rough crosses made from fruit boxes and branches mark the graves.

From the buckboard he misses the body—as brown and

desiccated as the claypan—and might have driven over it. But from his higher vantage point on camelback Mahomet Mahomet gives a whistle. The body is splayed out in the clay, stuck like an ant in amber. It used to be a man named Lester Drake who suffered heatstroke and delirium riding in the box seat on the Cobb and Co coach and reeled into the bush chasing visions of water. Water sparkling in the sun and rippling from the easterly wind, wide water needing only the swells of surf to be a convincing ocean.

Coming toward him, Mahomet Mahomet and his camel appear to Felix Locke to be walking on water. And as they meet at Drake's body the sheet of water seems to close in behind them.

Mahomet Mahomet helps him to prise and pull the body free. In the struggle against suction the noise of its resistance is like the camels breaking wind and the front of it comes away.

Locke's hangover this morning is not a throbber but the sort he prefers: helpful to tranquil meditation. The contemplation of landscape, the taking of logical steps, the calm focussing of poetic ideas. Helpful to meditation but not to exhumation. And not so good under a glaring sun. He takes a breather while he ties his handkerchief over his nose.

'So much for being in the box seat,' he says.

Accustomed to Melbourne's two or three centuries each summer when the gritty brown northerly scorched the city and bay and turned the sun red at noon, Inez had anticipated heat, desert days shimmering around the hundred. But then the thermometer under the coolest tarpaulin of the main hospital ward hovered for three weeks at a hundred and fifteen. The red earth outside radiated heat so intense that flocks of budgerigars fell from the sky like balls of green blossoms and the breath was squeezed from her lungs.

She couldn't breathe air that was hot enough to stop birds' wings. On her regular treks back and forth to the excreta heap and incinerator she had to concentrate on taking the air in tiny sips simply to stay conscious. After a moment the nauseating reek of excrement and smouldering dressings and detritus would rise up and club her senses, and the clouds of glistening flies would rise as well and dive on her meagre moisture before it evaporated. And all the metal instruments and tin billies and dishes were too hot to touch without gloves, and her patients burnt their buttocks on their bedpans.

Six tents strung together on the flat behind the Prince of Wales Hotel—this was the hospital started by the Sisters of the People and run by Matron Beatrice Shand, a Nightingale nurse with a distaste for amateurs but a desperate need of staff. The undenominational Sisters attended to the sick without charge. With more heat and more people this summer there was more diarrhoea and delirium and death, too.

More than one fever was beginning to grip the goldfields. Matron Shand anxiously looked for, and too often found, the telltale red tongue tip, the glassy eyes, the swollen abdomen, the rose-coloured spots on the chest. Men behaving like crazy deaf mutes and raving at night. There was gold fever and there was what Matron Shand thought could be an epidemic of typhoid.

In the middle of this heatwave and water famine an old prospector called Alphonse Brazier found a forty-ounce gold nugget shaped like an elephant at Siberia, eighty miles north in waterless, trackless country. After the stampede that followed, six hundred foolhardy prospectors with equally thirsty horses rioted at the Thirty-Five Mile Soak when they were rationed to two tablespoons of water a day. The strongest and best-armed took the water, and the rest cut their horses' throats and drank the blood and, still insane with thirst, tore off their bloody clothes and stumbled into the mirages of the desert.

With eight camels carrying three hundred and fifty gallons of condensed water, Mahomet Mahomet and the Afghans rode to Siberia and, following the meandering trails of dis-carded trousers and empty waterbags, miraculously saved all but a dozen men. Mahomet Mahomet refused a government reward or even expenses. He declared, 'These men are the sons of God and therefore I have saved them,' and in a cacophony of beads and cowrie shells and brass bells, and hacking groans from camels and naked, peeling men alike, deposited the sick survivors at the hospitals of the Catholic Sisters of St John of God and the Salvation Army Hospital Corps, and fifty of the sickest men with the already over-loaded and understaffed Sisters of the People.

So, after working fourteen sixteen-hour days in a row, Inez agreed to pose for Axel Boehm. Of course he had been on hand to photograph the elephant-shaped nugget and the return of the gallant camel train. Tipping his topee to her, his offer still hanging in the air like a whiff of his aromatic hair cream. It wasn't as if it would take too long, she told herself. A photograph was not a painting, after all.

It would be her first outing. Her first day away from mining accidents, coated tongues, watery stools and heatstroke. Above all, away from doing and acting.

She had learned, in her tiny corner of the nurses' tent, to wash her hair and her whole body with only a cupful of brackish water. Melbourne seemed light years away, but her feeling of anticipation during her spartan sponge bath was suddenly keener than before any Melbourne Cup or Government House ball. (And after those frantic sixteen-hour days in the desert she could cinch her waist in to eighteen inches!)

Standing outside under the tent fly so her hair would dry in the hot air, she half-noticed a line of bulldog ants moving along their tunnel just below the surface of the sand. Here and there the tunnel's crusted roof had collapsed, exposing the glistening artery of ants as they hurried to and from the rubbish heap. Scurrying there empty-handed, struggling back with their heavy individual loads of human detritus.

She turned away from the red nerve of ants and shook out her hair. In her preparations, her body, and then her mind, wished only to consider the glorious passivity of allowing a healthy man to dance attention in the shade.

The studio of Axel Boehm is surprisingly neat and spacious and, beneath its tin roof, relatively cool. He leads her through props and scenery, shrewd backdrops of sandy desert and ferny verdant bushland and the mock headframe of a mine shaft.

'For creating illusion,' he says airily. Though she notices his hands are trembling.

'Illusion? I thought the camera told the truth.'

'Truth?' he says, sitting her down. 'I want something more than truth.'

Even if he has to cheat to get it, she thinks. Now he's rattling on about how his studio helps to isolate people from their environment.

'So they become symbolic of themselves,' he says.

Inez can't take that in, or the vaguely threatening, isolating, 'they' that he's apparently applying to her as well. She's beginning to feel like an object, abruptly suspended between the tense realities of city bankrupt and goldfields stretcher-case. But then . . . it's coolish here, and while this dangling sensation, this detached languor, is unsettling, it's preferable to illness and poverty and heat.

In a swoony fatigue she watches and half-listens as the German sounds off on this sharp contrast between his aims and those of his customers. Relishing talking to a woman. Showing off in a silly boyish manner, gesturing, pacing on his long, stick-insect legs. She guesses he had a cruel nickname as a boy.

'People want a precise record of personal and commercial life, and then complain if the likenesses are unflattering,' he tuts. How could they foolishly believe the camera caught reality just as it was, ignoring the vast difference between their human vision and the camera's monocular, unblinking eye?

It didn't seem so unreasonable to her.

'The thing is,' he confides, 'people come to me as they would go to a doctor or a fortune-teller. To find out how they are.'

'So they're dependent on you.'

He smiles. Waiting for her to arrive, he'd anticipated the look (and smell and feel) of her, the insolent upper-class tilt he remembered in her top lip, the faint purple shading under the eyes. But there is already something different in her face. A subtle shift has occurred. Not just the sharpening of fatigue and climate and work and diet. The levelling, the democratising of her features, has begun.

He looks slyly at her hands. Yes, efficient short nails now, rimmed with dust. Browner, more capable fingers.

Maybe there is a fascinating photographic serial in her changing features, an evolving narrative of Inez portraits? Serving tea, he asks, rather excitedly, 'How are you finding your work here?'

She draws a deep breath and runs a hand over one of his props, the sculpted head of a young woman. 'Exhausting, of course.' She strokes the cool forehead, the closed eyelids, the hair falling smoothly to the right and left of the parting. The head feels like cold water, soothing to the touch. 'This piece is quite lovely.'

'Yes, a cast of the death mask of the famous *Unknown Woman from the Seine.*'

As her fingers fly off it, he hastens to say, 'In Europe many people have casts or reproductions of her.'

'From a real dead person? We aren't keen on such things in Australia.'

He says crisply, 'You should not be frightened. This is beauty. *L'inconnue de la Seine*. Look at her.'

So, challenged, Inez looks. The unknown woman is very young, maybe still a girl. Pretty. Her mouth is gently pursed. Below her peacefully closed eyes (closed, Inez realises with a shudder, against the cold river water, closed also in order to see only an inward image), below these serene eyelids and high cheekbones, around the edges of her sensual lips, a small smile of expectation and pleasure seems to stir. A smile that calls or whispers of a glimpse of something intimately known.

'The last thing her eyes saw was the bank of the Seine, then the waters of the river, and then she closed them, and then the cold shock came, and the dizziness and suffocation and numbness.'

He's actually smiling while saying this.

'Now see these photographs I have taken of her.'

They are worryingly close at hand.

Inez forces concentration. Again, the unknown woman seems to be approaching something that offers happiness. But now in her appearance, and the way his prints reproduce it, there is an added uncanny element of seduction and temptation. While for Inez—ever since her father looped the rope over the Toorak willow branch—there can never be a soothing quality in any representations of death, or even thoughts of it, she must admit this face radiates something almost bewitching.

Surely this isn't his seduction technique?

It turns out he also collects books of death-mask

photography. *Of course.* But leafing through these volumes at his insistence, Inez *is* struck, as he has promised, by the uniformity of the faces, whether brimming with youthful health or emaciated by grave illness.

Yes, she agrees, the burden of strife and change and mortal existence has been erased from their features. The women all look like the Virgin, the men like saints.

So? She isn't frightened exactly, just bemused and disconcerted. Is this art? The European way of doing things? Hanging over the serene religious images is the pervasive smell of his hair cream. His aroma is on the pages of the books, the prints, her cup and saucer, and therefore on her own lips and fingertips.

She can taste his smell in her lungs.

'The way I see it, death carries out a massive retouching operation,' he says.



Not frightened, but disconcerted, Inez is surprised then to find herself posed sedately on a chaise longue. There is nothing macabre about having a sulphur-crested cockatoo dancing up and down your sleeve. Its claws gripping her wrist, her forearm, its grey bullet of a tongue tasting a button now and then. A beating wing ruffling her hair. Peering at her out of its crocodile's eyelids, fluffing up its yellow crest and screeching 'Hello?' with the rising inflection of a querulous schoolteacher.

'Why the bird?'

'It's tame. You say *kiss* to it. It will make a good photograph.'
The cockatoo nibbles her knuckles. (That huge eagle's beak! Those talons on her arm! Its strange rising-and-falling weight.) While, uncaring, this idiotic photographer potters with his equipment.

She's grumpy enough to call out, 'Did you have a nickname as a child?'

Under the hood he pretends not to hear. As soon as he has taken the photograph he smooths back his hair and, rather grandly, hands her one hundred pounds.

'Oh.'

She's frowning and rattled. She thrusts the flapping bird back at him and, her hands shaking at her handbag—she can't open the clasp fast enough—she wrenches it open, shakes out the bundles of Colonial Bank of Victoria notes on to the chaise longue. As if making a simple currency exchange. *Why does she feel like this?*

She has to excuse herself to powder her nose, gather her wits.

The outhouse is relatively clean, for these parts. Newspaper squares hanging neatly on a nail. Smoothed wooden seat on the bucket. A dry dirt floor. And something catching the sun rays coming under the privy door.

In the sudden heat of outdoors she feels giddy. Can this be right? A semicircle of gingery-red curls. A fine fleece of scissored pubic hairs glinting on the floor.

This is like being in a heat mirage. She's hurrying back across the yard. Too dizzying to look at him slanting now in the studio doorway, yearning towards her, all uncomfortable arms and legs and acute foreign angles. His red hair hastily re-combed. The sickly-sweet redness.

He blinks at her curt farewell. As she stamps back in the dust, she longs to draw her image back from the lens. The thought of him possessing it makes her shudder.

But before she gets carried away with primitive ideas of her soul being stolen from her, she considers—and this is somehow disconcerting, too—that it's not exactly the most intimate or sophisticated of images.

The photograph, in fact, will be regarded at first as whimsical, if a little *curious*, and later become popular as a jolly and even patriotic picture-postcard: *Woman Kissing Cockatoo*.

During the water famine all winds from the south and west ceased to blow. Instead of faint evening intimations of cooling sea breezes, teasing hints from the Indian and Southern oceans, there was only the easterly wind, all day, day after day, surging out of the inland deserts to blister the skin, eyes and tongues of humans and animals and toss and whirl the heaps of loosened dryblowing dust into a vast red dust-cloud.

With each hot day the stench from the faeces and rubbish piling up in backyards and around the camps grew fiercer. And the accumulated human and animal filth encouraged more flies, as every bush or rock—any mound or declivity giving the slightest privacy—was used as a latrine. People grew sick and desperate.

During the water famine some miners bribed Aborigines with whisky or tobacco or trousers to find them water. Others tied them to trees in the sun and fed them salt meat until their thirst forced them to lead them to their tribal waterholes in the remote granite outcrops. These the miners drained or their animals made foul and muddy.

The desert Aborigines told a tale of their spirits discussing the best punishment for an oaf who had polluted their water-hole: 'What do you wish for the one who muddied our water?' 'That he become a stutterer and never be able to speak a clear word.' 'And you?' 'That he always go about dumb with his mouth gaping.' 'And you, my brother?' 'That he never take a step without breaking wind.' But for the leader of the salt-meat water thieves they retaliated with a symbolic spear in the throat.

During the water famine the dust storms came up with the

sun and went down with the sun. A howling red wall all day long. Abandoned horses and camels lurched out of the dust storms, crazed and frothing with thirst, nightmarish beasts trampling campsites and charging any unprotected water.

During the water famine an expedition containing four British members of the Royal Society, three Aboriginal guides, a Chinese cook and four Afghan cameleers, dragging behind their camels two longboats once used for harpooning whales in King George's Sound, disappeared into the eastern desert in search of a mythical inland sea.

During the water famine those miners who couldn't afford the rising price of condensed water, much less fresh water transported expensively from the coast, cursed their dry throats and conjunctivitis, tore at their itchy eyes and died from thirst. Or went mad and ripped off their clothes and committed suicide. Or died of typhoid. Or died of suicide *and* typhoid, like one of the three young Hallstrom brothers owning a condenser plant cooking water out on the salt lakes, who all developed fever. Archie died there at the lakes, Byron disappeared, raving, into the west, and the third boy, Marius, suffering from sunstroke as well, was brought by friendly prospectors to the Sisters of the People.

This was after the chaos of the Siberia goldrush and there was no room for him. So, in Inez's first month, the nurses took Marius Hallstrom into their own tent, into Inez's corner, where Marius's friends cared for him in shifts while the nurses were on duty. Inez could hardly disagree. To an untrained amateur nurse these Nightingale nurses with their historic and mythical traditions were as cool as the midnight condensation on a kidney dish.

On the third night the youth's delirium subsided enough for Billy Cornwell, the exhausted friend on watching duty, to finally relax in sleep. Inez came off her own shift to find Billy snoring deeply, while on her own bed lay Marius Hallstrom, his throat sloping open to the windpipe and a scalpel in his dead fingers.

It was impossible to overestimate the mysterious maddening effect of the water famine. Prospectors routinely drank urine and animal blood and lake water so salty their kidneys collapsed. A wood-carter lost his reason and drank a pint of lime-green paint that had fallen off a wagon. A cyclist with only a mile to go to town drank his machine oil.

But it went beyond the simple lack of life-giving drinking fluid. The lives of the Europeans were made strangely incomplete. Suddenly the hotels' billiard rooms were thronged with players day and night, men queuing in the street who had previously never held a cue, men attracted to billiards because the baize was the only greensward they would see.

Without their unconscious but eternal watery rituals for banishing the spectres of death, cooling passion and killing the phantoms of the night, their souls seemed wounded and deficient.

During the water famine the numbers of typhoid cases doubled, quadrupled, became a flood. With the stunned, guilty demeanour that came from officiating at funeral after funeral of men younger than themselves, Felix Locke and the clergymen were conducting mass burials every day.

But while prospectors could pick up gold nuggets shaped like angels and eagles and elephants just lying on the ground, they could forget funerals. While gold could be shaken from the dust or crushed out of the quartz in batteries and mills rumbling day and night, while two incredibly rich mines— the Londonderry and the Wealth of Nations—had fired the financial world's imagination, the mining world could ignore typhoid fever.

The editor of the *Goldfields' Gazette,* Walter Ravine, warned against this fatalistic attitude. His editorials tried to stir the community out of its apathy. 'Typhoid is not the will of God,' he thundered. 'When men refuse to recognise the ordinary rules of health and cleanliness, and endanger the lives of their comrades, it is unjust to lay the consequences to Providence.' A week after his last *Gazette* editorial hit the street, Ravine was dead of typhoid.

The water famine was another matter. The miners agitated for the government to solve the water problem. As optimistic diggers themselves, they couldn't see past drilling. The Government geologists insisted the terrain was unsuitable, the watertable unstable, the water unpotable. The miners were impatient. The Goldfields Water Scheme, C.Y. O'Connor's ingenious plan to pump water from the coast, was still languishing on the drawing board. Progress was the thing. Why not bore deeper for better artesian water with the new diamond drills?

Political pressure brought a new drilling contractor,

Lorenzo Foss, with his heroic mien and a moustache to match, who managed to strike bore water ten miles outside town. Wild cheering greeted the first Foss water-buckets to come up, and then a roaring cacophony as the bullock teams and horses and camels charged them and tipped them over. The mining warden, Joe Finnucane, yelled so hard trying to maintain order that he burst a blood vessel in his eye. Cursing teamsters struggled in the dust to drag back their thirsty animals. When they finally regained control of the supplies, the water was found to be undrinkable.

On the causes of typhoid, even Europe's foremost scientists were said to be confused and divided. Polluted milk, said one theory from abroad. (There were no cows for a hundred miles of the goldfields!) Infected urine, said another. Bacteria-laden air, said others. British doctors in India, more imaginatively, put the occurrence of typhoid down to the breaking of virgin soil.

A not too dissimilar view was expressed by the goldfields' Catholic priest, Father Godfrey l'Estrange, who blamed the 'animal vitality' and 'licentious behaviour' of typhoid's youthful victims. 'It is no coincidence,' said God-the-Odd, as he was immediately nicknamed, 'that young men lose their *innocence* and their *health* together when they come to this place.' The *Miners' Daily*, on the other hand, blamed the new green wallpaper in the post office. Hadn't the post office staff all succumbed to typhoid? The new wallpaper, which had originated in China, must be infectious.

As for the best treatment, the cold-bath cure—a four-hourly immersion on a stretcher in a bath of cold water—was the medical favourite. But impossible in the circumstances.

Massage was suggested as an alternative. Press advertisements claimed that a bottle of Clement's Tonic would revive even a severe case of typhoid. Many took tincture of opium as a painkiller, and Bile Beans, Doan's Ointment and Dr Williams' Pink Pills for Pale People. But the popular miners' remedies were whisky, quinine and raw onions, which accounted for the violent breath of most patients brought to Matron Shand's hospital. To the Sisters of the People, savage onion-breath came to mean typhoid.

Support for the infected-air theory came from the eminent Perth surgeon and physician Dr C. Hector Mann, in an article in the *Australasian Medical Gazette*.

'Only by wearing a cotton-wool respirator can the real danger be avoided,' said Dr Mann, but he agreed that was difficult in the climate. So he recommended that all food should be overcooked and all water boiled. (The miners' habit of adding whisky to all liquid as a preventative measure he dismissed as a fallacy.) Most importantly, he stressed, everyone should be supplied free with a bottle of disinfectant—concentrated solution of corrosive sublimate in hydrochloric acid, coloured with methylene blue—with directions for use.

The Mann view was challenged in the next issue of the *Gazette* by the acting health officer of the goldfields, Dr Jean-Pierre Malebranche. Dr Malebranche pointed out that because of constant water famine and the consequent high cost of water, the people had built wells and tanks to catch the rare rainwater. As the miners mostly lived in tents crowded together, with no sanitary provisions, the pollution of this catchment water was inevitable.

'Round every clump of scrub in the hills,' he wrote, 'you see a collection of faecal deposits, and the drainage from these is collected by residents lower down. It is usual to see cesspits and wells lying side by side, forming, as it were, the two barrels of a gun.'

As Malebranche told Felix Locke over whiskies at the Prince of Wales, 'It all boils down to the old saying: Don't shit where you drink. Any poodle or cocker spaniel knows that.'

As Malebranche said to the prostitute Violette, in their own language, as she sponged him with eau de Cologne, in lieu of water, at Madame Rioux's, 'They have no legends here to cope with elemental things.'

He was thinking of the many rivers which had come into being through the urination of Gargantua. During his walks, the giant and his bladder had inundated the French countryside at random.

'I refer to the white people, of course. I've heard that northeast of here the Aborigines construct votive rainbows over dead snakes to appease water gods.'

Violette made a dove-like noise in the roof of her mouth. She was humming, as always, and dabbing, and letting the old language wash over her.

Malebranche's voice was low, the confiding murmur of the favoured customer. How satisfying he found it to speak French every Monday night. How pleased the girls were, too, to hear it spoken. It was like slowly slaking a great thirst. (Actually, he spoke French also on Thursday nights to Sono and little Oyoni and Yoko in the next street, but of course he was not understood.) It was his language for pleasure, and he was speaking now for the pleasure of hearing his language.

'Did you know, Violette, that in times of drought in Transylvania virgins sit naked on a harrow and pray, and that the Tamil women of southern India tie frogs to winnowing fans? In Africa, of course, the sole purpose of twins' existence in some tribes is to chant dirty songs to incite the rain god to ejaculation.'

This caused Violette to blink and titter, to pause in her sponging and humming and glance inquiringly at the doctor. But he spouted on contentedly.

'And in the goldfields? It's not just the drought which is affecting attitude. Absent in any British aesthetic celebration of water is a certain lightness of touch. Taking the waters lacks any romantic inspiration.'

Here he lapsed into a brief reverie of his student vacations on the Riviera, of sensual days in Menton and Antibes, where bathing and wine and girls and food and music and art had somehow come together by the Mediterranean.

Life, as he recalled it with a sigh here in a heatwave in a tin-walled goldminers' brothel in the Antipodean desert, used to be like those fanciful and charming old French paintings of bathing-houses which invariably revealed a voyeur—with the connivance of the winsome female attendant—spying through a hole in the wall.

His words streamed around her. Violette was recalling the more recent past: the weekly bath nights she and Juliette and Madame Rioux had conducted before the water famine. From an article in *The Ladies' Doctor* ('in order to be naked without being seen, bathwater should always be clouded') Madame Rioux had had the brainwave—once they stopped giggling—of clouding the tawny, rotten-egg-smelling bore water with powdered almond paste, when she could get it, or bran or flour or resin when she couldn't. Dissolved beforehand in spirits of wine and then cast into the bath.

Violette missed those bath nights. In the relentless heat, with luck, she could spend half the night submerged. The men liked it, too, roaring out of the water stained with iron and looking and smelling like big silly biscuits. Macaroons begging to be eaten. After a gold strike, of course, the bath was French champagne.

At a time when a Zeiss lens is treasured, when fine lenses for microscopes, telescopes and wet plate photography are a popular acquisition for the leisured classes as well as the professionals who use them, the tiny creatures living in water have become not only visible, but almost common knowledge.

Malebranche has a first edition of Johann Eichhorn's *Natural History of the Smallest Aquatic Animals*, published in 1781, which devotes itself to the invisible world and whose author 'sought to know God in his smallest works as well as the glory of his vast heavenly bodies, the smallest showing just as distinctly the perfection of their creator'.

Like Eichhorn he seeks to know. But, unlike Eichhorn, he sees under his microscope lens . . . potential murderers.

He is listing and classifying the diverse microscopic creatures—the *infusoria*—in samples of salt water, condensed water, bore water and putrid faecal run-off water from diverse sources around the town. Yes, and even the rich broth of *infusoria* in surreptitious samples, taken before the water famine, of Madame Rioux's brothel's bathwater.

For him, like any seeker of knowledge, time ceases to exist under his lens. In a drop of water he, too, sees a world in which monsters seethe and pass, and whole dynasties rise and fall between the minutest crumbling joint of a decomposing gnat.

But, amazingly, Dr Malebranche is more or less alone in searching for the microbe, the creature, the infusorian animal, which is, perhaps, the *typhoid*.

Dr Malebranche arrives each dusk to cast a melancholy eye over the day's admissions. Felix Locke comes by early each morning to pick up the bodies. In between is the Nightwatch of Delirium.

Matron Shand's hospital: only the kitchen is a sheet-iron building. The wards and the nurses' and matron's tents are made of hessian, with doors at each end and no windows or floors, and a hessian fly over each tent. The typhoid patients lie on and under wet blankets—no sheets—on stretchers made of cornsacks tacked to a frame. More hessian. There are other beds, spring-mattress stretchers stacked outside in the yard, but the mattresses to go on the wire frames haven't arrived. Like many other items they are on the road somewhere.

Hessian doesn't muffle, much less contain, the sounds of delirium.

The mad twelve hours.

As the dusty purple sun sinks over the coast, over civilisation, the duty nursing assistant, Inez, lights a candle in a bottle as her duty lamp, places another candle in a hole scraped in the ground in the middle of each tent, and waits for the muttering to begin. For the *poor typhoids* (more like *vampires*, like *zombies*) to come alive. To lurch up and begin their raving.

What is it about nightfall, she always wonders, that brings on such glistening madness, such glassy-eyed transformation of personality in the typhoid wards? The hallucinations and chattering teeth. The deafness to reason. Why is fever so touched by night? Can she blame the absence of light, the moon, the effect of flickering on a fevered brain? The distorted ghostly shadows thrown by her guttering candle as she moves from bed to bed?

What is it about night, too, that brings on suicide? The *poor typhoids* requiring not only constant care—two ounces of condensed milk and condensed water every two hours, and their coated mouths to be cleaned with glycerine and borax—but, at night, constant vigilance. To keep them and their ulcerated intestines as quiet as possible when all they crave is to be threshingly noisy and craftily self-destructive.

Bear down on them, tie them down, keep them living. Not like eighteen-year-old Marius Hallstrom. One minute sleeping like a humid baby in his rosy spots. The next, lying back happily with his throat open on her pillow.

And outside, only fifty yards away, nightfall brings on more ranting, more crazy noise. There, in the bar of the Prince of Wales, men are roaring wildly with health and money. Throwing it away, drinking, singing, gambling, fighting, flirting, shrugging off their real lives.

The delirium dies with the dawn. The hospital falls silent with exhaustion. At 6.30 a.m.—the early hour is meant to keep death from healthy people's consciousness—the undertaker arrives to pick up the bodies.

The easterly wind introduces itself this morning with a whiff of stale beer and whisky from the pub. Then it slides over the stretchers and ruffles the damp hair—ginger, blond, black, brown, curly, straight—of the recently dead. As if to emphasise how boyish these *poor typhoids* are. And how perverse the disease. As if to remind the nurse and undertaker that it favours the young and robust.

Felix Locke is yet to find a way of dealing with his hospital calls as he has learned to deal, at the other end of his professional processes, with the cemetery. The art of distancing. The distancing of art.

This is his cemetery ploy. Whenever the minister is conducting a mass burial service for young victims, Locke picks a dune to stare at. He looks at the dune and narrows his focus until he finds a perfect segment of sand-dune detail. No weed stem or animal track is allowed to mar its surface. Here the desert atmosphere is written: calm, nothingness. Like the sheet of empty paper before a poem, it will be what he makes it.

Then he makes his mind like this sheet of dry dune sand, this moonscape across which nothing but the wind may pass for hours or weeks. The only movement, as the wind rises, is the thinnest streaming of sand from the dune crest, like spindrift blowing back from a wave, and the occasional slide and trickle of gravity. And in his mind he writes on this page of sand a long streaming breathless sentence until the service is over.

Like the sea, too, the blown sand renews its gentle curves and rippled harmless surface when they move away.

Maybe there is a way of dealing with the hospital call. Loading bodies onto the hearse, he smiles at the exhausted young nurse, Inez, standing under a tent fly, squinting into the glare and rubbing her dark-ringed eyes.

'Nice day for it,' he says.

She snorts with laughter—out of surprise, emotion, fatigue. The easterly is already picking up heat and stench and grit and momentum. Drought roars again across the continent. The ore batteries thunder and grind. Bright stinging sunrays slant across the hotel and hospital yard and stripe the withers of the undertaker's horse.

'Looks like it'll stay fine,' she says.


Is it possible that the dark act of driving a full hearse back to the mortuary during an epidemic can still allow a chink of pleasurable light?

In the night he had dreamed he was playing a flute with a golden mouthpiece. Tunes came out like birdsong. Felix Locke, relishing anew his love of women, their way of instantly changing the scheme of things, taps the horse's flank and actually trots up to his funeral parlour.

How plans, schedules, orthodoxies, careers, lives all swing on their changing moods and prescient caresses, their soft agreements and implicit acknowledgments! And on the pressing urgencies of their flesh and childhoods, their forbidding self-interest.

Inez. An Australian girl. A nurse. Humorous, capable, ironic. Who could be more understanding or matter-of-fact about the undertaker's role? The other day Malebranche had said something worth passing on to an optimistic, philosophical sort of girl: 'The water in our blood will be cloud one day. And was a glacier aeons ago.' That put things in perspective.

'Nice day for it,' he repeats to himself.

Dust spins in the sun as the undertaker jumps lightly from his hearse.

Coming off duty at seven, Inez wakes her replacement, Blanche Brill, a freckly Nightingale nurse from Leeds, and sits in her corner of the tent sponging her face with half a cupful of condensed water. She wipes her hands with disinfectant and then washes them with toilet soap and the remainder of the water. She would like to cry, as she often tries to when coming off duty, and tries again this time, but cannot cross the threshold, cannot raise the final necessary impulse any more.

She makes herself a cup of tea and drinks it slowly outside as crows flop heavily onto the rubbish heap with appropriate retching cries. She turns her head so she can't see what they have found there. Then she brushes her hair and changes into the dress she was wearing when she arrived in town.

Abruptly she undresses, powders herself, and puts on the dress again. She dabs some cologne on her pulse points.

The sun already has a concentrated sting to it. Before she can change her mind, before the street becomes busy and the pall of dust hangs over the town, she hurries to the studio of Axel Boehm.

She knocks. She can't, and doesn't, say anything.

❦

That night she went with him to photograph men cooking water.

Ninety-one condensers ringed the shores of the lake. She counted the ninety-one fires burning under them. All night long bent figures stoked the burning wood while others wearily splashed back and forth, drawing salt water from the lake.

These men kept their hats on at night, she noticed, and no matter what time new parties of men arrived at the lake, they immediately started work, unloading the tanks and firewood from the carts and boiling the water (three or four or five times the salinity of sea water) in a tank and condensing the steam. Axes rang frenziedly through the night to feed the fires. Flame-haunted, shiny faces anxiously checked the boilers for leaks, waiting to taste the result. Praying that it was drinkable. Thirsty horses whinnying as they also waited.

He moved around the shore below her, through the saline mud, lugging his cameras, tripod and case of plates, his magnesium lights. Now and then his accent snapped up from the shore and he was lit up by the intense white flash of a magnesium flare. No one had the time or curiosity or energy to look at her, sitting there on a lump of rock breathing salt and sulphur and woodsmoke while the granite exhaled the day's heat under her thighs.

Her thighs flickered suddenly against the granite. He had played Mozart's clarinet concerto for her on the gramophone.

Surrounded by fire glow, the lake was the colour of varnished rosewood, or burgundy by candlelight. A decanter of burgundy catching the deep light on the sideboard in St George's Road. A fire burning in the dining room fireplace;

her father pouring the supper wine. Blood, she knew now, was wine-dark in a glass.

Who or what was she now?

The fiery shore, his intense white lights, made the sky and earth even blacker by comparison, dimmed her night vision, subdued the stars. Night penetrated the water like an old remorse. In the dry air of the water famine the sparks streamed up and levitated over the lake like gusts of mad angels.

# BLACKWATER

THE SMELL OF DRYING SHARK overpowers the scent of cloves. The shark smell invades the cabin and her senses and her dream, which this sweaty, rolling night happens to be of a handsome white horse, a wise creature that can fly and talk and is stressing on her the urgent need to adopt the urchins of Naples and teach them the art of massage.

When the smell intrudes, just before its force wakes her, the horse looks disappointedly at its suddenly decaying flanks and moulting wings, then at her, and says, 'I notice you are killing me.'

A day out of Mombasa and their Union Castle steamer *City of Edinburgh* has already called at Port Said, Suez, Port Sudan and Aden. But Africa only begins for her after Mombasa when, still twenty miles from the island of Zanzibar, her dream catches a moment's exotic whiff of cloves and spices (and in a second creates this beautiful animal around the fragrance), then, over and above the smell of cloves, the overwhelming stink of dead sharks.

The smell comes on the breeze from the great open vats of sharks salting and drying twenty miles away at Zanzibar, but when, awake now, she peers out of the porthole the dawn ocean is smeared with the dried-blood coloured sails of Arab dhows carrying more sharks down to Zanzibar.

To Angelica the smell heralds Africa. Later she will believe that the first overlaying whiff never actually left her senses. For a time whenever she drifts into the first stages of sleep she also has a recurring feeling of loss and guilt for the beautiful but rotting winged horse.

She mentions the dream as they climb into her lower bunk. Even travelling together as an ostensibly married couple allows for only a cramped saloon cabin with two single, tiered bunks. From Marseilles to Naples they had slept entwined in her bunk—both at night and during their daily siesta. But by Port Said, as it became warmer, they had begun to sleep touching only at the hip or shoulder, straining politely apart towards the cooler edge of air or bulkhead. By Suez, separating after lovemaking with sweet, sweating apologies, they would claim their individual beds.

'Try to dream the horse well again,' Will suggests. He's hardly awake, but awake where it's necessary. At the ship's bar of an evening he has made the acquaintance of pink gin and appreciates not being able to think yet. Operating by instinct. Pushing in with the dozy lubrication of sleep and their surface moisture. Rolling with the creaking ship. 'Maybe you can cure him.'

The shark smell is lodged in her sinuses. 'I can never make dreams do what I want.'

'I can. I'm actually asleep now.'

'We are melting.'

Even at 5 a.m. their bodies are squelching as if they had dropsy.

Rolling with the ship, dreamily licking the salty stream of the neck and breasts and bitter armpits as they move.

She hadn't looked at all surprised. 'You must take it,' she'd said of O'Connor's offer.

'There is nowhere on earth further away,' he'd said, unnecessarily. He was pleased and embarrassed at her genuine enthusiasm—and, uncomfortably, missing her already. Of course the distance was part of the attraction. Halfway round the world! He'd already made up his mind to go.

'But you?' he said.

'I'm coming with you.' As if it had never been in question.

He was relieved and touched and, in this grateful mood, thought the moment right to give her the gypsy ring plaited from river rushes. He dropped it silently in her palm. From carrying it in his pocket these past weeks it was a little frayed and flattened.

'What is this?'

'Village lovers use these rings instead of the wedding ring.' He shrugged. 'It's just a country gesture.' Then he looked at her. 'Why do you want to come?'

She was looking curiously at her finger. She thought of her card with her gift parrot, its shorthand inscription unnoticed.

'For change's sake. To get away from *Charley's Aunt.*' She smiled. 'Maybe to be with you.'

He thought of the river rushes where they had first made love. Didn't she see the connection?

'Good,' he said. 'That's wonderful.'

Her father had wept as he farewelled her. It had awakened dramatic echoes in Ham. Of course the farewell at the water's edge is the most theatrical and heart-rending of partings. The classic myth of death conceived as a departure over water, the image of the boat as floating coffin. But the vessel was only the Dover–Calais ferry, the weather was fine and the Channel calm as a dewpond.

They would travel by train to Marseilles and board the *City of Edinburgh* there.

Ham had worn a dramatic greatcoat to signify the seriousness of her departure. Something also suitable for a gusty wharf. An emphatic collar, epaulettes. His chest pushed out the lapels. It was unfortunate that the day was unseasonally humid. She had cried, too.

Will had said his own farewells at home. His parents' quiet grief, the way they stared at him like a pair of sad martens— dark-ringed bewildered eyes glinting out from their den— had disturbed him but hastened his leaving.

As he left, his father's arm was around his mother's waist. She even waited a moment before inching away from it. Both of them seemed to have shrunk. Even Sarah was pale and wan. They placed his budgerigar on the mantel by the white otter and the holy water. He saw this for the important gesture it was. He was travelling a long way, after all.

By Dover he was again eagerly anticipating the journey.

Sailing down the east coast of Africa to Australia had been O'Connor's suggestion. 'It's not as popular a route as the west coast, but it's more direct and more interesting for people in our line of work to experience the canal. And of course there is Inyanga.'

It was less a suggestion than an instruction. And, as it happened, unnecessary. Will had an ambition of his own to fulfil.

The Union Castle Line operated a monthly East Coast passenger service from Europe to Portuguese East Africa via the Suez Canal, then a fortnightly service on to Durban and Cape Town, from where other monthly steamships plied to Australia. They took their five daily grains of quinine, put on their new khaki colonial-wear and their solar topees against sunstroke and disembarked at Beira. They travelled west on the Beira & Mashonaland & Rhodesia Railways' boat train across the narrow strip of Portuguese East Africa, through the shrieking, dripping Amatongas rainforest and across the southern Rhodesian border to Umtali.

The railway was new and the country still unaccustomed to it. In eighty miles they rose five thousand feet and saw the rare flash of a departing leopard. Wart-hogs scattered before the train, holding their tails like signallers' flags. Baboons nipped and pinched their children off the line. Will and Angelica were agog. Like the baboons, they kept squeezing and pinching each other at new sights. All the scenes of life and death and territorial conflict, but none more than their own adventuring natures, impressed them.

He liked her taking in all this creation and weighing up their place in it. It made him self-conscious but proud, their being a species pair in the scheme of things.

Following O'Connor's directions they got off at Rusapi Station, the depot for the Inyanga District, then travelled by coach another sixty miles into the Inyanga Range, wild mountainous country rising ten thousand feet above sea level, and still covered over sixty square miles with the remains of structures erected in remote times by some long-forgotten people.

Here, in O'Connor's view, was the whole point of Africa: the mysterious aqueduct terraces of Inyanga. As he had said, 'It's important to see mankind's visionary feats so you can weather the inevitable mundane minds and cock-ups.'

Vultures hovered proprietorially over the terraces. Angelica had always imagined the worst of vultures, imbued them with ugly natures, but these birds launched into the air currents with a heavy, thoughtful grace, bobbing and soaring like old widowers taking to the dance floor. Will was more caught up in the grace of the aqueducts below them, their sinuous crossing from hill to hill. He visualised the forested mountains before their ingenious construction, their origins in downpour and mountain stream and dam, the reasoning and labour and wild travails of the ancient engineers.

Twenty thousand years old? More? They predated the arrival of the Bantu, if not the Bushmen, and were built by people who thoroughly understood irrigation. The aqueducts were two feet wide and two feet deep. They had no paving or constructed sides and in spite of natural obstacles their levels were exactly carried out, with not an inch of fall wasted throughout the length of their courses.

'These are a marvel.' He believed such precision was beautiful. The marvel was repeated over and over. On the summits of a hundred hills were a hundred stone forts, each encircled by terraces and, twining round its flanks, an aqueduct. And on the downs, in the valleys and on the lower reaches of the hills, positioned approximately every fifty yards, were the remains of stone shelters. He imagined teeming populations and thriving agriculture. Everything was efficient and exact, striking to the eye and in harmony with the terrain. Above all, lasting.

On the paths, leopard pug marks overlay and mingled with bare human footprints and the old spoors of many beasts. The air was as sharp as a carnivore's breath.

He was breathless from excitement, exercise and altitude. 'This is *art*.'

Wherever he looked was a sign of importance. Huge straggling grape vines, lemon trees, figs, cottony shrubs, all sprouting from the dusty terraces. He gestured at the plants and trees. 'These are a clue to the mystery of the aqueducts. Most are of Arabian and Indian origin. Archaeologists assume that long before Christ there was an Arabian civilisation here and that it recruited labour from India.'

But she was looking at the vervet monkeys leaping on the terraces, the sunbirds flicking after insects in the crumbling stonework, a determined dung beetle rolling a ball of manure across the path. She was looking all around at different signs—bones and dung and copulation and the marking of territory.

They drank sundowners under a big-rooted, pungent tree at the coach station camp. A party of sunburned Rhodesians joined them with their gins and quinine water. One of the men occasionally punctuated the conversation by leaning down, picking up some dried animal turd, breaking it open and sniffing it before continuing drinking. Dour and laconic bush types, the Rhodesians bluntly corrected their idea that animals were plural. It was a herd of *elephant*, four *lion*, half a dozen bloody *monkey*. In Africa where animals abounded, where animals made the landscape, animals were strangely singular.

With the sunset, hundreds of small, red-beaked birds came instantly to life and started flying in frenzied, chattering loops about the big-rooted tree, and simultaneously defecating everywhere, so that the camp soon smelled like a poultry yard and the African drink waiters padded past with birdshit in their hair.

'Red-billed quelea,' the Rhodesians said. Quelea, singular. As night fell, the chattering hubbub and throbbing wings of the swarming birds fell into a regular rhythm and sounded like ocean waves rolling in.

'This is nature,' she said.

On their train journey to Salisbury he read to her from the *Royal Geographical Journal*.

> *At one time, in a not very remote geological period of the continent, the Zambezi delivered its waters not eastwards, as at present, but southwards into a depression known as the Kalahari Desert, which afterwards became filled up with sediment, thus necessitating the enforcement of a new escape route.*
>
> *In a country where few rivers flow all year, the Zambezi is an anomaly. The flood time of the Falls occurs after the rainy season is over, and continues well into the dry season. This phenomenon*

*is due to the existence of swamp and marshes along its own
banks and the banks of its tributary streams. These swamps or
'sponge areas' take the first four months of the wet season to
become soaked and full, and do not start to yield their waters
until the start of the dry season . . .*

'Look,' she interrupted, and pointed at animals—impala,
wildebeest, zebra. Circling, moving, displaying, spraying.
Staking out their backyards on the dun plain. She had little
interest in geological features or the background of things.
She liked a figure in the foreground to give the scene perspective. An animal would do.

'The examination and reading of dung holds the secret of
Africa,' she said.

'Who says so?'

'Those Rhodesians last night. They also said wild animals have
bad eyesight. That's why everyone here wears khaki, so they
think you're a bush. If several people stand close together they
believe it's one big animal and think twice about attacking.'

'It's where we are going that holds the secret of Africa. One
of the wonders of the world.'

'I'm looking forward to it.'

'Angelica, this is one of my great ambitions.'


On the leg to Bulawayo he read out David Livingstone's own
description:

*Of these Falls we had often heard since we came into this coun-
try. They were called by the natives* Mosi-oa-tunya *(The*

*Smoke that Thunders)* or Shongwe *(A Seething Cauldron).*
*After twenty minutes sail in a canoe from Kalai we came in sight*
*of the columns of vapour rising exactly as when large tracts of*
*grass are burned in Africa . . .*

*Half a mile above the Falls, I left the canoe and embarked in*
*a lighter one, with men well acquainted with the rapids. By pass-*
*ing down the centre of the stream—in the eddies and still places*
*caused by many jutting rocks—they brought me to an island in*
*the middle of the river, and on the edge of the lip over which the*
*water rolls.*

*There was danger of being swept down by the fierce streams*
*which rushed along on each side of the island, but the river was*
*now low and we sailed where it is impossible to go when the*
*water is high. Though we reached the island, and were within a*
*few yards of the spot, I could not perceive where the vast body of*
*water went. It seemed to lose itself in the earth . . .*

A yellow-haired passenger drinking from a flask began to sing
'The Rose of Tralee' in Afrikaans. A phalanx of African waiters,
including a man wearing a huge red sash saying WINE WAITER,
wobbled down the corridor with trays of English cuisine.

He looked across at her and spoke.

'At the very edge of the precipice Livingstone lay on a jutting rock to lean over the abyss below. He carved his initials
on a tree which is still standing. He said: "This is the only
instance in which I indulged in this piece of vanity."'

'You would need to be vain and obsessed to be an explorer.'

'He was a very practical man but when he saw the falls he
became gushy. He wrote, "On sights as beautiful as this, angels
in their flight must have gazed."'

'I like him more after hearing that.'
'Peering over the precipice can be a great thing.'
'Didn't his wife give her life to water, too?'

On the way from Hwange, when the train stops at night for water at some pan known only by its number, they insist on getting down with a grumbling guard and stretching their legs beside the carriages.

In the darkness everything compounds the intense and suspenseful feeling of walking in Africa. Their explosive footfalls on the quartzite railbed. The glowing eyes of spring hares caught in the swing of the guard's lamp. The unknown stars of the southern hemisphere; the Southern Cross lying on its side, far away down the night sky toward the Cape of Good Hope. Lions coughing in the mid-distance. And, fifty yards ahead of the engine, a small sand river, a gleaming channel of fine white quartzite sand and, in it, the huge luminous skull of an elephant.

Made alert and silent by the night and the deliciously increased fear of wild animals in the dark, they feel brave and skittish back on board. After two nights spent apart in the Beira & Mashonaland & Rhodesia Railways' regulation ladies' and gentlemen's sleeping compartments, they are frisky with lust.

'I blame Africa,' she says. 'All the ruttish life out there.' She chatters like a vervet monkey and her hands under the travelling rug are as cheeky as one.

'Then we could as well be eating each other.'

'Have you noticed the main urge, even ahead of sex or hunger, is territory? While the leading gnu or greater kudu—the big boy—spends all his time patrolling the fences, the shrewd number two chap gets the ladies.'

'Then I know where I want to be in the pecking order. Not the greater greater kudo but the lesser greater kudu.'

He bribes a porter to give them a sleeper together. The porter is nervous being part of such a proposition but eventually pockets the five shillings and leads them to a tiny staff compartment near the guard's van. By the time the train starts around the high and zigzagging basalt gorge of the Zambezi they are slithering down in the humidity of the dark woods.

A faint mildew smell rises from the sheets like a mist of algaes from damp sand. When he is over her, one of her fingers gripping his damp chest scrapes his nipple. In the rocking moonlit booth he investigates this rasping finger, rolls it between his own thumb and forefinger. She is wearing the ring made of reeds.

Later she says, 'Tell me nice things.'

He makes up a story of her white horse flying them over the falls. The horse sees things through the excited eyes of Dr Livingstone. This is the island in the river. See the tumult of the Zambezi, the flowering orchids sprouting from the constantly dripping trees, the permanent double rainbows, the thundering chasm.

She easily becomes a child and receives his fantasies seriously. When his Livingstone data runs out he takes the images framed by the carriage window, like the green and yellow shooting star just flaring by, and presents them to her. That comet up there is for you, those wild animal eyes burning green and red out there.

He tells many tales of the horse, and finally acts it while their bodies meet and grip in tears and sweat, until they are as drenched and snorting as coursers. She rides him as if she could wrench both his character and the spirit of Africa from him.

They are still awake at sunrise, giggling and murmuring like children, in awe of the noise they have made. The moon is still high in the west as the first birds wake—silver parrots sweeping like gusting leaves through the river trees, shrieking in the strange moonset over the steaming falls.

He would remember the portentous feeling that swept over him when they first walked along the path to Devil's Cataract, towards the boom of falling water, the dense clouds of spray, the great jets of vapour shooting into the sky and hanging over the falls like a pall.

For once he shared his feelings with her. This sunny day he was more open, more moved than she had ever seen him. They stood there saturated by spray while ferns and evergreens dripped and dragonflies swarmed and metallic-crested and hornbilled birds flapped away. Even when he was silent his thoughts shone on his wet face, the open secret that as far as he was concerned here was the start of things.

'I wanted it to be like this,' he said. He meant, but couldn't say: here is the volatile spirit of life.

*And to have you here in this sequence of our lives.*

He had hoped for just these emotions. He'd hoped for once not to be disappointed, to be simply awestruck, and was satisfied.

His hand glanced her arm as he murmured, unnecessarily, 'Old African legends say these are the primeval waters of myth, containing the seeds of millions of beings.'

She raised a quizzical eyebrow. On the slippery, waterlogged path she had to support herself for a moment against a big ebony tree, its dark, crenellated leaves a thick canopy over their heads. The tree prevented much light from reaching the ground and, instead of the usual dry tangle of undergrowth, a rich humus lay under their feet. Between the tree's mossy buttressed roots a pink orchid shone out of the rot, and she bent and picked it and rose again quite slowly.

'Are you all right?'

She was sniffing the orchid. 'It doesn't have a smell.'

No khaki colonial-wear today; she wore a simple blue cotton dress. He thought how pale she looked against the suddenly bright material, and took her damp wrist.

'Not enough sleep,' she said, and smiled. 'Look—footprints!'

The tracks in the mud were of waterbuck and baboon, hippo and leopard and little scratchy tracks that could have been mongoose. They had been told to expect these prints but not, by day, the actual leopard or hippo.

Amid rainbows, they walked on by the falls and stopped

again in wonder at the water leaping clear of the rocks and falling in a thick unbroken fleece into the deep fissure. As the water plummeted, it broke into huge separate pieces of water, all rushing in the same direction, each shooting off sparking rays of foam all the way to the bottom of the chasm.

She was thinking, *How momentous it all is, how heroic*—and how, suddenly, she craved a landscape with less drama.

Now they were on a drier path, walking arm-in-arm past the Main Falls and Livingstone Island—where the intrepid doctor had hung over the lip of the abyss to view the tumult below—and Horseshoe Falls, and Rainbow Falls, to Danger Point. Approaching the point, they saw more smallish tracks, like human handprints, a scuffle of them in the sand, and round a bend in the bushy path a troop of baboons squatted in the sun.

They were feeding on fruit from a large Cape Fig tree which overhung the path. Some sat in the tree eating and shaking figs down on those below. Others were grooming. Nine or ten young ones rolled green figs about like toys and played recklessly on the rocky edge of the point itself.

Most of the baboons jumped into the tree when they saw them. Three big adults, however, remained squatting on the path, munching figs with an incurious air, their supercilious heads only half-turned towards the interlopers. A big female continued to groom the biggest, most imperturbable male while he ate.

'I need to sit down,' Angelica said.

'Not here.' He took her hand and turned back along the path. A hornbill shrieked in the spray ahead. Behind them the fig tree sagged and thrashed with its loosely clinging harvest of baboons. The roaring of the falls registered on him again, the clouds of rainbowed mist, the surging force, and they had gone perhaps thirty feet when she screamed.

Things moved so fast he saw the recent past. The big male baboon was scuttling like a spider. It was on her back, hands gripping, feet clinging to her hips, rocking up and down.

Will's own roar surprised him. The way he loomed, snarling, over Angelica and the ape. The fact he would have bitten its throat out. And that she stood there and did not fall. But the baboon slid off her almost immediately and stood upright for a moment, showing its fangs and—its fingers regretfully caressing the hem—reluctantly releasing a handful of blue dress, its shiny red skewer bobbing indecisively, before sauntering in several insouciant, face-saving stages back to the tree.

She wasn't harmed, not even scratched, and seemed to quickly recover her equilibrium. But her cheeks were flushed and he noticed how prominent her pupils appeared.

All his own nerves and muscles were twitching and his heart was thundering. Snapping a branch against his knee, he swung it in his hand, and his eyes glaring back along the path as he hefted it were mad and almost hopeful.

Her voice was so thin and dry it was hard to make herself heard against the booming of the falls. She had no moisture or resonance in her throat.

'At least it wasn't a leopard,' she said. 'But he thought you were.'

Under two lunar rainbows they drank champagne by the Zambezi.

Will had thought she would be on edge but she was surprisingly languid. She seemed to him to be seduced that night by the lunar rainbows of the full moon. How could such a strange and lovely phenomenon not lead you to believe that underneath its fierce bluster nature was indeed reverie and languor?

'They're very otherworldly,' she said, sipping champagne. 'Like rainbows in a dream.'

'You said once the otherworld was your cup of tea.' He leaned over and kissed her bare shoulder.

Her skin was cool and fragrant and densely female against his lips. Her unfamiliar dreamy mood aroused him, the flowing lines of her shoulders and back and upper arms. Moonrays arched over them, and he thought of light eternally refracting and reflecting through the exploding droplets. All this dramatic *son et lumiere* sparked off by a crack in a sheet of basalt.

'And my experience of the exotic was rather more limited then,' she said.

There was no hotel at Victoria Falls, but during the monthly incidence of the lunar rainbows the railway company prepared an 'African supper' for its passengers. Consomme of impala, crocodile cocktail, roast of wart-hog or Egyptian goose served at sunset on a raised landing by a quiet creek and reed bed of the Zambezi. A champagne toast to the vivid sunset, another to herald the arrival of the night-rainbows and, between these events, the bravado of dining on some of the same wild creatures filing down to the river's edge before them.

As the moon rose, vervet monkeys used the moonlight to

dart across the deck, snatch from plates and upset sugar bowls. Natives topping up champagne glasses threw shadows across the tables. The river flowed only feet away. He was drinking champagne with gusto, and in the optimistic warmth of the evening it seemed to him not impossible that all living forms could rise up out of that deep, heavy water.

As Angelica slowly sipped her champagne, however, she felt her mood changing with the miasmal humidity settling in the dark ferns and blood lilies. This creek was only a mile above the falls, but so subtle and slow it could have been a hundred miles upriver. Damp mud and algal smells, the mineral rot of driftwood came to her.

She thought abruptly of Kate. She saw Kate suddenly as an Edgar Allan Poe character. Poe favoured water that was deep, dormant and still—full of black suffering. She thought: death associated with water is more dream-like than death associated with land. The pain of water is infinite.

Poe's water images usually followed his main preoccupation, a reverie of death dominated by the image of a dying mother. The fact that this had occurred to her gave her a start.

It had been a long while since she had allowed herself to think of her mother.

She stared into the bush and drank more champagne without tasting it. When she was little, her father was always quoting the raven nevermore. 'Mr Poe' was his funny lugubrious voice. She thought of Ham rampant and full of claret at the Sunday lunch table. Oozing roast meats, hooting guests. Her mother laughing gaily, hanging on his performance. Her mother confiding to her in the kitchen in waves of gin: 'You know during *The School for Scandal* he rogered Ellen Terry.'

Will said, 'I bet the natives don't eat crocodile. I think there is a rule: Don't eat anything that eats you.'

'It tasted like lobster cocktail,' she said. She heard her voice as if it were someone else's. 'Surprisingly mild.'

He watched the moonlight softening the strong planes of her face.

'The wart-hog was the same as pork,' he said. 'Crackling, apple sauce and all.'

Shapes moved just within the limits of her vision. Elephants silently materialising. Rows of zebras without fuss. Little sidling jackals. Giraffes angling down to drink. *Sorry, elephant, zebra, jackal, giraffe singular. When I was a little girl I had two dog and three cat. Countless guineapig. Three Shetland pony. The aviary was full of bird.*

'I'm glad you're here,' he said.

Beyond her range of vision things buzzed and occasionally trumpeted in the waterberry and monkeybread trees. Nearer lay the shape of a hippo carcass, swollen mauve in the moonlight. It was a female, she knew, stranded like a seaside toy on a sandbank. Bile-lemon crocodiles sinking down to feed on her.

She felt the pulling-away sensation, the rush.

'We'll never forget this,' he said, stroking her arm. 'Do look at those rainbows.'

She felt a gush of blood.

In their compartment they slept most of the way to Bulawayo. She slept on to Salisbury, too, and when they made love on the Salisbury-Umtali leg she lay damp and still, not passive so much as pulpy and dormant, a continuous framed rectangle of prickly tree-crowns, buzzards, steely clouds streaming past her eyes while he jerked and shuddered inside her.

He apologised for the haste. 'It's been three days.'

'*My boy*,' she said, patting him. She was able to slide out from under him, glad of the quick end to it. His body as he self-consciously washed himself from the carafe was giving off an odour like the cargoes of salted sharks on the way to Zanzibar.

A hundred miles from Umtali, her senses were far beyond acute. She noticed she was still spotting, and she was shocked by the hot gun-metal smell of her brown blood.

The water in the carafe smelled acrid and swampy, the dust on the varnished windowsill seemed as rich as loam, and she had to keep the window closed against the impossible proximity of animal spray and dung dust and carcass rot. She ached for boiling water and disinfectant. She could *hear* the smells and stains of Africa, their high sour whine and guttural buzz.

The crumpled ball of cloth wrapped in a copy of the *Rhodesia Herald* reverberating under the seat.

The opaque smear of baboon drops on the blue fabric.

She paced and fretted with her churning thoughts: leave me alone, take notice of me. He was calmly reading a book called *The Matabele at Home*. It was when she looked up at him with pink-rimmed eyes and asked, like a strange child, 'Could you please tell them to drive the train more slowly?' that he took notice.

He watched her open the window and throw the blue dress from the train. Into Africa. Saw it catch on the gesturing branches of some thorny African acacia and disappear.

'We're leaving far too many fingerprints,' she said, closing the window quickly. She wet her handkerchief from the carafe and rubbed at those prints on the latch whose whorls seemed about to lasso and choke her. Her eyes glittered as they glanced about for more things to clean.

In Salisbury they had bought two Shona sculptures of emerald soapstone, heavy and cool, really far too cumbersome to lug across the world. The sculptor, a bright-eyed young man who spoke some English, told Angelica her statue was called *The Impala Child*. Will's, he explained with much flickering of his fingers, was *Woman Turning into a Bird*. Soon she lay along the seat with an arm around each sculpture, trying to absorb their green, marine cold into her body, alternating her burning forehead against their sheen.

Blackwater fever had taken firm hold by the time they crossed the Odzi River into Umtali.

In the Africans' wards each patient has his or her 'bottler' by the bed, a relative who sits there simulating the sound of water with his thumbs on a little hollow-boxed water-piano.

The liquid sounds of Africa flow into the Europeans' ward, and to her the mingled burbling of the bottlers sounds like gadflies and creates dream-memories of warm days in the meadows.

The whole Umtali district is crisscrossed by the upper tributaries of the Odzi—the Odzani, Umtali, Sabukra, Dora and M'pudzi rivers—and the river people cannot sleep without the patter and gurgle of running water. Not just any water but their own familiar stream. So each bottler plays a special rhythm.

In the hospital at Umtali, assisted by the bottlers' sounds, she, too, sleeps. Almost in a daze himself, Will stays by her bed watching her tossing in waves of delirium, wiping her face, cleaning her mess, fanning her with a damp raffia fan to the thrumming of the water-pianos. As days pass it dawns on him that the African bottlers are *speaking in water*. Speaking in the many sounds of water to the patients and each other.

He supposes they speak about the white woman with blackwater fever. Perhaps it's because they make it clear to him with their trickling and pattering sounds that water is the mistress of smooth flowing language, of continued and continuing language, of language that softens harsh problems and gives a uniform substance to the differing rhythms of life, that he feels almost fatalistically calm.

They are playing in the river after a late Sunday lunch. It's really only a stream at the bottom of the meadow behind their summer cottage. Silly, dank King Neptune hair of duckweed and reeds trails over his face and ears. She and Kate are climbing him, squealing, standing on his knees, using his thighs as a ladder, sliding down his sleek back, balancing on his shoulders. He easily throws them off and ducks them. Rubs his scratchy face of weeds and whiskers over them.

He's chuckling, too, as he holds her squirming beneath the surface. But King Neptune goes too far. She's panicking and spluttering. She's only a child pressed into the river ooze by his big hands.

All around them is that soft, gurgling buzz, like the patter of rain on newspaper. Unlike the noise of any other fly: the appreciative sound of the gadfly's love.

Especially its desire for florid, full-blooded victims. Its dirty grey-brown body lands on his bare back and creeps up to the creases of his juicy neck and stabs deep. Even though she's under water and he's holding her there, she wants to warn him, to shout, but of course she can only babble. The gadfly is swelling with blood as her father fades and shrivels, and it stays there, so engrossed in its feast of blood it doesn't see the hand raised to swat it.

*Whose hand?* It can't be hers, she's *drowning. Kate's?*

Strange that she feels the sting of the slap.

'She's back again,' a distant voice says, coming closer. Will's tired, red but younger eyes looking into hers.

# ENTROPY

THEY CROSSED THE INDIAN OCEAN with the Roaring Forties in their ears and coat collars. Three weeks from Africa, four months since England, they sailed into the Southern Ocean. Only Antarctica lay further south. This alone is enough to make Will feel accomplished and adventurous, and when the *Oceana* steams into Albany, a little mail-packet port on the rim of King George's Sound, a wide sandy bay on the southern coast of Western Australia, the optimism of pioneers and explorers floods his soul.

On deck, he takes her arm and leans into the breeze. Salt mist drifts in their faces and dusts their lips. Smells of coal and kelp, whale oil and eucalyptus waft on the air. He feels ready for anything. Since Africa slipped over the horizon her fever attacks have not recurred. Their arrival at last in this newest of places, her pink colour in the sharp air, fills him with hope.

Mistaking their steamer for a whaler, a school of pale sharks pilots them through a swell into the harbour. Standing at the rail, Will can feel through her layers of clothing the buoyancy of her breast against his side.

'All this ozone! At least my lungs feel well here,' she says.

He leans into her breast and wills this healthier person to prevail. He's tense with excitement and the grandeur of opportunity. He winks at her.

'Your lovely lungs.'

Her thinner body rocks slightly back and forth from him to the rail. As she gazes towards the land she's touching him, not touching, then touching again. Soon, unable to tell if they are touching or not, he welcomes her hair flying against his cheek.

'Very scenic,' she says. 'I feel things have changed, don't you?'

'Yes.'

As usual every wave below them is apparently distinct but intrinsic to the limitless whole. But now there is a green and white shoreline for the waves to bounce against, a stretch of land to bring visual relief, a border to control and balance the infinite.

He takes it she means a change for the better.

'Yes, I do,' he says again.

There had been moments in the past three weeks when standing alone at the ship's rail looking out on the hills and valleys of unending water he had allowed enticing fears to suggest themselves.

Calenture, it was called: the impulse, well known to sailors, to jump into the sea. It had not been excessively hot, he hadn't felt feverish, but he'd found himself every day imagining the sea was a limitless green field and to leap into it a seductive and refreshing idea. Rather, he'd found himself imagining what it was like to imagine this were so. To pretend he had the impulse. But it amounted to the same thing.

He indulged many morbid thoughts. The most desolating sight on the planet: a rapidly diminishing ship's stern. Then the intolerable loneliness of treading water, the terror of limitless depth, the intense concentration of self in the middle of the cold and choking immensity. The sinking down.

Why indulge them? Why retreat to an eleven-year-old's self-pity? Perhaps because one night, after a week at sea, she'd said, turning her face to the bulkhead again: 'I'm afraid I'm in hibernation. I want to shelter from the physical for a time.' And added, 'It's no fault of yours.'

He'd simply touched her bare hip. Trailed his fingers affectionately along the curve. He felt stupid now and began to murmur, 'But I'm not . . .' The thing was, she was still sleeping naked, sprawled on the lower bunk with only a thin sheet twisted around her legs.

Simply patted her.

'I'm not ready to be touched.'

A congested sound came from him. He wanted to hush her before she went too far. He heard himself say some odd words: 'I'm not impatient.' After all, he was a mature twenty-three.

Wasn't water supposed to calm, to soothe, to release inhibitions? But the sea had doused her fervour along with her fever. She slept night and day while he sat on deck reading Marcus Clarke's *For the Term of His Natural Life* and paced and drank. At dusk she would surface, blinking into the haze off the high swells and, after a turn around the deck before supper, they would stand together at the rail watching the unfamiliar sight of the red sun sliding into the sea.

'The male sun sinks into the female sea,' she said, one pink and greenish evening in the middle of the Indian Ocean.

He thought about this.

'Sometimes it looks like a whale, sometimes a swan,' she said. 'But definitely male.'

'I can't see it as a swan. A whale or a turtle maybe. Males are more turtles than swans.'

He pulled his neck into his jacket and made a turtle face. Although he was hurt he was generally behaving with the genial, middle-aged dignity of a labrador pushed from the hearth.

That night in their cabin her hand touched his wrist and she said quietly, 'It's just that I don't want to be acted upon.'

'*Upon?* You mean *with.*'

After a while she said, 'I could still touch *you.*'

He didn't act. He waited. He obeyed. She solemnly undid some of his buttons. So he undressed. He may have wondered why she sprinkled him first with eau de Cologne, then talcum, before giving him a light massage, but she couldn't tell him he smelled of dried shark to her.

Under the perfume and powder he was all knots and tension in the neck and legs and shoulders. She was still clothed, of course, without the strength to press or knead him firmly, but she made an effort to relax his thighs, trying to use her diminished weight to stretch and open the pelvis–thigh connection, and even rocking for greater effect.

He lay naked and still, with his eyes closed, willing her to at least drop her hair on him, but she did not.

When he opened his eyes, hers were closed. Her face was angled away toward the porthole. She was an expressionless profile, present but barely there. In the rolling and creaking of the ship she was just a bunched backhand butterflying of the fingers, acting quickly upon him, and as he came he felt self-conscious and shamed.

If it's momentarily disconcerting that no one is at the wharf at Albany to meet them, the day is sharp and bright and he's keen to stay cheerful for both their sakes.

He stays cheerful when they discover that the boat train for Perth, the capital, doesn't leave until next morning, and that they will need a hotel room for the night. (Engineer-in-Chief O'Connor's new steamship harbour at Fremantle, a more convenient twelve miles from the capital, is still under construction.) Finding neither porter nor cab, Will pays the harbourmaster to store their luggage in his shed and they set out, following the harbourmaster's laconic directions, to walk the half-mile uphill into town.

The road of crushed rocks and seashells, smeared frequently with some flattened furry or scaly animal, sways under their sea-legs. A crow pecking at a wallaby corpse starts to flap away as they pass, but decides against it. While their shoes slide uncomfortably on the shells, a clump of barefoot children, rushing past them down to the harbour with fishing rods and bounding dogs, scamper heedlessly over the jagged surface.

As they grow warmer with the climb they attract sticky bush-flies, and they keep swiping at the cloud settling, scattering and immediately resettling on each other's damp shoulder blades. Thus they stumble over the limestone threshold of the first hotel on the road, impressing themselves on the publican and drinkers as a hot, overdressed and quaintly flapping young English couple.

The red-faced publican is loath to leave his seamen cronies to attend to them. 'Emma will look after you,' he grunts, whisky in hand, and to sly, off-stage laughter a deeply sighing chambermaid, as if granting them a great personal favour, shows them to a room.

The bed is rumpled. At his frown, the girl says, 'The sheets will be clean enough. The last man only slept in it one night.'

So their first night in this most remote part of the world passes with Angelica lying fully dressed and covered by her cloak on top of the bedclothes while Will tosses fitfully under the covers on the sagging mattress. Remote but strangely familiar, this little port, as below them in the street men laugh and shout in several British accents and sing and vomit into the night.

Whenever he glimpses her pale motionless profile she seems to be awake, but he can't be sure. All night she lies prone and pale as a statue. Once, woken by a shambling fight on the crunching seashells of the street, he thinks he sees a small smile on her lips and takes it for amusement at their situation, or even a good dream, but it might have been moonlight.

It's still early morning when they board a train on the new Great Southern Railway. The bare clay and yellow sand and splintered tree stumps of the railway cuttings are still raw scars in the thick bush. Through high eucalyptus forests echoing with the carolling and screeching of birds, past an occasional small, lush dairy farm or orchard, they travel the two hundred and fifty miles north and west.

After travelling a hundred miles, Will thinks the Chief has exaggerated. He has never seen such high, thick timber. Desert? This temperate, well-watered place of olive-green?

A bungalow has been provided by the Department of Public Works in South Perth, across the Swan River from the city. A long white sand-spit, crowded by day with resting seagulls and shags, pelicans and black swans, spears past their front gate into the river. Stands of bamboo and paperbark trees separate their low-lying back garden from ten or twelve acres of Chinese market gardens and, beyond, the city's zoological gardens.

The lions wake them each morning. The house is airy and spacious, with a wide verandah to catch the sea breeze. At dawn its thin lattice shakes with the lions' roars, their moaning rhythm reverberating over the cabbage and beetroot beds and through the bamboo and paperbark trees and into their dreams.

'Who'd have thought we'd have our own piece of Africa?' he says on the first morning. He looks anxiously for her reaction. His own scalp is still tingling but she seems calm enough.

'Now we don't need an alarm clock,' she says.

Woken daily by the lions, he forms the habit of a dawn walk along the sandy shore. The river before him is really more than a river. Between their bungalow and the town a mile north it's an oval lake. Beyond the sand-spit it turns west into a wide estuary five or six miles across, winds placidly for twelve miles, creating bay after bay as it goes, before suddenly contracting into a narrow, swirling sea-mouth at the Indian Ocean. Throughout its whole length and width at this hour, almost to the horizon, its silken grey surface is intermittently ruffled and shirred by schooling fish.

Most mornings as he strolls around the rushes and paperbark trees of the bank, thin Aboriginal boys are wading in the river, fishing with boomerangs and spears. Hundreds of swans are fishing, too, and with their dark, wet sheen and thin angularity—and with their necks looping from the surface like sinuous arms—they seem closely related to the dark, darting boys.

Although it's still officially spring the weather is becoming warmer each day. Spring slides imperceptibly into hot summer. One warm morning he wades into the shallows, drawn by water so smooth his impulse is to knife into it, to break the glassy skin with the precision of the swans and the Aboriginal boys, without sound or splash.

The river flowing around his thighs is colder than he expected. But he dives in and thrashes about until that moment of ecstasy when the blood recovers from the shock and the water temperature miraculously rises around him. Little blowfish dart about his toes. Velvety brown jellyfish bob by. The water is brackish with ocean salt and thick with life. Algaes, planktons, minute weed-shreds. He will gradually learn the names of the river fish—tailor, mullet, whiting, flounder, kingfish and cobbler—but this morning the only one he recognises is a stranded octopus carried in from the sea and left in a rock pool by the night's high tide.

He returns home wet-haired, bare-chested, his shirt bundled in his hands, charged with a skittish, boyish energy from his swim. Angelica is eating marmalade toast. She notices his flushed face and the sun's rays coming through the lattice accentuating the pallor of his skin and the blue veins of his chest. A joke plays around his eyes. Around the ribs and shoulders—everywhere but his teasing eyes—he looks sixteen to her.

'Home is the hunter,' he says, and shakes the shirt over the breakfast table.

The octopus slides in stages from the shirt, gravity finally defeating its hold, and plops on to the cruet. It entwines the cruet, absorbs it, abandons it. It's the size of a dinner plate and missing a tentacle. The other arms sidle tentatively over the cutlery, grip things, release them. In the absence of a crevice to hide in, it finally draws up defensively against her tea saucer.

He expects a squeal, at least a catch of breath.

She puts down her toast. What is this bony youth about, standing there grinning and shivering, with the sun patching his milky-blue chest and his hair dripping down?

She reaches out and allows a line of suckers to fasten on her hand. The other tentacles also enfold her wrist as she hoists up the creature like a Gorgon's head over the table. She looks at Will curiously—she has never noticed his chest so thin or the veins so close to the surface before—and walks from the room wearing the octopus glove.

Through the lattice he watches her quick progress across the verandah, across the front garden, the road, the sandy river bank. She kicks off her shoes, wades into the shallows and pushes her arm into the river, swirls it about, and after a moment she straightens and walks back to the house.

He used to tell himself it was just her nature and upbringing. Her blood. Her profession. That she could jump so quickly from one role to another. From humorous to solemn. *After all, she is an actress.* In the middle of lovemaking he would be looking at her expression, waiting for her features to be transformed. Not knowing whether he was kissing Portia or flower seller, tragic heroine or strumpet. He doesn't know any more what the real *her* is. Much of the time she is simply expressionless. Has she changed entirely or has another Angelica become dominant lately?

*After all, she is an actress.* His old impressed-but-mystified feeling has become plain confusion.

After the octopus joke, travelling on the paddlewheel ferry to the city, to the Department of Public Works, he sits on deck recalling her in the days when they made love, or even kissed on the mouth. Whatever role she was playing, she always closed her eyes. Even when she massaged him. What he had put down to swooning now seems a dogged refusal to face up to love.

He turns his back on the sun's glare and looks back towards the bungalow shimmering in a mirage of quivering light. The sensation is like the warning of an approaching migraine headache. He's struck by the bright, blunt morning, the ferry's swirling coal smoke, the steady, capable drumming of the paddlewheel, the diced jellyfish bouncing in the wake—the realistic, pessimistic here-and-now.

He has caught her latest mood. He thinks how easy it is for the grandest adventure to be negated by a look, a remark, a silence. Maybe worse than missed opportunities are those not missed which should have been.

Her blood. He can't say the word he's thinking, even in his head. Her other inheritance.

The river had dictated the position and design of the capital. Placed on the rim of a remote continent of immense space, the town had nonetheless been drawn up seventy years before on a tight English urban-provincial grid pattern, with narrow main streets running along the river flats parallel to the river.

Jostling his way through the crowds along a narrow footpath of oyster shells and sand, Will saw how the early planners had actually created two towns within the one. There was the lovely town comprising the elegant and wealthy St George's Terrace and Adelaide Terrace and their bisecting streets, with their macadamised road surfaces, Governor's mansion, river views, shady Cape lilac trees and stately commercial buildings and residences. And the three streets of hotels and shops and boarding houses and small businesses running behind them seemed bustling and prosperous, if only because of the narrowness of the limestone roadways.

But directly north and east of these pinched city blocks the road turned abruptly to dirty sand. Here, in an old mulberry plantation far from the river and the social whirl of the Governor's parties, was another town for the poor, sick and homeless, for the refugees and immigrants and the thousands of would-be or luckless gold diggers. A stinking, crowded camp of tents and lean-tos whose refuse drained into the sand and whose inhabitants, those lucky enough to escape typhoid, were driven mad by the bites of sand fleas and bush flies.

This city represented both joy and frustration. He desperately wanted it to mirror his own grand visions, to look back on Europe and Asia and Africa, and forward across the river to the future.

What he wished was to impress her with it, and with his place in it.

He walked up from the ferry wharf through a sea of men's hats, a cacophony of voices and clashing musical instruments. From the brewery the rich aroma of hops wafted in the bright air. At any time of the day or night the streets were thronged with crowds of men on their way to or from the goldfields, drawn to the hotels from whose balconies spruikers and loosely corseted barmaids and sentimental Irish tenors and fiddle players attempted to entice them inside, while at the same time the brass and tambourines of the Salvation Army strained to draw them in the opposite direction.

The easterly wind blew against his back. The early planners had also paid no heed to the prevailing winds. Sea breezes sweeping up the river turned those streets running north and south into fierce wind tunnels, while the longer east-west boulevards (he was now morosely climbing west up the hill of St George's Terrace) efficiently trapped and retained the hot, gritty winds of summer.

In his present mood, arriving in the already sweltering brick offices of O'Connor's Department of Public Works, Will could see why the Chief's band of imported engineers scoffed at their unimaginative predecessors. And at all politicians and newspaper editorial writers since. In this colony of a million square miles, with its three thousand, four hundred miles of coastline stretching from the Timor Sea to the Southern Ocean, the Chief was responsible for, in the words of Premier Forrest, 'railways, harbours, everything'.

Fortunately his recruits were a loyal and enterprising team:

James Thompson, like O'Connor, from Dublin and London and New Zealand, F.W. Martin, W.W. Dartnell, Frank Stevens and A.W. Dillon Bell, from London via New Zealand, all experienced in harbour and railway construction, and John Muir, the engineering surveyor from Victoria. All were in their thirties. By at least ten years, William Dance from Hartbridge, Wiltshire, via Bristol, was the youngest.

They were all accustomed to ill-informed criticism of their grand and radical schemes. For spending too much public money. For being not from here but from somewhere else. But the Chief seemed able to ignore the sniping in the parliament and press. Having recently pushed the new railway east to the goldfields and dredged out his new steamship harbour, he was trying to concentrate on his goldfields water scheme. The parliament had adopted the scheme in principle, then taken two bickering, filibustering years to agree to buy the pipes to carry the water. Only this week had it finally passed the bill to contract the companies chosen to build the pipes for the water main.

Will was to become an expert on water pipes. From that morning the Chief would talk pipes to him constantly, in person and by telegraph, for three years. He would sing the praises of a radical rivetless locking-bar pipe new to the engineering world. It was invented by a Melbourne man named Mephan Ferguson and only recently patented. The beauty of Ferguson's invention, insisted the Chief, was that its design minimised leaks and offered less frictional resistance to the flow of water than the usual riveted pipes.

It had been tried only on a small scale. The longest aqueduct in the world, on an uphill grade, in the world's driest continent, would certainly offer a rigorous test of the revolutionary water pipe.

Implicit in the Chief's enthusiastic lectures to Will was the great good fortune of a brilliant inventor and the one engineer with the imagination and courage to prove the worth of his invention managing to find each other.

So after a busy workday in the strange novelty of a new place, in the intensity of a new project, Will returns home on the ferry that evening, the water and twilight united in cool harmony, and his mood is . . . hopeful.

He can taste the night and smell the perfume of the water. The night is calm and salty. The warm, weedy fetor of sunlit water has gone. The river and the night's offshore breezes have taken on a common fragrance of subtle algaes and blossoms and eucalypts from across the water.

From the ferry's bow he sees the bungalow's lights—first a speck, then a growing glow. Electricity has recently come here. The particular electric light across the narrowing strip of black water owes its existence to her. It's a symbol: it means Angelica. It's the verandah light facing the river which she has switched on as a welcoming sign for him, and it fills him with peaceful resolve.

She is bent over her tarot cards, fanning them out on a red silk scarf, the scarf itself spread smoothly out on the dining table.

Halfway across the Indian Ocean she had first produced the tarot pack from her trunk. She kept the cards bound in the red silk scarf. It had seemed to him an exotic, even over-vital covering for something so mystical and dreamy.

He saw tarot cards in the category of the female and secretive. Even now as he enters the room and kisses her cheek she protectively half-shields them from his intrusion with her hands and the angle of her body. Even trying to avoid looking at them, he catches a flash of the ominous magical symbols: wands, pentacles. He is a Baptist again and struggles to ignore this heathen witchery.

'A lovely evening,' he says. 'And a busy day.'

She smiles wearily, as if it were she who had laboured all day to bring water to the desert. To push water uphill.

He moves behind her chair and begins, tentatively, to rub her neck. 'What have you been doing?'

She sighs, then says, 'Listening, learning.' A pause. 'Writing.'

Beside the cards and red scarf is a pile of paper and three pencils with snapped points. Perhaps fifty pages covered in wavy scribbles. He had forgotten Mr Pitman's hieroglyphics.

The tip of her right index finger is still indented from the pencil.

'Just some notes,' she says.

The sheets of shorthand rustle in the warm evening breeze drifting through the lattice. The way she continues to lean over the table is making it hard for him to rub her neck.

When he stops, she straightens in her chair, quickly scoops

up the tarot cards, bundles them in the scarf and looks up at him with the greenish shrewd eyes of a stranger.

'I've been meaning to mention something,' she says. She shakes her head as if to clear it, and smooths back her hair. 'Your aura has become very ill-defined.'

He looks at her for a long moment. There is a moat around her. Cold, grey fathomless water.

'I'll attend to it at once,' he says, pouring himself a strong whisky.


His aura had changed from blue to grey.

For some weeks now she has seen auras around everyone, and she has seen spirits floating under the stamped-metal wildflowers of the bungalow's ceiling.

The spirits are white and gold and not the least frightening. Quite the opposite—they seem to be offering her silent support. The more encouraging and affectionate, the more golden and plentiful they are. On the other hand, the auras she sees around people's outlines range in colour from deep happy blue to a melancholy leaden grey. Of course their clarity, too, can vary from misty to sharp.

This evening, however, it's a different spiritual experience that has tired her. As his ferry pulled out from the jetty and chugged off into the sun and seagulls that morning she'd felt a compulsion to write a letter—to whom she wasn't sure. The ferry had moved off so slowly. She knew the boat was carrying too much weight—all the souls aboard were heavy. She couldn't grab up pen, ink and paper fast enough. She had just written *Dear . . .* when she threw the pen aside as too slow and cumbersome and snatched up a pencil.

And then—there was no other explanation for it—her hand had hovered over the paper, and an outside force had come into her arm and hand and begun writing. For a second or two he had written in his old man's spidery, if impatient, longhand the words *Isaac Pitman* and she had felt the weight and fatigue of his years—the crick in his neck!—in her heavy wrist and shoulders, then in mid-sentence—gleefully, youthfully—he had switched to his shorthand.

Oh, he had a lot to say, and in much faster, more proficient shorthand than she had ever managed—at least one hundred and sixty, one hundred and eighty words a minute he was going, her hand whizzing over the paper, whereas she had never progressed beyond a hundred words a minute at her fastest.

She wrote down questions and he answered them, sometimes so eagerly he didn't even wait for her to finish the sentence before jumping in. Soon she found it was enough just to think the question and he would answer it.

She wrote all morning in this spirit-hand, filling page after page until she thought firmly, *I'm too tired to go on*, and immediately the pressure lessened and she found herself writing in his old man's longhand again: *Angelica, dear, is there anyone else you wish to speak to?*

Her scalp tingled, a pulse thumped in her wrist. She was too wrung-out to answer, to write anything but *Tomorrow*. And she had slept all afternoon as the sun beat down on the tiles of the roof and the breeze strengthened and shifted from the east to the south-west and drove off the swans and pelicans from the sand-spit and whipped the river's slick surface into lines of blue waves.

When she woke the sea breeze had dropped and it was after dusk. Warm yeasty air flowed through the lattice. She was consulting the tarot to regain her equilibrium when he arrived home, his grey aura drifting about him like thin fog in the verandah light.

He has learned how Chief O'Connor deals with obstacles in the path of his water scheme.

O'Connor had decided on a site for his main dam on the Helena River at Mundaring, in the Darling Ranges. The dam workers had been digging through gravel and limestone and granite for six months and were down one hundred feet when on the north side of the river they made an extraordinary discovery. A granite boulder eight miles long and two miles wide was lying in their path, detached from the solid rock and overlaying a porous vein. O'Connor hurried to the reservoir site and spent two days examining the problem. The government totted up the cost and pressed him to abandon the site.

'We can remove the boulder,' he said.

Aside from the exhaustive work, this would delay the pouring of the concrete for the dam wall. So he installed an electric lighting plant enabling shifts of men to dig into the night. He commandeered five more drills. And in twelve months his men excavated down a further hundred feet to bedrock and drilled this gigantic boulder to rubble and chips no bigger than house bricks.

Will is at the dam site to hear this background story to the ceremonial pouring of the concrete. There to climb down into the vast hole and try to imagine a granite monolith as big as a city. And to envisage deep clear water lying over where they stood.

A fine day, as the Chief has prayed for. The cool, dry smell of stone dust in the air. Optimistic speeches have been made. Down in the fresh cavity, in the depths of strata of brown and yellow and rusty smears of iron, below a slice of deep blue sky, four barrowmen nervously abseil down the sharp incline to pour the first concrete.

The difficulty of the men's task is lightened by a clever invention of the Chief's: a concrete mixer he has made from a boiler casing, fitted with internal flanges and running on a conveyor.

A shot from a pistol, the barrowmen release a slow grey trickle, then an oozing surge, as officials clap sternly and workmen whistle their ironies.

Her conversations with the spirit of Isaac Pitman have given her a breath of herbs and garlic. Now she carries a notebook and sharpened pencils with her in case a spirit has something to say. And, wrapped in the red scarf, is the tarot to which she refers for a second opinion, on spirit-writing and most other matters.

He is worried about her . . . stability. But to voice his concern would make things worse.

Following Isaac Pitman's shorthand instructions she is using his old herbal nostrums to cleanse her blood of blackwater fever. She has stopped eating meat and visits Li Tun at the Chinese market gardens for dried barks and fungi and whiskery twists of root. She boils them up with long peels of yam and drinks the stinking broth. Will catches her examining her tongue a dozen times a day. Toxins rise to her surfaces: little adolescent pustules on her forehead, between her breasts and shoulder blades. Her hair is greasy, her thin face is all pointed chin, her bones start to stick out and all her body is pasty like her tongue and seems turned to air.

Next thing her breath smells of seaweed. She is boiling up kelp gathered from the shore into a green-black soup.

During these rituals her eyes avoid his. She leaves notes for herself in shorthand which are meant to exclude him, although he can tell the difference between her marks and scratchings and those dictated by Isaac Pitman.

Woken by vivid, violent dreams, she rises in the night. His thrown-out leg finding empty space, he comes into the dining room to find her bending naked over the tarot.

And unable in the night to hide his anxiety, aching to touch her, he whines like a child, 'What are you doing?'

She is in a fugue. For weeks she has the look of someone mentally and physically separated from her surroundings. In the face of her distracted intensity, sighing resentments and kelp breath, he is helpless.

So he crosses the river. He escapes into his work, into Mephan Ferguson's interlocking pipes, into the technical problems of temperature, heat and gradient, of caulking and hydraulics, of distance and the reckless openness of the landscape.

This is a landscape of such stark space and beauty that reason can only try to defy it. Small boys kneel on the ferry jetty burning ants with magnifying glasses. From these tiny squirming fires rise little plumes of smoke and the acrid smell of hot varnish. A dog barks all day at a stationary goanna with a blue tongue. A laughing bird shakes a snake five times its length in its beak. Pink trees with the delicate texture of moist flesh sprout from the sand; to touch their soft trunks leaves fingerprints. And all around the city bushfires burn, defining the sky and heat.

This is a landscape to easily make him curt and undemonstrative in return. White flowers, white sand everywhere, the sun glinting off the limestone and oyster-shell footpaths, can bring on headaches. So the eyes of newcomers are constantly guarded and squinting against the glare and its flickering surprises.

Bone-weary of moods and crazes, every day he's grateful to be able to cross the river.

He takes to recrossing the river several hours later of an evening. Instead of catching the dusk ferry home, he works late and joins his colleagues in the Weld Club for an hour or two. It relaxes Chief O'Connor to entertain his engineers over whisky in the Strangers' Room of his club and point out the basic mistakes of planners and politicians.

One Friday evening the Chief is in typical form, announcing cheerfully, as if it had just occurred to him, that the early planners had got the climate wrong. Because the Andes had snow at this latitude on the west coast of South America, they had decided it would be the case here. 'They forgot to take into account the small matter of altitude.'

His eyes are twinkling. He allows the chortles to subside before continuing.

They had also got the rocks wrong, concluding that there was coal here because of the prevalence of limestone. 'But of course it's coastal limestone from the Pleistocene Age, not Carboniferous like the mountain limestone of the Pennines.'

'Of course,' echo his engineers.

They had even got the trees wrong, mistakenly believing that if the trees were tall and green then the river flats must be fertile and productive.

'Even this place,' says the Chief expansively, of the red brick, Queen Anne-style club with its belvedere tower looking obliquely across the Esplanade to the river. 'Designed so the sea breeze blows into the members' room and the Chinese servants' quarters are hidden from sight. Meanwhile the chimneys smoke, the dining room's so stuffy you can't breathe, the drains clog, there's six inches of water in the cellar and the skylights leak on the billiard tables.'

Will seems to have been awake and anxious ever since he can remember. Ever since the pre-dawn zoo noises had set his heart thudding weeks ago. He's drinking too quickly.

'I like the trees and rocks here,' he says.

He feels bound to defend the misinterpreted trees. He voices his admiration for the tall, olive-green Swan River mahogany or jarrah, the grey-green tuart, the darker Swan River cypress. He likes the bloodwood or marri, too, and the blue-grey tinged peppermint tree, 'like a less droopy English willow'.

He's expansive and vocal. Just this side of overwrought.

There are many guests in the club that evening, sunburned and enthusiastic from outback adventures. Lord Percy Douglas, the aristocrat turned explorer and mining entrepreneur. A young American mining engineer, Herbert C. Hoover. The author Rolf Boldrewood. They are introduced. Will downs his whisky and tells the amiable, winking faces how from his verandah the treetops look like an ocean swell rolling and tossing in the sea breeze. His waving arms describe a surf of hissing bamboo, an ocean of eucalypts, voluptuous and edgy.

'In the wind their trunks groan and spasm like women coming,' he announces to the Strangers' Room of the Weld Club.

The room is still. Someone snorts. The Chief clears his throat. He pats his shoulder like an uncle.

As for rocks, Will says the pale limestone cliffs give this strange, bare coast the look of the moon.

'I'm a moonraker myself,' he adds. 'A drowner. The last of the line.'

❀

She couldn't describe to him how she felt disassembled. It wasn't so much being far from home, living on a windy sandspit by a river in the Antipodes, that was affecting her. It was not, although Will could not believe this, to do with him.

She felt it when he was present and when, like this evening, he was late returning from the city. In a way the feeling made her oblivious to him. It was a feeling that her soul had left her.

She was desperate to fill the vacuum. So she was quite calm and firm in her intention as she left the house and pushed through the barrier of dark bamboo and paperbark trees and climbed over the back fence into the darker market gardens.

Here the wind dropped and her feet sank in sighing heaps of fishy seaweed mulch. Sighting along a gleaming line of cauliflowers, she picked her way to the shed where Li Tun and the other gardeners lived among piles of hessian sacks and wooden crates. By day, when she bought herbs here, the shed just smelled of stale sweat and shallots. Now the smell was sweeter and more acrid, like boiling yams. Li Tun and three older men lay on sacks smoking pipes. A young man was steaming rice in a pot. Something cooking seemed to give off whiffs of semen. A plucked swan, neck lolling, hung from a hook.

Li Tun, grunting, took it she'd come for more herbs.

'No ginseng,' he said. He didn't get up.

The men stared at her. Their leathered faces were faintly lit from below: a lamp on the floor shadowing their eyesockets. Tight skin shining across their cheekbones and foreheads. Skulls came to mind.

'I want to buy . . . opium.'

She took out some money.

At the dining table she took up a pencil and looked out at the bright lamps of the crabbing parties on the jetty, the distant creeping lanterns of the prawners in the shallows, then back to the paper in front of her. She held the pencil over the paper and began, tentatively, to write.

It wasn't her soul back again, but it was a definite light, tingling presence, and through her it began to write with increasing strength.

*Darling,* it began.

Remorseful the next day, he asked her to come outdoors with him. A Saturday picnic. On the ferry she was quiet, but followed him out on deck and allowed the air and the slapping momentum of the paddlewheel to shake out her indoor cobwebs. They sat at the bow and raised their faces into the breezy sunlight.

He took her up to Mount Eliza from where the city and the river and the smoky eastern ranges all stretched within their frame of view. Picnicking to magpies' warbling and the gentle thud and scratching of animals moving through the bush, she seemed almost herself.

The grass beneath them, the smell of the sun on her hair reminded him of the Avon river bank. The willow tree, the chirping insects, the bed of rushes under their bodies. The way she had first kneeled and touched him. Their happy tongues on each other.

He moved closer and touched the warm hair. Ran his finger up her parting.

'You're bluer today,' she said. He took this as good news for his aura. Her eyes were not evasive, her movements no longer skittish. She nibbled an everyday sandwich of potted meat.

'It must be the sky,' he said, 'or my headache.'

From their vantage point it wasn't hard to imagine the sky leaking over its borders. Its individual particles of pigment gleaming sharply blue. This sky was not a neutral ceiling for the landscape. It was a force. It pressed on the low hills, forcing them to make a horizon with the river.

'Idyllic,' she said.

He was so grateful and aroused and hungover he could have made instant love under the peppermint trees, or fallen asleep. He brushed her hip and was startled to feel the sharpness of her pelvic bone.

'I'm glad you're back,' he said.

Her smile was bright and unfamiliar. Her hand on his wrist—the way it entered his sleeve to stroke his veins and hairs—was arousing, but her creeping fingers seemed thinner, bird-like and insistent. When she saw the effect they were having on him she giggled and lightly smacked his wrist.

This was a new side to her: coquettish.

But at the moment he would smile at any whim. He watched her carefully. He saw her lift her chin to the sun and toss back her hair like someone being an actress.

In the sunset Angelica stands naked in water to her thighs. She has discovered a particular cool current streaming here from a tributary in the ranges that she says is fresh enough to bathe in. He sits on the bank and watches the tips of her hair brushing the water as she wades into the river.

The movements of her body seem to ignore him. At the same time, as if not completely discouraging a voyeur, they subtly acknowledge his presence. This is the relationship of the performer and her audience. When she's deep enough she faces the shore, still without glancing at him, and swings the heavy fall of hair at him and then lowers it into the water. The last sunrays glance off her shoulders as she bends. Her breasts dip to the surface. The water laps at her sleek pelvis. Then she straightens up, still facing him but not looking at him, and briskly gathers up her hair and squeezes out the water.

Her waterfall of hair.

Now she bobs and bends again. She drops her hair in the river with a wide looping movement and then straightens again and flings it in a sweep of sparkling droplets. Her mouth is open, almost smiling, as she tosses back her head. The sun is setting over the river mouth and her white body moves in the eddies of swirling evening fish. The darkening backcloth of Mount Eliza looms behind as she swings her arms before her. She bows her head and catches her cascade of hair and holds it like a first-night bouquet.

He sits stunned, moved by the performance and by her restive beauty. He had forgotten she was such an actress. Then he claps his hands and turns as if to share the sight of the show with the whispering audience of paperbark trees. The men from the Chinese vegetable gardens are watching avidly from the leaves.

They are making hissing, clicking sounds, like bamboo stems crisscrossing in the breeze. He calls out, 'Hey!' but they are already rustling off into the bushes, hissing through their teeth, clicking their tongues, a couple of them rubbing their crotches and glancing back slyly as they go.

Before she is out of the river he's wading in, knee-deep, holding out the towel for her.

Back home she moves towards him, flirtatious as a new lover. Pungent hints of caged animals and vegetable combustion stream inside on the warm easterly. And with the whiffs of ammonia the indignant squeals of some bothered zoo beast.

She has prepared a pipe. It has a bamboo stem and she offers it to him with the actressy smile of the picnic.

'Smoke this with me?'

He's astonished. She may as well have asked his mother's son, the boy from the Ebenezer Chapel, to join the pagans. He looks at the pipe, then at her. He nods.

Lights blink on the dark water. She is in charge, laying cushions on the verandah floor. They lie side by side and share the pipe. Organic and inorganic fantasies seem to pass between them and mingle in the moonlight. From a sandy sunlit hill, a view of apes scuttling in the poppy beds and cabbage rows. For a time—a minute? an hour?—he massages her body. He is magically able to do this from a distance. And to observe the desert and garden zephyrs drifting through the lattice and playing over their bare skin.

The warm air graces his lingering touches. It buoys him up. It sustains a stroking carnal act of great lassitude. Limitless depth and time.

He sees, hears, himself murmuring, 'At last.'

And, while dreaming he is dreaming, there appears at the jungle verge of these animal, vegetable and mineral dreams a close-at-hand and repeatedly coughing lion. The lion's skin is made up of a multitude of pale dots. He tries to stir himself but cannot, and waves it away with a languid hand.

When they eventually wake on the verandah in strong daylight the wind is sharp, the lions have long ceased roaring and Hammond Lloyd is sitting in a deckchair in a white linen suit, drinking a cup of tea and looking down at them.

He places his cup and saucer on the floor and his jacket falls open, revealing a pistol in a pigskin shoulder-holster. For what seems minutes no one speaks. Someone's breath is whistling, a mucousy catch in the throat.

Angelica and Will are drawn up, all goose-fleshed limbs together, on the same small brocaded cushion.

'I am here,' Ham says eventually, 'in a play.'

'You have a gun,' she says.

'A precaution for the wilderness. For the natives and animals.'

'You surprised us.'

'I coughed several times and moved loudly about. But you were not in this world.'

'Well,' she says crossly, and her breasts quiver as she waves in the direction of the sand-spit. 'You will have to move about in the wilderness while we dress.'

He gets up slowly. 'When you are ready, I have things to say.'

Will is numb. He has a headache and his mouth is dry.

As they gather up their clothes Ham is sighting along his pistol barrel at a swan.

It seems Western Australian gold had inspired not only the investors of London but the London stage as well. After commissioning the noted colonial photographer Axel Boehm to photograph goldmines and miners, mining camps and goldfields scenery, and paying him one hundred pounds for a selection of negatives, the theatrical impresario Sir Augustus Harris, the lessee of Drury Lane Theatre, had instructed the artist Theodore Bush to draw inspiration from the prints and repaint his theatre into a 'Panorama of the Golden West'.

This elaborate redecoration was to acquaint Londoners with 'authentic atmosphere' for a production of *The Princess of the Golden West*, a drama inspired by the discovery of the Londonderry gold reef. It would play to packed houses at Drury Lane, and now a Harris protégé, Marcus Doyle, had— rather bravely—brought *The Princess of the Golden West*, with the great Hammond Lloyd from the original cast, to the Golden West itself.

The famous visiting actor doesn't look enthusiastic at the prospect. He's pink and hot but declines to take off his jacket. If he did, Will wonders, would he remove the shoulder holster?

Ham looks solemnly at Angelica. He is yet to acknowledge Will.

'Your mother has passed away.'

Her calm is astonishing. 'Yes. When exactly? And from what?'

'Three months ago. A paroxysm of the brain. For the best, Little Root.'

'I guessed it. I know she is happier now,' she says. 'The important thing is she won't take disorder on with her.'

'*On*, Sweet One?'

'To wherever she is.'

'I had her interred in Bath. I thought the asylum cemetery was inappropriate.'

Surely she should be weeping, or arguing, by now.

'Did you see her before she died?' she asks, just as calmly.

'You know, Rooty,' Ham says, staring out across the water. 'Our dear Mummy was mad as a hatter and never too ecstatic about the vagabond life of the theatre.'

Something occurs to him then. He is gathering her up in his arms, pressing her face to his lapels and moaning while his tears suddenly stream down.

'She was not like you and me.'

Since the opium pipe of the previous night they have not been alone. Eventually, late in the evening, Ham leaves for his suite in the Palace Hotel. They wave him off on the last ferry, turn away from the white-suited figure on the stern and walk home along the sand. From a crabbing party in the river comes a splash, a yelp, a snatch of laughter. She doesn't resist Will's arm around her.

'The gun!' He laughs. 'I thought I was dead.'

'I thought both of us. I hope he doesn't hurt himself.'

'It's my balls he has in his sights.' A sudden thought. 'You know in England he had me followed?'

'Not always *had you followed* as such. Sometimes it was him.'

He draws her against the soft trunk of a paperbark tree. Its bark strokes against them like loose skin. Many questions are making his heart race, but he is also keen to turn the mood back to the intensity of the verandah.

'Actually, I thought: shoot me now. After last night I don't care!'

'It was a dream.'

'Yes!'

'I mean, you dreamt it.'

'What?'

'You were miles away. You weren't inside me. I should know.'

He steps back from her. A pile of crab and mussel shells crunch underfoot. He almost stumbles.

'It's a pleasant effect of the opium to give men the fantasy of entering.'

He can hardly talk. 'You've noticed this confusion often?'

She doesn't speak, just passes like a superior apparition from the waning light of the ferry wharf into the darkness over the sand.

Appearing in an improbable play a long way from home, with an uncertain director, before an uncritical audience, Hammond Lloyd was at his worst, his performance grandiose and histrionic. *The Princess of the Golden West*, a melodrama about honour and fortune lost and regained, was a huge success.

His every entrance was applauded by a grateful first-night audience prepared to overlook the play's many implausibilities for the rare and flattering experience of seeing a famous English actor represent its own story. Even a bizarre version of it. (The Princess turns out to be a large gold nugget.)

'Didn't he get away with murder?' Angelica says to Will.

'They lapped it up.'

'The naughty boy, he needs a tight rein. I blame the director.'

The opening-night party at the Palace Hotel. Local dignitaries, new gold barons and society matrons are drinking French champagne and fawning over Hammond Lloyd. After five curtain-calls and three glasses of champagne, he is magnanimously sharing credit with the other actors, kissing and lavishly praising even the lowest-ranking members of the cast.

From the chattering throng he spies them. He beckons.

'Oh, God,' she sighs.

Her dress bares her arms and shoulders. As she moves off, Will has an urge to stroke her, to grip her familiar but strange smoothness from behind. Shower her shoulders with kisses. Hold them back. But he follows them, craving that dense, sweet skin.

'Darling girl! Do join us.'

In the few steps it takes her to reach Ham's side, he sees the shoulders realign themselves and become those of some actress.

Something she had said about herself before the theatre still bobbed in his mind. They had been strolling to an early supper. Along Adelaide Terrace the upper classes were making the usual evening celebration out of watering their gardens. The young ladies of Perth liked to dress up and show off their ability to water their lawns and flowerbeds simultaneously with the popular new flexible hosepipes.

'What a stupid waste, pouring water into the sand,' she said. 'It just runs away.'

'That's the point,' he said. He loved the smell of moisture on this summer grass. 'Keeping up an English country garden on arid sand in a hot place with little water is so difficult that everyone wants one. It's a desirable social asset.'

'It's perverse.'

'It's the element of difficulty that makes life interesting.'

'I'm tired of tests,' she said. Just a few hours later, uncomfortably shuffling around the brittle hubbub of the opening-night party, his viewpoint has changed. He is also tired of tests, of constantly pushing uphill. He feels like giving in to gravity for a change.

Her remark keeps coming back to him. As they had sauntered among the sweet atmosphere of dampened couch grass and dewy tea roses, its vehemence had made his skin prickle.

'I want to be selfish,' she said.

They sit quietly on deck on the midnight ferry to South Perth, his arm resting along the rail behind her head. His fingers stroke the rail. When they encounter a bump in the varnished surface, a congealed drip, they worry at it and pick it off, then recommence stroking and smoothing. She sits lightly beside him. Champagne is on their breath. Her perfume drifts toward and past him. Their bodies don't press, rather they tip against each other.

There had been a scene in the play where Ham, playing an aristocratic prospector down on his financial and romantic luck (but not for long), stood in a make-believe stream panning for gold. Will recalls it and laughs.

'The audience got a good chuckle out of the babbling brook.'

'What do you mean?'

'At Ham panning for gold. There are no streams in the goldfields. No rivers.'

'A minor geographical point.'

'Not at all. That's the whole reason I'm here. Why *we* are here. The complete absence of streams in the desert is why we are in this place, why we are sitting here on this ferry now.'

'The drama is the important thing.'

'*Drama.* You've never considered what it is that I do, have you? What engineers do? '

She looks at him steadily. Her face is expressionless and the dark masks her eyes. 'Tell me what it is you do, Will.'

His takes a deep breath and speaks very slowly. 'We change the order of things. And that is as dramatic as life gets.'

She stands up then. A strange smile is on her face. 'An ant changes the order of things. A cabbage. Even an actress.' Then she moves away from him, like any good actress, into the patch of light spilling from the saloon.

She sits on a bench and takes out the tarot pack from her evening bag. The light spills on her bare shoulders and collarbones. Her hands are hurriedly shuffling the cards and starting to spread them on the bench.

'No!'

He is beside her quickly, scooping up cards. Her hands flap at him in protest, her voice is guttural with rage, a growl, but he gathers them up in several swift movements and throws them over the rail into the black water.

Chopped up jellyfish and white cards glistened in the moonlit wake of the paddlewheel. He smelled algae, and hops from the brewery. He looked back at the lights of the receding town, the lights of the hotel of tipsy first-nighters. The king-fish lamps of fishermen glinting on the far bank. The stark mound of Mount Eliza rising up behind them.

'I'm surprised the tarot didn't tell you I'd do that,' he said.

Jellyfish and tarot cards swirling off together in the dark. She looked at him like the bitterest enemy.

'Why did you come here with me?' he asked.

'To escape.'

'And have you?'

She kept staring at the expanse of river, at the tarot cards streaming in the wake. Her hair was out and blowing across her face like a veil.

She is feverish. The fever has come back, with its own insistent reveries, its own point of view.

The memory of him rising from the river of her childhood. His face and shoulders running with duckweed and reeds. King Neptune. Laughing and chasing her, going too far with his snuffling snatches, grabbing her before she can reach the bank. Snorting laughs and bubbling lips catch her, bury their scratchy Neptune beard in her neck and cheeks.

Is it now, the present, as they walk down the gangplank and he follows her from the jetty, along the sand and silently into the river? Yes, it's while she's wading heedlessly out into the black water. Careless of the nips and stings of crabs and cobblers. Needing to cool her fever. Ignoring her soaking dress and leading him into the river.

Anyway, it's with great ease he peels the dress from her, pulls her close, lifts and surprises her, enters her in the shallows of the river.

His pushing is cold, then warm. It sluices water into her. Is she willing or unwilling? Both. Is she to live or die in this moonlit water? Does it matter?

So not helping or hindering, just floating with the moon in her eyes, bouncing in the small waves they make. Meanwhile curious blowfish gently nibbling. Jellyfish sliding against her sides, flounder spinning away like saucers, mullet flicking by.

She feels each particle of algae clinging to her skin. Her hair floating in the tide. In the thick coolness her bones feel straight and light. Water inside her warming to the temperature of her blood. She and water. Part of each other, like the river subtly joining the sky.

While he clasps her thighs and keeps her hoisted on to him.

She can hear him sobbing *I love you* beyond her bobbing breasts. That boy Will from the Roman bath inside her.


Withdrawing, he is phosphorescent as he stands.

The remainder of that night he spends by her bed with glasses of water and damp towels. When her heat swings to convulsive shivering he brings her blankets. When she vomits and voids her bowels he washes her. When she settles he gently plucks shreds of seaweed from her pubic hair and specks of algae from the down of her face.

Her eyes regard him seriously as he tends to her.

'I love you,' he says. The second time in hours, or ever.

'Yes.'

She falls asleep through the lions' first roars.

Too late for him to sleep. The sun comes over the ranges as he starts his ramble along the shore. Swans appear from the pink edge of the horizon, skim into the shallows and settle on the spit. Low tide. The spit is fully exposed, the water so shallow he wades out a hundred yards into the channel before it's deep enough to swim, then it's suddenly so deep he can't touch bottom. The flutter of sails. Yachts pass. Then fishing boats and flat-bottomed timber boats hauling sandal-wood. A pelican's heavy belly passes over him. Below, cold currents twist around his ankles. A childish tremor of fear says her ghosts are whispering down there. He can't bring himself to open his eyes under water, to look down into the depths.

She is still sleeping peacefully when he returns, and when he leaves on the ferry for the Department of Public Works.

At the next low tide he has a vast expanse of time to study the growing contrast between the white of the sand-spit and the black of the adjacent bungalow. He stands in the bow on the evening ferry home. In the absence of the verandah light, the house is submerged by the dark mass of bamboo and paperbark trees.

He has never heard his feet go up the steps before. Clattering through echoing rooms.

What signs of her existence in the trellised bungalow by the Swan River? Do these count? The bamboo opium pipe, a cool soapstone statue, some tangled hairs on the dresser, a ball of screwed-up notepaper. They do not say Angelica.

His shaking hands unfold the notepaper that his brain says her hands have touched so recently. But no message is revealed. Only a couple of mocking shorthand squiggles.

That night he wakes from unhappy dreams, his searching arm and leg finding wide, cold space. A start of sudden dread. The shock increasing as he remembers.

The bed still smelling of her fever. His face in her pillow inhaling the dampish indentation of her head.

He gets up and inspects the house, every cool, empty room. *Just in case.* Maybe she's frowning over her tarot at the dining table. There *are* sounds of life in the house. Cockroaches scuttling, river rats tunnelling in the soft limestone of the foundations. In the ceiling, possums scratch and thump. Stale, malign nature.

On the verandah he fills a deckchair, facing the dark hump of Mount Eliza on the opposite shore. Nodding imperceptibly. Grasping at straws. Thinking that if the ferry was running at this hour, and if someone on deck, a particular young woman, was looking in the direction of the bungalow, she would see the verandah light and consider it welcoming.

He waits two days before walking down the hill from the Department of Public Works to the Palace Hotel.

The suite is the grandest in the hotel, with dual balconies on the top floor corner overlooking both St George's Terrace and William Street. At noon, in his best dark suit, it's not hard to march along the corridor and enter the rooms behind a chambermaid carrying linen.

The famous actor is sitting on the sofa in his shirtsleeves and braces drinking a pre-lunch gin and quinine water and reading the *West Australian*. He doesn't look up, even as Will shoos out the maid and closes the door.

'Where is Angelica?'

Ham looks up then. A mutual thrill, a charge, runs between them. He slowly removes his glasses and says: 'Dear boy, you have ten seconds to leave here.'

He has never seen Ham wearing glasses before. An undershirt shows at his neck. He notices there is no shoulder holster. He smiles.

'This is not a play. Where is she?'

In a rustle of sliding newspaper, Ham stands then, the sky and river merging blue behind him, and rocks on his toes. The room is quiet. From the street below comes the rumbling of beer kegs being trundled from kerb to cellar.

'My dilemma is whether to lay criminal charges against you or just shoot you.'

'Please yourself. I must see her.'

There is a closed jarrah door to one side and he moves towards it and reaches for the handle.

'She is not here,' Ham says, producing the pistol from somewhere and firing it.

He knows instinctively she is there, even with the noise in his head. Or will be there when he opens the door. Although his right hand clutching the handle is shot through, his reflexes continue to turn it and open the door on to the sight of her standing in a white nightdress just now being patterned with his blood.

His own ghostly face stares at him from the bedroom mirror behind her. He notices his hand only because of its effect on her. There are prominent veins there, and his hand is spraying her body and the room between them.

'Hello, you,' she says. She doesn't seem the least surprised. 'Are you all right?'

He feels insane. He laughs and swings his numb hand like a club and blood fans out over the bed.

'It's not as if I use my right hand!'

'He takes extreme measures for me,' she says.

Her mouth moves uncertainly. The hair that tipped the river's surface, that hung down her naked back as she waded, has been cut short. She stands, motionless, for a moment and then brings a towel for his hand, wraps it up and kisses him lightly on the lips.

'You need a doctor.'

'You have blood on your face,' he says. 'Are you coming back?'

She wipes her face on a hotel pillow. Her smile is sad, her mouth still set in a crooked line. Now he notices her pallor under the smears of blood. Her eyelids are pink and swollen and she seems not so much smaller as more concentrated.

'Are *you* all right?'

She nods, then shakes her head.

'Life is too dramatic, Will.'

The big men come into the room then, two thick-armed cellarmen in their leather aprons, with Ham hovering behind them, and they bundle him down the corridor and down the back stairs, swearing at the blood on their clothes, and throw him out into the hot noon street.

The Chief is a formidable sight cantering on his grey hunter out of the dawn mist. Through the shallows and across the spit, scattering swans before him. A thin and straight-backed six-footer, all his control coming from his hips, the early sunrays shooting off his spray, he looks something of a centaur.

The bungalow is built on fine river sand, and the way the drumming hooves make the walls reverberate and the windows rattle, a cavalry regiment could be charging up. One of O'Connor's young daughters rides behind him on another grey. As they pull up, the horses are snorting and streaming with sweat and water, rolling their eyes at the first roars and the sudden whiff of carnivores.

From the verandah, from the chair where he sees the sun come up every morning, Will watches them walk the horses up to the house.

He stands in the doorway, his mouth without moisture, his head aching. He has no choice other than to go outside into the new light. Another day. A steamy haze lifting over the water. On the jetty, black shags meditating like nuns. On the spit, swans drying their wings in the breeze. *Odd, the whiteness they hide under their wings.* He goes barefoot down the steps carrying his bandaged hand in front of him like a shield.

As Chief O'Connor dismounts, Will sees his fine cordovan leather riding boots are stained by spray and salt. His daughter's face is pink from exertion. It's a twelve-mile ride along the bank from their home by the river mouth at Fremantle.

'Good to see you up and about,' O'Connor says, as if he were just a neighbour dropping by.

He nods. 'Good morning.'

'Can Bridget and I trouble you for a cup of tea while these fellows take a breather?'

So civility forces him to break his firm intention and lead some human beings inside his house. A place of soured dreams, leaden auras, this bungalow whose absent spirits echo in his head.

If he wasn't just happening to be riding by, it was certainly O'Connor's habit to start the day with an early morning ride and, in summer, a bathe in the surf. He often spent much of his workday in the saddle.

Indeed, first in Ireland and then in New Zealand he'd found a good horse essential to the job. And during the early stages of his steamship harbour at Fremantle, when dickering government funding was restricting his staff numbers, he'd appointed himself engineer in charge of construction and was on site, on horseback, most of the day.

He'd brought in limestone by cart, and granite by night train from quarries in the Darling Ranges, and built long protective breakwaters north and south of the river mouth and protruding out into the Indian Ocean. Then he'd built a bridge and railway line across the river. He blasted and dredged a channel thirty feet deep through a rock bar across the river mouth which had defied engineers and planners for seventy years. He had the bucket-dredge *Fremantle* working twenty-four hours a day, six days a week, and his submarine blasting had the property owners of Fremantle screaming for peace and compensation. His harbour works finally covered three miles of land, river and ocean and he patrolled all this territory and construction on horseback.

On Moonlight he was a familiar figure to the labourers and tradesmen building the new harbour. And also to the colony's fishermen and coastal traders, boat builders and timber haulers. Always cantering along the breezy shore, or fording the river where the sea and river tides came together, even plunging into the sandy surf to inspect the progress of the harbour dredging or the breakwaters.

He liked to sit on his horse on the headland and eat a ham and pickle sandwich, share a Mount Barker apple and relax by watching water mingle with other water.

As a boy he'd ridden to hounds with his uncle, the master of the Meath hunt. Riding had brought him pleasure ever since. He had the Irish love of a good horse, and the firmness and gentleness to persuade Moonlight, even the more reluctant Prince, to climb a gangway to board ferries for works inspections on Rottnest and Garden islands. He enjoyed hunt club picnics and race meetings. Only this spring, carrying twelve-stone over a two-mile course—and his familiar colours of shamrock green overlaid with Irish harps— Moonlight had won the Fremantle Hunt Club Cup.

But, as Will had guessed, this morning's ride is not just for the fizz of river spray and horse sweat on his face. While they sip their tea the Chief is eyeing the bandaged hand.

'Three weeks now, isn't it? How is it healing?'

Will makes a noise, in disgust or maybe self-pity. Anyway it seems to come from him.

'I can't write or draw plans.' He looks down at his bare feet. 'Or even tie my bloody bootlaces.'

'You can walk and talk, can't you, and drink beer and make decisions?'

In the early quiet of the verandah a biscuit snaps in the O'Connor girl's teeth.

'I want you to be site engineer for the pipeline.'

Still Will doesn't speak. During the night he'd had an opium dream of Angelica. Her eyes and lips were turned down at the corners. He'd brought her gifts of precious jewels to make her smile. In the dream he felt protective and patted her cheeks to cheer her up. So exquisite was the skin of her cheek against his fingertips it made him cry with awe and pleasure. Stroking her was such a thrill he couldn't stop. Even when his hand began to bleed. She didn't smile, but neither did she leave. She stayed. He stroked her until eternity with bleeding fingers and was almost content.

When he tried to wake, he felt split in two. One part of him wanted to wake, the other didn't. Eventually the waking man made the sleeping one grip a sharp-edged diamond in his palm so the pain would wake him. He came to with a start, of course. Thinking: *The season of the play is over. She's really gone.*

In this state of flux he feels as if he's dying every minute. Something of his substance constantly falling away. He finds it hard to take in information on other topics. How long has O'Connor been speaking?

'Pretty soon those bandages could come off. I want you to take the pipeline to the goldfields.'

They get up to leave soon after. Will sees them off, asking himself if he feels any different than before they came. Worse, if anything. See, that was the trouble with human contact.

As he gets back on his horse, O'Connor calls out: 'Don't be too flattered, son. This is a raw place. The bastards are gunning for me. I have a lot on my plate and I'm too short of engineers to waste one.'

They ride off past three Aboriginal boys skylarking and splashing off the spit. O'Connor waves cheerily to them. The smallest boy, the only one wearing trousers, is learning to swim in the shallows by doing the dead man's float. Will flops down on the sand and allows the early sunlight to fall on his skin. For some minutes he watches the boy practising the dead man's float. Time and again he stays face-down in the water for only a second or two before jumping up, spluttering and hitching up his soggy trousers.

He'd learned to float in the Avon. He remembers his father's patience on a summer afternoon. Curious cows peering from the bank. Swallows skimming the surface after gnats. A kingfisher's flash of blue. The squelch of mud beneath his hands and knees so loath to release their grip.

*Let us gather by the river.*

Dead man's float: the first sign that water requires not only mastery from humans but surrender.

Sitting there on the damp sand, he suddenly removes the bandages and a sickly smell flies out. His fingers are swollen and the hand is puffy and white, as if too long under water. His scar shines like sun on a shilling.

He tries out his fingers. Of course they are too stiff to move. Still half-cupped, frozen around the shape of the handle of the bedroom door in the suite in the Palace Hotel.

Pelicans wheel over the spit, and in the shallows shags dive, disappear, resurface. The small dead-man's-floater splashes on, dabbing himself into the frothy shallows. Persevering but still pulling back from the brink.

The boy, the birds. He has the vague notion that swimming would exercise his fingers, so he walks fatalistically into the river and begins to swim out into the deep. But it's not the cupped stiffness of his hand striking the water, or the throbbing ache, that worries him. It's that he starts choking. He stops and coughs and clears his throat and wipes his streaming eyes. He takes a breath and begins to swim again, but the choking sensation returns. His chest feels cold and tightly stretched against the grey water. The taste of the opium pipe comes into his mouth. And when he stands, gagging and hacking up pale bubbles, the water presses around his chest and throat and he feels compelled to cough or die.

There is a pattern to this. When he starts to choke, when his lungs tell him they are filling with liquid, he is thinking of her.

Returning to work, he notices a strange phenomenon. He feels oddly calm. Another thing, in this past month of absence and opium the colours of life seem to have moved to the extremities and disappeared. Maybe they are so bright he doesn't see them any longer. Maybe this hazy panorama is all his eyes can accept.

The sun is a dull light behind phlegmy clouds. He leans on the ferry rail peering down into the river. Orange algae specks compressed by depth have turned the water black and rich as stout. Jellyfish undulate below the surface as if swaying under glass. In their translucent but individually patterned globes the urgent faces of unborn babies press up against the ceiling. Grinning skulls, weeping children, sly women with almond eyes.

The invisible sun bores into his skull, but he knows he needs to stay outside in the fresher air above the river. In the submarine mood of the saloon there is the danger he might start to choke.

When the ferry docks at the city wharf, the leached piles rock back and forth and black shags and white gulls flap away. He is the last passenger off the boat. By then the engine has shut down and the surface is slick again. Bird lime is on his sleeve. He scratches it off with his good hand and walks down the gangplank across the oily shimmer of water.

This is what absence is: deep reflecting water like this, a black mirror. His feet strike the land again. He sets off mechanically, pacing steadily up the hill back to work.

All is chipper in the city. Once again he is observing the requirements of the city, of professional men and of bright, noisy daylight. But he's not fooled. He knows what is the only point of day. To see a loved woman bathing at sunset.

The water scheme has suddenly surged ahead. On his return to the Department of Public Works he finds another ceremony is coming up, more official speeches. Another stage in the construction of the pipeline to be celebrated before the press and important guests.

He thinks perhaps the Chief and the manufacturers are publicly celebrating each juncture so the latest indecisive government—the fourth in four years—will be locked into the project. Just like a section of Mephan Ferguson's steel pipe.

Mephan Ferguson has come to an agreement with the metal-working firm of G. & C. Hoskins to make the sixty-six thousand pipes necessary for the project, and they are giving a formal luncheon party to celebrate the manufacture of the first three pipes at their factory at Midland Junction.

The company has come up with a gallant idea for the occasion: to engrave the first pipe with the names of the Premier's wife and the wife of the Minister for Public Works. And of engraving the second pipe with the names of the Engineer-in-Chief's wife and the wife of the Under-Secretary.

There is a problem with the third pipe. On this one the company wants to engrave the names of the wife of the parliamentary Opposition Leader and the wife of the on-site engineer. Before the ceremony Will is sounded out on the matter.

'I'm too young to have a wife's name on a water pipe,' he tells the Hoskins people. 'Leave me out.'

'It will look uneven.'

They say it's an honour. He tries to think but his head is thudding. He sees the names exposed to the sun and wind and crow droppings, the gaze of random sheltering kangaroos and dingoes for a century or two.

'Write the name Angelica Lloyd.'

'She is?'

'My fiancée.'

A fiancée is acceptable. They ask him to write down the name to save the embarrassment of a spelling error. It's for posterity after all.

No doubt they wonder at his stiff fingers, the gruesome scar. His hand shaking so for such a minor effort.

Of course a bullet striking flesh has a terrible and forceful effect. There is a jagged tearing, ripping and stretching. A bullet fired across the room from the showy octagonal barrel of an actor's Tranter six-shot .45 is violent but fortunately fairly slow.

This bullet went through the prominent veins and thin flesh on the back of his hand, below the middle and index fingers, leaving a hole an inch across. It severed two tendons, fractured the second and third metacarpal bones and was lodged there until he flicked it out with his pen-knife in a half-swoon onto the deck of the South Perth ferry.

Then stumbled home like a wounded bear to his cave.

It left him with two numb fingers that wouldn't fully straighten and a puckered scar like a coin. And some minor clumsy habits. He couldn't scoop up water to wash his face without poking himself in the eye. When he tried to put his hand in his pocket it got snagged up. And he couldn't tuck in a bedsheet without catching his fingers.

But despite the wound, despite himself, he gradually found he could write and draw plans and tie shoelaces, although it took a greater effort. He could do more or less everything else.

(He could write letters to her, and did so for a month. He did not really expect a reply and there was not one.)

He could easily cup the bowl of a bamboo opium pipe in his wounded hand throughout the night.

In eight weeks the wound had healed and the pain was gone. The explosion inside his head also eventually went away. What remained was the vision of her in the white nightdress, in this bewildering context. His blood on her face, the rueful smile, her short-haired head shaking no. No to reality, to the memory of loving attentions and laughing intimacies. To firm declarations.

*I just know we were together.*

What remained was his hand permanently moulded in the gesture of opening a hotel bedroom doorknob.

# STUDIO PORTRAIT
# WITH BICYCLES

A FTER FOUR YEARS of water famine, the government at last sent ten thousand gallons of fresh water from the coast in two hundred and fifty 40-gallon steel drums on O'Connor's new railway. Halfway to the goldfields the water express was stranded by the leading edge of a tropical cyclone which swept south from the Timor Sea, flooding the track and the flat western desert for a hundred square miles.

People later spoke in awe of those first huge raindrops which left pockmarks like teacups in the red dust. In the goldfields the torrential rain soon flooded the houses and hotels, washed away the hessian and canvas miners' camps and overflowed every available receptacle. Every tank and bucket, all the dams and abandoned pits were filled. Millions of gallons ran off into the sand. In the deluge the Cobb and Co mail coach was swept away. The driver could just cut the lead horses free and ride them to safety, but the horses yoked to the pole were drowned. Those prospectors cut off by the floodwaters from food supplies stayed alive on pearl barley and dried beans. In the short life of the goldfields no one had imagined such heavy rain could fall.

Two weeks after the deluge began the sun burst over the sheet of clotted red water spreading to the horizon and turned it purple. Only the camels, reasserting their eminence over the railway, their nostrils and humps barely above water, could make the crossing to the goldfields. In the claypans and in the chains of submerged salt lakes which had linked up along the courses of ancient rivers, the eggs of desert frogs and transparent shrimp responded magically to the rare moisture and hatched in their millions. Flocks of swans and ducks, egrets, herons and ibises appeared in the crisp sky. The birds gorged themselves in the receding waters while glistening succulents and crimson creeping pea-flowers spread over the red shores.

In the newly formed creeks and lakes the miners and barmaids and prostitutes held swimming contests, boating picnics and shooting parties of great hilarity and alcohol consumption. The strange turn in the weather had made both men and women excitable and reckless.

Sweltering in his cream suit, Axel Boehm was on hand to photograph many of these novel moist occasions. He captured the miners splashing like toddlers and delighting in their nakedness. Their chests and buttocks gleaming with the blue-white of skim milk. Their heads and forearms as dark and shiny as big-city coffins or rosewood pianos.

Although the humidity made his work more uncomfortable than usual, he gruffly ducked their cheerful splashings, resisted their tipsy calls to have a beer and a breather. To shed his clothes. To grab a slippery woman and dive in. He pleaded pressure of work. There was too much photographic potential in the muddy fun and mayhem.

They needed no encouragement to pose for him. Look at that wobbly human pyramid of nine naked miners! That old bare-arsed prospector carrying Ruby Nattrice, the singing barmaid, on his shoulders! That leering woodcarter posing with a black swan's neck protruding from his trouser flies!

Around the lustful water parties, more birds—crows and galahs—now came in clouds to feed. Full of food, they were even easier to shoot. Bloody bird-down smeared the creek banks and barmaids returned to work with sunburned cleavages and wearing pink and grey galah feathers in their hair.

The deluge had somehow changed the emotional climate. Unlikely people became intense and passionate and unrealistically optimistic.

Take the reclusive sixty-year-old Californian prospector, Frank Knapp. Stimulated by the wet flesh of a weekend swimming party, he followed Ruby Nattrice back to town, and while she was at work let himself into her room behind the Duchess of Kent Hotel. Ruby was by now a longstanding popular attraction at the Duchess of Kent, singing and playing her catchy tunes on the piano while balancing a pint of pale ale on her chest. Her screams on finding a naked Frank Knapp drinking champagne in her bed brought drinkers running from the bar.

Frank Knapp was astonished at the change in demeanour and attitude of the shoulder-riding nymph of the water picnic. Hadn't her moist, muscular thighs gripped his ears until his head boomed and he saw red sparks? Didn't he have a glass of champagne poured ready for her, and an interesting proposition to put?

But she kept yelling. Frank Knapp had no inkling that his prank had touched a raw nerve with Ruby, that she was recalling brains on the sheet-iron wall and young Taffy Evans' head peeled like a banana.

He pulled out his last card. When his proposal of marriage was treated with the same shrieking disdain, Frank, offended and emotional, pitched the bottle at her. Ruby fell screaming with a glass sliver in her right eye. This was when the mob dragged him to the bedroom floor and stove in his forehead with her porcelain chamber pot.

In the commercial side of town, meanwhile, previously conservative businessmen suddenly took the rainfall as a constant, like gold or the new railway, and planned rapid development. Talking *Progress* they began to form clubs and erect buildings which would last: impressive offices of granite and red clay-brick with galvanised-iron roofs and overhanging verandahs of imported hand-wrought iron. At the same time a rent appeared in the miners' camaraderie of earlier days when both labourer and lord, smeared with the same dust, had drunk together. A consciousness of social status was stirring.

A smart set rose mysteriously, literally from the red earth. The smart set came up with the idea of compacting the newly moistened ant beds to provide a surface for tennis and cricket and croquet games. Emboldened, they moved on to the jarrah-wood floors of the new Hippodrome where they held roller-skating parties presided over by a 'Professor' Seguy, a Frenchman who was a skilled skater and spoke five languages.

Next thing the smart set were attending natural science lectures and *conversazione* evenings run by their new Art Society. Then, as members of the new Orchestral Society, they held their first charity concert and ball at the new corrugated-iron Mechanics and Miners' Institute hall in aid of the

Children's Fresh Air League, to raise money to give disadvantaged miners' children a summer holiday on the coast. Before long they were planning the first University and Public Schools Dinner, which attracted social attention for its variety of imported foods and French wines and for excluding the Scots and Irish. That every other nationality was excluded went without saying. 'University' meant Oxford and Cambridge.

Every species was heedless and thriving in the new fertile inland. Late at night, when the pubs eventually ceased their bellowing, the rare noise of the frogs, like the bleating of demented sheep, kept the town from sleep.

In the rare humidity of the myriad creeks and streams trickling through the backyards of the town and the refuse of the miners' camps, the typhoid also thrived.

The floodwaters mean that work on O'Connor's aqueduct is delayed yet again. But the deluge teaches an important lesson: that once every forty or fifty years the desert floods. So where ancient water courses, as well as valleys and gullies and salt lakes, have to be crossed, the pipeline will have to be laid on high trestle bridges. Elsewhere O'Connor wants it to be laid on stanchions in high-banked trenches, to minimise expansion and contraction in the desert heat and cold.

As well as keeping the water scheme on course and on time, the site engineer has to supervise the digging of the trenches, and the building of the timber trestles, and especially the caulking of the sixty-six thousand separate pipes into one pipeline.

Will has seven caulking overseers to assist him along the length of the pipeline. One of them truly stands out—a middle-aged Yorkshireman named Dudley Bright. It's Bright who every evening seeks out the highest point in the vicinity of their current camp on the pipetrack. A sandhill perhaps, maybe a granite outcrop, even an old ant hill. Carrying a narrow leather case, he climbs this rise and stands on the crest securing his footing and facing into the sunset. At the precise moment when the last ray of sun hits the horizon he produces a cornet from the case and begins to play.

Sometimes on the flat plains the pipeline itself is the highest point in the landscape. Then Dudley Bright heaves himself up on the trestle, climbs up on a rapidly cooling length of pipe, to blow his cornet. He's a dark, serious sort of fellow, slow and red-jowled. The day's clanking and hammering is suddenly over. Men stop their murmuring. In the cooler air the sound of Dudley Bright's cornet is as sharp and startling as condensation on steel pipe, as the fresh dark, as the smell of damp turned earth.

The tune he plays each night is 'Sweet Marie'. The nightly notes of 'Sweet Marie' have become part of the project, like hauling or bolstering, as vital as the caulking process itself.

As for the caulking, each pipe has to be joined to its fellow by a simple thimble ring packed with lead. Every twenty-eight feet along the aqueduct's three hundred and fifty mile length there is a joint to be caulked—the pipes' length having been determined by the length of the railway wagons hauling them into the desert. The wagons are thirty feet long.

The caulking is done by hand. The work is hard and exacting and encourages bad tempers. The pipes absorb the sun. Long before noon a flick of sweat sizzles as it drops on steel. The caulkers have to work in exposed conditions, handling molten metal in cramped and twisted positions, often lying on their sides and backs. Hot lead scorching through clothing and leather aprons can burn their groins and bellies.

On the aqueduct there is no place for sloppy work. A caulker is a special sort of skilled labourer: steady, sober and physically strong. A man who can work with minimum supervision in a small team strung out along a remote stretch of pipetrack. That's the ideal. In the harsh reality of the climate and countryside who could find one of these paragons? Few of Will's caulkers have any experience. Drawn from other states and countries and occupations by the lure of gold, most are failed prospectors—boozers and misfits unused to hard labour.

They have to be scrutinised, bullied and inspired to work effectively as a team. The overseers are expected to coax them along, to impart a sense of the importance of the caulkers' work to the success of the water scheme. By day Dudley Bright is barely adequate as an overseer. He lives in his own dour world, dull-eyed, with a constant string of spittle in the corner of his mouth. He stands too close, and he spits when he talks. Despite Will's seniority, whenever his overseer looses spit on him, he agonises over whether to wipe it off or leave it.

But at dusk Dudley comes into his own. His cornet playing brings his caulkers together. At the end of the day his 'Sweet

Marie' lifts their spirits. They love the whole procedure. By late afternoon they are all pointing out to him the best hill for his evening recital. At knockoff time a hush falls as he strides forward with his cornet case. As he climbs the rise they regard his stocky frame as almost heroic.

'Up he goes,' they murmur. 'Up goes Dudley.'

Suspense hangs in the lemony light as the sun slides down, as he shuffles and positions himself on the crest. The pipeline stretches back to the west as far as they can see, thin as a hair. It's longer than yesterday. It's a cord linking them to the sunset, to where they have come from and to everything they have already accomplished. The sun is falling fast now as he takes the cornet from the case. The brass glints as he raises it to his juicy lips.

The split-second joint explosion of sun and sound.

Dudley Bright's caulkers' gang reaches the outskirts of the small wheat and sheep town of Merredin. The gang camps that night by a thinly timbered rise just west of town. As dusk approaches, Bright strides alone up the gravelly hill. Casuarinas and stunted banksias struggle up the stony slope. Magpies carol and dive past him, and pairs of green parrots whizzing home before nightfall. He straddles the hilltop as usual and takes out his cornet, nobly faces the setting sun, pops his lips and raises the mouthpiece.

A clear tenor rings out from the casuarinas.

Bright's eyes slide around to find the voice. But his chin remains upturned to the west. He starts to blow.

Another deeper, richer voice joins the first. The bass and tenor harmonise. They are singing 'Write Me a Letter from Home'.

At the bottom of the hill, men begin to stir and mutter. The cornet falters on 'Sweet Marie'. New voices start to join the sentimental harmony. 'Write Me a Letter from Home' swells over the stumbling cornet notes.

'Machine men!' yells one of the caulkers.

Men are already snatching up their wrenches and hammers, swinging buckets of lead and charging clumsily up and down the incline. It's an hour before Will and the police get there from Merredin and break up the fight. The old hand-caulkers versus the new machine-caulkers brought in by an impatient O'Connor.

Will's telegraph message is terse. *To avoid disruption to schedule please inform of any change in caulking procedures.*

The Chief's message comes back. *In future we will use the new Couston Electric Caulking Machine instead of hand labour.* A revolutionary machine invented by one James Couston. Another marriage of minds between engineer and inventor. At other sunsets in other places the fights between hand-caulkers and machine-caulkers will continue for weeks. On the pipetrack and even in parliament. But the machine does the work five times faster.

Dudley Bright misses the next week's sunset performances. The old hand-caulkers—plain pipetrack navvies now, labourers nursing their bruises and scabbed knuckles—want him to play his cornet again of an evening. Even the machine-caulkers don't really mind.

'Forget the singers, Dudley. Just a joke. "Sweet Marie". Solo.'

The seventh evening he carries his leather case up a nearby slope. His face is stern as usual. His chosen hill this time is the side of an old gravel quarry, a steep, crumbly rise. The hand-caulkers follow him uphill through the pink dust motes. On the gravelly crest he looks across into the sunset, raises the cornet and plays 'The Last Post'. The notes as cold and pure as ice. Then he swings his arm back and throws the cornet into the gorge below.

Down the incline the hand-caulkers rush, skidding and sliding through the gravel, breaking into a slithering jog, then all joining in a shambling run, their momentum carrying them down to their navvies' picks and mattocks, the inevitable sledgehammers, and to the new Couston Electric Caulking Machine straddling the pipetrack.

As the goldfields prosper so does Axel Boehm. Like others he can thank O'Connor's railway for his good fortune. Aside from his successful commissions and field photography and his portrait and newspaper and magazine work, a modest speculation in mining scrip has, with the railway's booming effect on shares, brought him enough capital to establish a new photographic studio next to the Windsor Castle Hotel in the centre of town.

The studio is also doing well. The reason is simple. Boehm has shrewdly applied to his commercial portraits his fascination in the changing effects of climate, fortune and occupation on human features.

He knows his clients—even the roughest miners—have no great wish for their features to be sharpened, levelled and aged. So he ensures a visit to his studio will take at least ten years off them. He employs retouchers, women with a sensitive hand, to remove the ravages and blemishes of time and place and labour—and illness—from his portraits. (But he forbids them to retouch his customers' 'character lines'.) He keeps a wide selection of wigs and cosmetics on hand, including jars of the popular Pascall's red gloss. As he jokes to Inez: 'The cheek paint is more for the barmaids' entertainment than aesthetic purposes.' His monochromatic photographic film is, of course, insensitive to red.

Anyway, his clients are charmed by it all. They are flattered at the lively curiosity he brings to photographing their weddings and balls and other social rituals. To attract miners drawn to town for their evening roistering he even keeps the studio open until nine o'clock. The studio boasts a skylight and a glass wall to allow in the daylight for indoor work, and dressing rooms where his customers can change into their costumes of choice. He provides many props and subtle disguises and elaborate backdrops.

The Irish and Americans and Germans and English favour a casual stance in front of a craggy background: rocks and gnarled gum trees—with a stuffed wedgetail eagle and goanna, if they wish—to show off an image of hard-won prosperity. The Italians and Greeks and Spaniards prefer to puff up their chests before a mine's thrusting poppet head. The current vogue among the Japanese laundrymen, on the other hand, is to pose formally with their bicycles against a soft rural backcloth. Better still, with a nonchalant kid glove on the handlebars of one of the three showroom-shiny black Raleighs, with their unworn Dunlop tyres, supplied by special arrangement (Boehm provides the photographs for the firm's annual calendar) with F.X. Corr and Sons, Supreme Bicycle Dealers to the Goldfields, around the corner.

Today he poses three laundrymen—chins proudly raised, hair parted and brilliantined back, each brow and mouth a grim line—in the black three-piece suits and watch chains of cold-climate diplomats. Bicycle-clips crisply subdue their trouser cuffs. Their chosen background is a winding stream, ploughed fields, a green wood, and a cobbled lane meandering off behind them towards a steepled church. Occasionally he wonders what impression their relatives in Tokyo and Osaka have of their lives in the Western Australian desert. (Are they aware these stalwarts live chiefly off the earnings of three other photographic subjects of his—Sono, Yoko and little Oyoni?)

With subterfuge, light and chemicals Boehm can turn a

dusty dryblower into a mining magnate, a laundryman–pimp into a cycling statesman.

It's with the same careful attention to detail that he presents himself.

Inez didn't know how to take him at first. His habits and pre-sentation. His courtship routine. This was back in the exhausting days of the water famine when, off-duty, she would flee from the heat and the rantings of the *poor typhoids* into the relative cool and peace of his old studio.

'This is new to me,' she'd said, of what was happening to her. She tasted the thin bile of his champagne in the back of her throat.

'It's my way of doing things,' he murmured. 'It pays you a great tribute, remember that.'

'It seems as if I'm open while you are closed.'

He blinked at that. He cleared his throat. 'Doesn't it please you to be so appreciated?'

The heat was mounting in her cheeks and mottling her neck. She nodded and closed her eyes. He was certainly gentle.

The slow, relentless rhythm. His strange whispering voice. The rustle of his cream trouser legs when he subtly changed position. The odour of his pomade.

His stroking, his gentle probing, had begun at her temples and forehead and eyelids and was now at her waist. Considering their outdoor work, the chemicals and equipment, his fingertips were smooth and cool and made her shiver. Their smell, of course, was sweet.

Buttons, clasps, hooks, melted under his hands. He was no thick-fingered fumbler. Fabric dropped away. With him she was always on a divan, bed, chair, chaise longue. His proficient fingers moving slowly over her body. Her clothes pooling around her on the floor.

After the first day or so she'd allowed a languid wrist to accidentally brush his flies. He jumped. Coughed. A hard mound there behind the cream trousers.

Quickly edging his pelvis away, regaining control. Those hands, his sleek head bending over her.

Waking to see his trouser legs and tripod standing back a few paces. A narrow space of air between them. The black hood looming. Her next overwhelming thought the memory of the Unknown Woman from the Seine.

The face of a young woman about twenty. She has a plain hairstyle. You can't see her eyes, and her eyes can't see, for she is dead. Suddenly Inez would like to think that the girl did not go into the Seine gladly. The emotion which followed her initial despair and the brief horror of drowning now so evident on her face.

Shivering at the memory of her cool drowned inner smile. Inez drawing her own bare limbs together with a cry.

His flushed face appearing from the folds of the hood.

'Inez, it's only your Axel. Who adores you.'

Felix Locke, in provocative mood, drains his beer glass and declares that the most memorable event in the past five years was the arrival of fish.

'I'll never forget it,' he says. That first consignment of snapper, jewfish, kingfish, whiting and oysters all packed in ice, pulling up in a four-horse spring van outside the Prince of Wales. Two hundredweight of fish carried three hundred and fifty miles overland and all sold in ten minutes.

From the balcony of the Prince of Wales they are watching the town's latest procession, in honour of the first Goldfields Mining and Industrial Exhibition. Thousands have travelled from all over the country—and from London—to attend. A special train has brought dignitaries from Perth. At the station the Afghans presented the Premier with an albino racing camel.

Locke has to make himself heard over the retreating stridor of brass bands and the fainter moan of bagpipes turning the corner ahead. Red dust raised by the squads of passing feet floats up and settles on their skin and clothes.

'It was the whole marine shock of it,' he says, recalling the streets suddenly emptying. The town steeped in the stinging aroma of frying fish.

Axel Boehm says, 'It hardly compares with the arrival of the telegraph and the railway.'

For forty minutes they have watched the clumps of marchers and dignitaries and standard bearers streaming past the hotel. Despite their jugs of beer they are feeling hot and bored. Boehm's tripod is set up in the corner of the balcony he uses to photograph parades, and every ten minutes or so he disappears under the hood to photograph the procession.

'Anyway the oysters didn't make it,' he recalls.

They have already seen and heard the Kilted Bagpipers, the Original Pioneers, the Town Band, the Bavarian Band, the Brown Hill Banjo Band, the Fire Brigade, the Governor's carriage, with escort, the Premier's carriage, also with escort, the Engineer-in-Chief and Staff, and the Mayor and Councillors and their Invited Guests. Pedalling past at this minute, tinkling handlebar bells in unison, is the sixteen-man Cycle Corps. Looming up behind them are the sturdy members of the Miners' Trades Association. Still to pass are the marchers, each with their two standard bearers, from the Art, Athletic, Benevolent, Billiards, Caledonian, Cambrian, Catholic Benefit, Christian, Cricket, Dramatic, Debating, Football, Gymnastic, Hibernian, Liedertafel and Literary societies. Bringing up the rear are the people themselves: the Citizens' Carriages, the Working Miners, the Children's Corps, the Afghan cameleers—on sixty camels, riding four abreast—and, in the very back, a Selection of Aborigines of the Region in new art muslin loincloths.

Boehm pours more beer from a jug into his glass. 'And the fish all had cloudy eyes.'

'Listen, it was compelling, that sudden smell of the sea right here in the desert,' says Locke. 'I wrote a poem about it.'

'Many of the customers were compelled to come and see me the next day,' Dr Malebranche recalls.

'I ate a perfectly good snapper,' says Locke. 'Axel missed the photograph, that's why he's denying the importance of the fish.'

True, the arrival and dispersal of the fish had happened so quickly that Boehm had had no time to fetch his equipment.

The coming of the telegraph, on the other hand, the mile-long string of camels passing through town, had given him plenty of time to set up his tripod. A hundred and sixty camels, tassels and beads swaying, bells tinkling, carrying telegraph poles and wire spools, pulling houses on rollers, laden with water tanks and machinery, had taken an hour to pass the hotel's verandah.

'The coming of the telegraph,' he says.

'No, the arrival of the railway,' says Malebranche. 'Then electricity.'

'The fish,' says Locke.

'The railway didn't make much of a picture,' Boehm recalls. 'Smoke. Officials. Ladies in hats. Everyone has seen a train pulling into a station. Not so many have seen a mile of camels end-to-end.'

'The arrival of the fish would have been a wonderful photograph.' Locke shakes his head sorrowfully. 'Great human interest.'

'*You* are an authority on human interest?' Boehm says.

'You should have been at the New Year soiree of Madame Rioux,' says Malebranche.

'As usual we'll take your word for it,' says Boehm.

'She put on champagne and hired the Bavarian Band. When they played 'The Gay Parisienne' all the French girls started a wild cancan and the Japanese girls began a sort of Hawaiian hula.' Malebranche thoughtfully sips his beer. 'That was human interest.'

Locke looks up from the out-of-step ranks of the Dramatic Society—strolling thespians in dusty pantaloons self-consciously declaiming *Hamlet*, holding Yorrick at arm's length. A sun-burned Ophelia marching sturdily riverwards.

'Notice no one has mentioned gold,' he says. 'Not a single discovery.'

'Gold,' Boehm says in a flat tone.

Frankly gold is losing its novelty for him as a subject. He sees gold every day. People pay for their portraits, like everything else, in gold. And while his most lucrative business is mining company commissions from managers eager to record progress for their company directors in London, it is also the most boring. Of course the mine managers totally lack imagination. Their favourite subjects are the installation of new machinery or visits to the mine by VIPs, where they line up everyone from the visiting Lord Suchandsuch to the mullock-raker's fox terrier in solemn hierarchical rows.

To capture vistas of the goldmines he still has to cart his cameras and tripod and cases of glass plates around mine shafts and over tailing dumps. *His chafed thighs! Those . . . straps forever cutting into him!* Despite technical advances everywhere else, field photography here is just as uncomfortable an undertaking as ever. And as risky.

The system of magnesium flares he devised to enable him to take photographs down the mines is proving an . . . unpredictable . . . light source. Stories of these flares of his, every seventh one of which is—a ridiculous exaggeration—rumoured to explode with disastrous consequences, are beginning to give his wide-eyed underground subjects—pictured as the rocky womb of the earth envelops them—the wary, stunned look of newcomers to hell.

He drains his glass, belches and says to Locke and Malebranche: 'Gold has been done to death. The arrival of water will be the celebration to see.'

'Water,' sighs Malebranche.

'If we live that long,' says Locke.

The sun and beer are starting to give Malebranche a headache. In the street below, gymnasts tumble and cartwheel in the hot dust. He thinks of the poverty-stricken typhoid hospitals and the thousands of pounds wasted on endless official self-congratulation.

'Senseless jubilations,' he says.

Axel Boehm had, in fact, already begun recording water's gradual arrival. He'd made several forays west to the pipetrack and photographed it inching closer. Each time he was surprised to find the workmen so intense and surly, on the edge of madness or mutiny. Fights seemed about to break out.

It made it hard to slip into his usual role of anonymous eyewitness. The foremen, too, were full of silent umbrage. Even the young English engineer in charge was vague and curt.

The responsibility of taking the pipeline uphill into the desert seemed to be affecting them strangely. The engineer and his men appeared to be fighting against entropy. Against their own disorder as much as water's natural lazy tendency to flow downwards.

On the pipetrack he saw and heard odd things. Labourers flicked hot lead on his hat and suit and stared at him with the wolfish, knowing eyes of convicts. As if daring him to take the picture, they flexed and flashed and pissed and squatted in front of him, and one smirking fellow masturbated openly at noon in the trench in the pipeline's shadow.

Regarding photography: the ignorant don't realise the extent to which the photographer is in command. Not for the first time Axel Boehm assumed control by withdrawing from the proffered subject. By calmly ignoring the potential photograph. Dusting himself off and focussing instead on pleasing static juxtapositions of machinery and skyline, camels and clouds. Whistling a bit of Mozart. Retreating under the hood. Placidly choosing his moment.

*You don't exist unless I say so.*

It was when they had forgotten the five-legged, hooded intrusion that he quietly photographed the red-eyed men with scabbed faces coming in from the desert. Hugging the pipeline, putting their ears and cheeks and lips to the steel surface as if it were a woman.




To judge the goldfields purely from the stamp of those citizens and organisations parading past, visiting dignitaries would never guess this was a place of great mortality. And great drinking and fornication, for that matter. None of the optimistic marchers celebrating the wealth and fame of the town's telluride ore and the industry of its citizens carried banners for the three main female professions of nursing, bartending and prostitution.

Of course by late evening when the fifty pubs were roaring with customers and the British prostitutes were staggering and shouting in the streets and the French women sauntered outside their brothels and sat in the doorframes in their high-heeled shoes of red satin and bright stockings and loose chemisettes that exposed their breasts and shoulders—and made clicking sounds with their tongues at every passing man—even the most blinkered visitor to the Mining and Industrial Exhibition would be aware of the last two professions. (The Japanese prostitutes, by contrast, were quiet and discreet. They hid from passersby and did not openly advertise their wares. Of course this had the effect of enhancing their popularity.) At no stage would rosy spots and raving delirium and haemorrhaging intestines come to mind. Not many would realise they were in the middle of a typhoid epidemic.

To avoid worrying visiting London investors, Locke was now expected to gather up the corpses late at night. Often he went on his rounds directly from the pub. The drink gave him a jauntiness helpful both in dealing with his morbid task and for bantering with the night nurses. And, incidentally, for masking his disappointment at his lack of success with Inez.

Of course he'd long known about Inez and Boehm. He was disappointed, but not as surprised as he might have been. She was with Axel. She was Axel's subject. (*Miss Gosper Arrives in the Goldfields, Woman Kissing Cockatoo.* He had seen both photographs.) After five years in this place what could surprise him now?

As he stacked young men's bodies in the hearse he kept up his cryptic joking with her.

More out of habit than optimism, he'd shout over the

ranting of the delirious patients, the *poor typhoids*: 'Come here often?' (How clever he was at masking his strange shyness with her, and her attractiveness to him. And how stupid and perverse. He hated his own jokey bullshit. He didn't want this platonic banter, he wanted *passion*.) 'Lovely night for it!'

She kept up her part of their routine. Dashing past with damp towels, subduing straps, a stinking bedpan, maybe a kidney dish of maggots she'd extracted from some prospector's suppurating Barcoo ulcer, she'd flick a damp strand of hair from her eyes and shoot back, 'Couldn't be better!'

He'd never felt so aroused by anyone. He adored the flush in her cheeks—the life, the passion, the confidence, evident there. She stood for good works without the piety. And the quirky mystery of her choices certainly added to the intrigue. Her circumstances and surroundings made her seem twice as alive. Umpteen beers and a couple of scotches in his bloodstream: it was all he could do not to put down the body he was carrying and take that quick body in his arms.

Of course carting the bodies back to the funeral parlour, his mood swung with the alcohol in his blood from lust to depression. The moon and stars in the clear sky made him ache with longing. Luckily the horses were alert. Every so often they had to manoeuvre the hearse around a body passed out drunk in the street. Lying behind him tonight under the tarpaulin, ten males aged seventeen to thirty. Compared to him they were noble and full of infinite sense, on a loftier plane. And another four hospitals to go.

A brightly painted woman cooed and swung her hips at him from Madame Rioux's. Then, realising who it was, she gasped and stood staring from the doorframe as he passed, her hand to her mouth. His answering wave was cursory. A dull pain was beginning behind his eyes.

Inez was just another skittish, superstitious woman who wouldn't permit these undertaker's hands to touch her.

Her hands caressed the skin of the dying, his the dead. The very same patients. The difference in their condition only a matter of minutes. Both pairs of hands were privy to the same intimate secrets. Why was that tiny step in time such an unbridgeable gap? Why did that hiccup make such a vast difference?

Violette came back inside the house looking drawn and anxious under her makeup. Dr Malebranche was sitting with Madame Rioux at her kitchen table smoking and drinking cognac. Violette sat down and crossed herself.

Malebranche had heard the hearse rumble past in the now quiet street, the horses' slow tread giving it away. He said, 'What's the matter?'

'The undertaker just went past!'

He blew smoke across the table. 'So what?'

Violette pulled her chemisette together, folded her arms across her chest. The skin of her arms was suddenly goose-fleshed and patchy. Her voice was faint. 'He beckoned to me.'

'He's a decent fellow, Felix.'

'He was staring at this house. His eyes looked right into mine.'

'*Merde*,' said Madame Rioux, looking at the clock. Half-past three. She screwed the top back on the brandy bottle and placed it out of reach.

Malebranche patted Violette's damp shoulder. Only a few hours before, after his own rounds of the hospitals, he'd been drinking with Locke. 'He probably fancied you,' he said. 'He's just a normal man, you know, doing his job.'

'Collecting the dead!'

'Someone has to do it.'

'He brings death. The fever of the rosy spots.'

Madame Rioux was yawning loudly and restlessly jiggling her brandy glass on the tabletop. The plague to deal with, and now the Exhibition's visiting excitement-seekers as well!

'Violette, you're crazy.' Malebranche snorted in exasperation and stubbed out his cigarette. He'd rarely felt so frustrated. The deaths kept increasing. His own puny search for the causes of typhoid was bogged down. The *infusoria* eluded him. He was suddenly shocked at the sight of his hand hovering over the ashtray. From tonight's bore-water bath with Violette it was wrinkled and white and glistening with salt.

He stared at it and shuddered. 'Felix removes death.' He almost shouted. 'He carries it away!'

Violette rocked back and forth on her chair and stared out the window at the black sky.

'Time to go,' Malebranche announced. He finished his brandy as he stood up. He was adjusting his clothing to leave when the young English customer who had been smoking opium with Juliette in the next room abruptly appeared in the doorway. He was naked and shivering violently and his eyes were bright and glassy. He was trying unsuccessfully to grip the doorknob, perhaps to help support himself. Even across the room Malebranche could hear his teeth chattering.

Juliette was holding him up with difficulty and making a nauseated face. 'This one is sick,' she said.

# THE LUNATICS' DOUCHE

IT'S NOT ALWAYS her in his fevers. Grey eyes glazing green. The pointed chin. Hair cascading to her thighs. The nightmare woman at her sunset bath.

Unfamiliar women, too, populate his dreams. But they erode in his arms, before his eyes. They lose their lips. Everything dries up. Ears and noses age and dangle like scrotums in warm water. Even so, you'd think nuzzling turkey necks, kissing faded eyes, would return them to their prime— fleshy, flirting farm girls and smooth-skinned washerwomen. But running sores break out across their skin and stinging insects sup on them.

He sweats and thirsts for love. He almost chokes once on a fat woman's tongue. Her breath tastes like hot tin and mustard. He'll warm to anything friendly. One glittery dawn he reaches out to love a citrus beetle on a lemon tree. It couldn't be a more enticing green; it's just its musky ooze that makes him gag. Another time a jolly dog stands above him panting. When it slobbers, its turd-eating breath alone is worth a yell. He goes to pet his budgerigar and dead pelicans' wings span the room.

Sometimes, in tears, he sees himself as a little boy with sleepy hair, and loves himself as son and father. Wakes gently picking scales of cradlecap from his own scalp. Kissing the softly pulsing diamond of his fontanelle.

No, his dreams aren't always of her. Bold Wiltshire night-mares arrive from yesteryear. Pig-hating horses screaming at the steam rising from horseflesh stewing for the sows. And his laughing father spreading chunks of raw horsemeat in the boughs of apple trees. Trees bursting with flesh and hens and rosy apples. Hens falling on the maggots of the flesh-fly with noisy relish.

He canters through the damp orchard of his bed and greedy oinks and clucks and horse's screams burst from his dry throat.

The high smell of horse urine wakes him that time. His father insisting on soaking everyone's boots for extra suppleness.

Even at his most conscious, mid-afternoon, he still lives in his throbbing head. Each pulse-beat is a rhythmic thought com-pulsively repeated. Sometimes he could swear he's smoking opium. *Slithery fish. Sloshy sties. Mucus in a spaniel's eyes.* In his mind he holds a pencil in his curled hand, writes hieroglyph-ics in the saucer of his skull. *Morning dew on horses' gums. Apes' red suppurating bums.* When he becomes aware of the nurse Inez sponging him down, he clears his papery throat and tries to scrape up the sanity and spittle to address her.

'Dribble of tots. Women's froth,' he confides.

'We'll have two ounces of glycerine and borax now,' she says.

Her hand strokes his forehead, prises open the flaky lips. His tongue is painted in curds. Its edges and tip are red. He gags a little and shares another confidence about moistures.

'Madmen's spit. Egg-white snot.'

'Yes, indeed.' She pats his arm, pushes hair from her damp brow. 'I want to clean out your mouth, William Dance, and have you drink something.'

It's mostly Angelica though. Two years down the track is nothing to a fever.

Fever's eyes are ash, her cheeks are flames. Fever dips a wet tongue into his every corner, buries her hot and restless face. Fever arches her hips up at him, her damp hair in his mouth, while he holds her moist breasts from behind.

Of course he responds to Fever. Loses himself in her luscious lips, wide mouth and eyes, flaring nostrils, sumptuous thighs. (In the beginning he couldn't find his way in, Fever's door was so narrow. Then it suddenly unlocked so wide she turned almost inside out.) But sadly now Fever has become all beak and wings and coiling neck. Fever pecking at his daydreams, hissing in his face, gutting him with lightning kicks.

Angelica directing the Lunatics' Douche as his swansong and making certain things happen to him.

Coming into town from the pipetrack he had felt strangely detached and languid. During the first day of the Exhibition his languor grew. His muscles turned as light and flimsy as tissue paper. The Chief and the Department of Public Works held a public presentation of the plans and progress of the water scheme while his lethargy increased.

O'Connor presided in the Mechanics' Institute Hall over his maps and models and miniature pipes and pumping stations. Will propped himself up against the iron wall watching the people of the goldfields nod soberly at this other tussle with gravity and nature. (As they left, however, they muttered to themselves, 'But will the bloody thing ever happen?') The visiting engineers and industrialists seemed suitably impressed. 'Bold but clear in principle,' was their reaction. (They couldn't have missed the pipetrack from the train.) 'Anyway, there's no feasible alternative.' As Will fought to stay on his feet, they shook his hand as well.

Later O'Connor spelled it out for him in the back bar of the Windsor Castle. 'It might be all beer and skittles here— they want the bloody water to arrive.' But in the city the attacks on him were getting more petty and malicious. 'They're not thirsty there and they don't let up. Every man thinks he's competent to make engineering and economic judgements. I'm supposed to be greasing my palm, stealing millions from the taxpayer. In parliament and the papers I'm the whipping boy more than ever.'

Will was so wobbly he could barely hold his pint of bitter.

O'Connor was weary, too, but fierce with tension. He rubbed at the neuralgic twinges around his eyes. 'I'm supposed to be nefarious, corrupt, a reckless blunderer!'

'Surely not.'

'And Forrest has gone into federal politics, so no bastard in parliament has the courage to stand up for me.'

By then Will was seeing geometric changes in his

surroundings. Wavering perpendiculars. Indoor mirages. He put it down to a touch of sunstroke and excused himself. In his hotel room he smoked a pipe and in its strangely cooling daze walked outside into the street still seeing fields of snowdrops. Feeling the touch of their ice-cold stalks and inhaling their bitter smell.

He wanted to retain that image. The glittering winter sunshine and the icy radiance of the snow! Searching for the luxury of cold, he went looking for the legendary watery ministrations of Madame Rioux's. As he told Juliette that night, he longed for dark earth instead of red sand, mud instead of dust, apple-faced girls washing sheets in grey streams. He wanted loamy puddles and dripping greenery.

'I want frost,' he said.

The very idea of cold was sensual. Cold was lusty. Making love after the theatre that midnight on the frosty grass of Batheaston common! Heedless to the cold and wet, laughing at their cold, tight lips, their teeth clashing like tombstones. Becoming aware of a man's shape watching them from the shadows, he'd grunted, 'Piss off!' and growled like a dog, but was in no position to do anything about him, not lurching helplessly in that specific moist oven-heat. (Angelica just closed her eyes and ignored the pervert.) And when they'd finished, the man wandered off snapping twigs in his hands and cackling bitterly to the stars.

He ached for ferns and moss and snow and her.

'*Neige*. I want *la neige*,' he murmured. '*Je veux la neige.*'

'*Quoi?*' Juliette said. The time he was taking! Just as well he'd paid the long-time rate. Just seeing him and his pipe swaying on the doorstep, Madame Rioux had demanded it.

Amazing, he said, now he wouldn't even mind the Levels. 'Imagine that!' he mumbled into Juliette's dimpled shoulder.

Then he was sitting up suddenly and ranting about the man watching in the frosty grass.

She grunted and pushed away and reclaimed her air space from this clammy body. Not understanding her client in the least, she had difficulty for once knowing exactly when a man's want meant demand, when sweat became fever, when maudlin turned delirious.

He began to shiver, then he vomited. He felt a disgust for food but a great thirst. He had a violent headache and repeated diarrhoea. His eyes were vacant and glassy. He was deaf and confused and he raved at night.

After three days his abdomen swelled and was painful on the lower right side. On the fifth day rose-coloured spots sprouted over his chest and abdomen like huge fleabites. At the same time he complained of a sore throat and pains in all his limbs.

It wasn't surprising that his stomach hurt. In such typhoid cases the lower half of the small bowel and the upper part of the large intestine are covered in ulcers.

'This is where death takes over,' Dr Jean-Pierre Malebranche explained briskly to the victim's employer. The Engineer-in-Chief had postponed his departure back to

Perth until the next day's train. The doctor said, 'If one of these ulcers penetrates the bowel it's all over.'

'What are his chances?'

'The typhoids have to be kept as quiet as possible to prevent perforation and haemorrhage of their bowels. This may happen in the third week. Or any time, if the wrong food is given or they aren't kept quiet.'

'My God.'

'If they survive three weeks they may eventually crawl back to convalescence.'

'Naturally I want the best treatment for him.'

The doctor looked carefully at O'Connor. 'I'm sure the nurses will observe their usual high standards of care,' he said drily. 'You know he's just one victim in the middle of a continuing epidemic.'

In one respect, of course, this victim was different from the others. This one he'd seen himself teetering through the bedroom door at Madame Rioux's, melting in his own sweat. This one's body, like his own, had glistened white with the salts of the bore-water bath. Ever since he'd pondered on the source of the young man's infection. Yet again he worried about the elusive *infusoria*. About where and how it chose to strike. But he felt tense and overtired and said, brusquely, 'I'm curious that you encourage your employees to live such reckless lives. I refer to his opium smoking and the old gunshot wound.'

The Chief blinked slowly, then glared at him. His eyes were tired, too, and fiercer. 'This is the frontier. We're all pioneers here, doctor.'

'We're certainly that.'

'I hope you appreciate the sad irony that this man is in

charge of bringing water to your town. To eliminate disease from your patients' lives.'

Malebranche sighed and rubbed his eyes. 'We'll do our utmost,' he said.

For the moment the patient lay mostly quiet on the hospital cot. The nerves around his mouth and closed eyes skittered under the sallow sheen of his skin.

In his head, trees whirled in the wind, rain sluiced down the roof, and parrots scattered from the thunderstorm into hollow trees. Lightning flashed through his eyelids. The river was a black sea battering the shore. Branches thudded against the bungalow like sledgehammer blows. Above him in the empty, echoing house the possums growled and hissed and scrabbled across the ceiling, sent mad by the driving rain.

Of all the nurses' touches, hers is lightest and coolest and registers most on him. Even when she doesn't speak and his eyes are closed his skin recognises her soft fingertips.

While capable enough, her touch is more tentative, not as brisk and cursory and professional as the touches of the others. There is another thing different about her touch. What is hinted at when her hands brush or clasp or bathe his flesh (and this is mostly in his daytime waking periods, when his skin is so sensitive, the nerves so close to the surface that it feels like raw flower petals) is that her touch is . . . almost grateful.

Not that the demeanour of Inez Gosper says this. It's just the hint in the pressure of her palms, their unconscious reacting to a faint flicker of response. Her fingertips speaking to his sick but still striving skin.

Her hands—her amateur's fingers, her woman's fingers—treat him as a patient rather than a victim. As a man rather than a *poor typhoid*. He responds to the equality in this. And the optimism.

As for her, she is *doing*—and getting a response. She's not in control so much as taking part in a mutual act. It's a vaguely uncomfortable realisation, but for once she feels there is something in this job for her.

Could this byplay be what the other Melbourne girls in the ship's saloon had chattered about? The *satisfaction*?

He wakes suddenly, wondering, 'What's that noise, that cool wind, in my head?'

'It's the tail end of the gale that went through this morning. Thank God you lot were prone and out to it. The top blew off the tent in the first minute. Then the kitchen roof-iron speared through here at head level. See, you're lucky, after all.'

'There's dirt and beetles on me. We're in the open!'

'Don't excite yourself. They're bringing new tents.'

'It's all right. I like to see dark clouds and feel the cool.'
'You should have seen it! The warning plume of dust. Then beetles swarmed inside the tents just before it struck and covered the walls like pepper. Camels and horses were tossed about. Raindrops as wide as saucers for a minute, then of course no rain at all.'
'You're the one who's excited.'
'It blew the rubbish heaps and dust away. I like things that clear the air.'
She smiles at him, then shivers.
'In the mine shafts they lost electric power for the cages. Can you imagine climbing up all that distance to reach the surface? From the centre of the earth, half-a-mile hand over hand, in the dark?'
'Yes.'

'Is that a bullet wound?'
'Yes.'
'Someone shot you quite recently?'
'Two years ago.'
'What dreadful thing had you done to them?'
'Just opened the wrong door.'
'May I touch it?'
'Be my guest.'
'It feels like satin.'

One time around, two, her finger circles his scar. Like a nursery game.

'Actually, I touched it once when you were out to it.'

'Drink this.'
  'What is it?'
  'A little condensed milk and water.'
  'Here I was expecting beer.'
  'And then some sago.'
  'My God, I'd love a plate of ham and eggs.'
  'Soon. After the red patches separate and go away.'
  'What week is this?'
  'The third.'
  'I can feed myself now, you know.'
  'It's my job.'

In the middle of the fourth week he wakes suddenly towards dawn from a light night fever. It's quiet except for the usual groaning and chattering of teeth. His body begins to tremble. An explosion of heat runs through it. He streams with sweat. As he kicks off the blanket he hears various inner sounds. A waterfall, the tinkling of bells, flutes tootling. A noise like the humming of bees or smoothly running machinery. No pain, but he visualises geometric shapes and the brilliant outlines of flames and waves. His head feels giddy and his mouth fills with saliva.

Either I'm dreaming this or I'm a lunatic. He has rollicking, singing visions. Energy seems to pour in a powerful current from his spine, his balls, belly, heart, throat and forehead. He can feel his blood coursing through his limbs. Outside the tent some night-bird's sudden choking call settles the quiet moans around him. Bodies flop finally into sleep. And soon he settles, too, calm and cool.

After a moment he sits up and pulls open his vest. A pale, unfamiliar chest frail as a leaf, the ribs poking out, sadly concave abdomen, clear skin gleaming ghostly in the candlelight.

Just then she comes through the tent flap into the ward.

'Look!' he calls out. 'Up I get!'

A dingo rustles outside in the rubbish heaps. A passing drunk shouts some gibberish. A patient moans and mutters back. Inez has a hand on his bare chest, lightly pushing him down.

'Wait until morning.'

Her touch stays on his new skin as she and her guttering candle move through the last hour of the night. He sits there bolt upright, a bold twig, sentinel of the *typhoids*.

He leaves the Sisters of the People, but travels only sixty yards. He takes a room in the Prince of Wales, next door to the hospital, while he convalesces. He's weak and emaciated. He could hardly return to the pipetrack yet. It makes sense, he tells himself, not to move until he's stronger. And it's handy to things.

The room opens on to the balcony. From there he can see the cobalt sky and the red land pooling together in the huge mirage on the horizon. The mythical inland sea. The tall poppet heads and smokestacks and mullock heaps jutting up in all directions. The white heaps of tailings shimmering in the glare. Crows and cockatoos flapping by below eye-level. He can see their wing joints working under the feathers.

During the day he takes the dry air on the balcony. He watches life go by. He eats a roast lunch of overcooked lamb or beef or pork, an evening meal of cold collations and sherry trifle. He drinks tea with five sugars to curb the salt. At night the light from the hotel bar below glints in the cracks and knots of his floorboards. The sounds are much the same: the ranting of the drinkers—men exchanging gold for alcohol—that much louder, the hubbub from his old colleagues, the *poor typhoids*, not quite so loud.

Some nights the celebratory and nationalistic songs and banjo and fiddle and piano-accordion music swelling up from the bar drown out the *typhoids* altogether, and he, like everyone else, forgets about them. Then, in a rare quiet moment between numbers (perhaps the barmaid is shuffling though her sheet music and the hoarse-throated men decide to take a break and gulp a mouthful of beer) a blood-curdling shriek, a devilish gurgling laugh, cut the smoky silence.

From the balcony he can see Inez moving between the tent wards, to the nurses' tent, to the rubbish heaps and back. The sun darts off the pans and dishes as she empties them. In the mornings she hangs the night's sweat-drenched blankets out to dry on the tin fence by the pub. She flicks back her hair and moves self-consciously.

She knows she's being watched.

He waves.

He knows her roster. Her first day off-duty he stays in his room all day. He doesn't want to be seen so obviously waiting on the balcony.

Two days pass. When he ventures outside the hotel for exercise—his legs still shaky, the sun beating on his dizzy head—he walks in the other direction, away from the hospital, towards the mirrored sea on the horizon. But only for a hundred yards.

In two days she knocks on the door of his room. She's out of uniform and holding a string bag of oranges.

'I have something for you,' she says. 'I wanted to wait until your system could take it.'


He lies back on the bed while she squeezes an orange segment into his mouth.

'Just half an orange today,' she says. 'Not too much acid all at once.'

She's still acting the nurse. She has neatly diced the orange and flipped out its pips and laid the pieces on a saucer. She eats some, too, at first sitting on the edge of the bed holding the saucer, then gradually inching into a firmer, more central, position.

He's intoxicated by the sweet spikiness of the juice.

'Are you spoken for?' he asks abruptly.

A breath of dusty air stirs the net curtains. She frowns, sighs, licks a sticky finger, eventually touches it to his scar.

'Are you?' she says.

'Yes.'

There is a spot high on her thigh she steers him towards.

'I could get more central than that.'

'No, that's right.'

Not wanting to lose herself yet.

She is in his room late on the humid Monday afternoon when the boy delivers the telegrams. She has sandalwood chips burning in a saucer. The day seems tight and swollen, ready to burst but unable to crack. Thunder rumbles in the eastern desert.

The first telegram is from O'Connor, informing him that the government wants to hold yet another inquiry—its third—into the conduct and completion of his water scheme. This time 'the instrument of tortuous delay' is to be a Royal Commission.

'This means you could be required to give evidence,' he warns Will. 'I hope your health is up to it.'

The timing of the second telegram that the indignant

telegraph boy brings up the stairs only half an hour later is—
what with its shocking revelations—most confusing. But a
weekend, with its Sunday break in telegraph services, has
intervened between the sending of the two messages.

In the overcast afternoon the room is dark. He takes the
telegram out on to the balcony to read it. Crows flop in the
hospital rubbish heaps. This message is from the Department
of Public Works regarding the Engineer-in-Chief's custom-
ary early morning ride along the foreshore.

A finger of sandalwood scent follows him out onto the
balcony.

'You've suddenly lost your colour,' she says.

Bridget O'Connor had woken with a cold. So she had stayed in bed and not ridden with her father that Monday morning. The start of another week. Early autumn in the crisp coastal air. The Chief saddled up Moonlight as usual, and Arthur Lynch, his groom, saw him cantering off at 6.30 towards Fremantle harbour. Then he turned south along the coast toward Robb's Jetty.

It was still low tide as he cantered over the shells and strings of kelp and crusted powder of the shore. As he neared the jetty, he rode his horse over the lip of the tide and through the line of grey waves into the Indian Ocean.

The breakwaters he'd built had altered the configuration of the coastline here, changed the surf, dictated how the tides behaved. Regardless of the wind or moon, the waves were now smaller and snappier south of his new harbour. And becoming chilly with the change of seasons.

He urged the horse further out to sea. He let the breeze take his hat. The water was over the stirrups and Moonlight began to swim. The Chief faced across the ocean, took a revolver from his jacket pocket and put it to his head.

'I have to leave here.'

She shakes her head. 'Not yet.'

Oranges on the dresser. The sweet aroma of sandalwood. Other things associated with her, presents she has brought him. He's amazed at the way they instantly represent the past. Lemon barley water. Glucose lozenges. Sadly leached by heat and storage: a tin of Swallow and Ariel chocolate biscuits illustrated with a snowy, sentimental European Christmas scene. Red desert peas in a beer glass. The changing cheery wildflowers she has picked from around the mines and mullock heaps. (Once arriving, smiling, saying, 'I found orchids in Siberia.')

Symbols of femininity and need.

Life was timing. That agonising moment when novelty became familiar.

As small children he and Sarah had eagerly picked the first primroses when they appeared in January. A few weeks later, when they shone in every bank and hedgerow and filled the copses, they ignored them. They could have been weeds. And in early March hadn't all the village children scrambled for the best violet marr? At the end of the month the blue and white flowers lay strewn on the road, dropped by bored hands.

She'd brought him something else. Gold in a Players cigarette tin. Little nuggets like golden raisins.

Rattling the tin, she'd said, 'You can get some nice cufflinks and tie-pins made.' Earlier, she'd asked, conversationally, 'Do you have any gold?' *Like, 'Do you play tennis?'*

'Not a speck.'

'I have some.'

The way she'd described it, she collected gold as a hobby. She said sick miners always brought their gold to hospital with them. Samples of rich ore, nuggets wrapped in rags or bags, hidden in their boots or billycans.

'They give us presents when they pull through.'

'What if they don't pull through?'

She'd looked off out the window. 'You shake out their clothes before you burn them. Of course it depends whether there's next-of-kin.'

He can't tell whether this charged and rumbling air is an approaching electrical storm or just the thunder of the ore batteries, the pulse of the goldfields. Like these surroundings, noticed for the first time.

Brilliantine patches on the pillow. Old tobacco smoke (hence her smouldering sandalwood chips) permeating the kapok, the blankets, the filmy yellowed curtains, the sliding musty curvature of the mattress. Those pendant bedsprings whose squeals had first brought forth answering thumps and guffaws from the bar below, then hoots and cheers. Finally a bottle of Moët sent up with a grinning barmaid.

'It would be a terrible shame to end this at the beginning,' she says.

The certainty of her touch. Lingering and hopeful. She would stay and hunker down in the desert with him. He knows this. Bartering gold to live. Eating oranges, fighting off the Barcoo sores of diet deficiency and the new bitter breeze humming along the telegraph wires.

He's dressing already.

This is like delirium again, seeing the panicky horse snorting into the swell, swimming towards the mirages of land smudging the horizon. Its hooves chopping frantically at the rising waves. Dragging him by one stirrup out to sea. Without instruction, however, instinct taking over. Its reins trailing and the surf surging over the saddle. The horse turning back to shore.

In the electrical humidity she stands naked in front of him. Her hands framing his thin face. He sees the line of her neck, a wisp of her hair, in geometric relation to the purple clouds behind them.

'You shouldn't travel yet.'

'I have to go.'

MARIONETTE JOYEUSE

HUNCHED OVER A SLIDE containing a squirming droplet of Madame Rioux's brothel's bathwater, Dr Malebranche considered for the several hundredth time that, in the sequence of life, water was related both to the uterine and seminal fluids into which life dissolved and from which it regenerated.

He'd seen this under his microscope in other samples from his visits to Madame Rioux's. Myth and science and sex coming together. (The prostitutes couldn't believe he took the used sheaths *home*.)

Of course the water of life was also mythically related to other vital fluids—ambrosia, amrita, mead for the warrior, soma, wine, blood—all symbolising the surge of the libido, the feeling of being alive, the continuous flow of vital interest to and from the unconscious. Sensations not unknown to Jean-Pierre Malebranche, thank God. Even now, even in this place.

Why then did it kill? And how? Or was he mistaken in this?

Was Father l'Estrange right in saying that this vitality arose from the animal passions and drives? (Implying that the vital fluids were guarded by monsters! The Devil himself!) That only if one's physical vitality were beaten down by prayer and abstinence could the pure, uncontaminated pleasures of life be enjoyed? He couldn't accept God-the-Odd's view that all those dead youths had had such a strong hand in their fates.

That they had died merely from being adventurous boys. But wasn't water supposed to warn the unwary? Like the pool of poisoned water in the desert which stopped you near its bank. Its eerie stagnant sheen silently screaming *go no further*.

The irony was that he came from the new generation of science, the modernists for whom water meant health and industry, even pleasure, rather than religion. Water to him was a sanitary, industrial and commercial product, a raw material, a secular source of hygiene and energy.

Of course he often married his belief in hygiene to his sensual nature. Bowed over his microscope slides now, deeply fatigued, he felt a real physical longing, a deep spinal ache from his sacrum to his shoulders, for the spas of Europe. For the romance of Baden-Baden, say, or Marianske Lazne. And, yes, a nostalgic twinge for the seductive ambience of a particular spa in Tokyo, with its *shoji* windows, *tatami* floors and a fresh chrysanthemum arrangement every morning.

Beautiful women not only bathing him in waters of several temperatures, but pampering him with delicately sculpted meals, each delivered with a fan and a Zen poem. Giggling charmingly, teaching him to play wind instruments and make prayer arrows.

Understandably, he sometimes optimistically mentioned these nostalgic enchantments to the Japanese prostitutes on Thursday nights. He'd murmured his approval, too, of their traditional douching habits.

Little Oyoni sitting in her humid tin and hessian room, the French language washing over her, her sullen boyfriend pacing the gravel outside, just looked blankly at him.

He was hardly writing anything these days. The difficulty of poetry, thought Felix Locke, was compounded by activity. There was too much happening around him. Too much flamboyant death and exaggerated life.

But applying his imagination to the usual grass stems and sand-dunes and salt lakes suddenly seemed too silly to contemplate. In the midst of two such fierce fevers, why waste words on scree and shale and talus? He might as well be a geologist or a mining engineer. Why bother giving rich inner lives to crows and beetles? Why view the tumultuous world in a pock of dried mud?

He was a romantic who was weary of nature.

He was bone-tired and sexually frustrated and drinking too much.

So he poured himself a long whisky, lit a Players and sat down and began to write a poem.

Felix Locke and Mahomet Mahomet had, earlier this thundery afternoon, brought back to town a body charred evenly down its right side and missing the right ear, sleeve, trouser leg and boot. Now Locke, Dr Malebranche and Boehm are sitting on the balcony of the Prince of Wales drinking their sunset whiskies in the rumbling air and discussing the effects of lightning on the human body.

'His heart stopped dead,' says Malebranche, staring off at the sun disappearing into the violent green, yellow and purple clouds. 'That's what does it, the electrical shock.'

'The lightning bolt through his skull didn't help,' Locke says.

'What must be the odds against a man being struck by lightning?' Malebranche continues, shaking his head in wonder. 'Think of the tiny population and the vastness of the land and sky. The insignificance of the individual in the landscape.'

'Look at it this way,' says Locke. 'It's flat as a pancake for hundreds of miles. Not many hills, very few trees. Anyone standing up is a lightning rod. And my fellow was a six-footer.'

'What a waste,' says Malebranche into his whisky. 'And it didn't even rain.'

Below them the noise from the public bars is spilling out into the street and booming in the hot electric air. A few cheers and catcalls ring out. Some searchers for the inland sea are dragging their whaleboat through the town. Two swaying and bedraggled English explorers, their Aboriginal guide and two Afghan cameleers shamble north, their camels' feet rising and falling in the dust with a steady and infinite resentment.

On the balcony they drink in silence for a moment. Eventually, Locke, nodding in the direction of the street and the slowly departing explorers, raises an eyebrow and says, inquiringly, 'Axel?'

The photographer is curled tightly over his whisky glass. The collar of his cream jacket is turned up. He seems to be crouched inside it.

'I can't be bothered with them,' he says.

When she came to the studio that night Wagner rushed to meet her halfway down the street. She let herself in. The studio was awash in opera. *Tristan and Isolde.* Romantic intensity on a dramatic scale.

Axel was lying on the sofa drinking schnapps with his clothes disarranged. His eyes sunken and his hair falling dry and floppy on his face.

'It is you,' he said. 'Eventually.'

'It is.'

He struggled to sit up, claw at his hair, arrange his clothes.

'You look pale, my goodness,' he said, rising to his feet, supporting himself on a familiar sculpted head. 'Your busy life.'

Inez stood staring at him. The strange unbuckled disarray of the trousers.

Misunderstanding her, his gaze fell on the white stone face under his hand.

'Oh, a young, unknown woman, hardly more than a girl, was pulled out of the Seine,' he announced. He coughed. He gave the sculpture a jerky caress. His accent was more pronounced, and high in his throat. 'A suicide, most likely. She was taken off to the Paris morgue. She soon began to attract attention there. Do you know why? She was remarkable.'

'Yes.'

'Why wasn't she simply cast aside like every other woman there? What was so remarkable about this drowned and nameless young woman that a death mask was taken from her?'

She sighed and sat down beside him.

'Tell me.'

❀

At first she treated Axel in his studio. It was cool and quiet. She nursed him as well as she could. After all, hadn't she tended hundreds of *typhoids*, worked the Nightwatch of Delirium for three years? For as long as she was able she did what she could for him. When in moments of pale and furious lucidity he investigated private flesh and perceived that bathing and a change of clothing had occurred during unconsciousness, he would lie back staring for hours at the thin cloud strings moving across the skylight.

Early on she had to put the inevitable question to him. 'Hospital?'

Knowing what his reaction would be. It would be the end of the life he had created. All his nightmares come true. Even with her he reacted as if his privacy was being assaulted.

He hardly deigned to shake his head. He wouldn't look at her. Something was missing from his eyes, but there was still fury there.

Only when he was delirious did the anger disappear. Then he spoke with clarity and in rudimentary prep-school English. 'Oh, may I go ballooning?' he asked sweetly.

'Yes, Axel.'

'I am a student from the Atelier Jung in Trier. Do you know my *Young Thespians Costumed for a Harvest Performance*?'

'Of course.'

'These are my travelling years. I can see prisoners chained to trees. I dearly wish to see the landscape from the air.'

When his condition reached a dangerous level she knew she had to admit him to hospital. She had no choice. She foresaw what would happen, but she was addled with fatigue and anxiety. For a moment she was hopeful that if she alone looked after him there she might be able to postpone the inevitable. But she would need to rest sometime. They were nurses—he would be found out in minutes. In her deep tiredness she envisaged the embarrassing flurry in the male typhoid ward. Snorts. Laughter. The terrible indignity must not happen.

As it turned out, Matron Shand took the revelation of the long masquerade of this prominent townsperson surprisingly calmly. After all, she had an epidemic and a gold rush to deal with. In these two competing fevers she had discovered many permutations of the human form and spirit.

Quite conscious but totally silent, his eyes closed firmly against himself and the stinging glare of the outside world, against its busy fingers and curious eyes, Axel Boehm was quietly admitted to the female ward.

The friends of Axel Boehm walked next door to the Prince of Wales. They slumped into chairs on the balcony. No one spoke. Inez looked exhausted. Her eyes searched about her and her hands were trembling. Locke poured her a gin and set the glass down beside her.

Dr Malebranche patted her hands. She looked forlorn and self-conscious and her question was faint and weary.

'You've always guessed the secret?'

They shrugged. Both Axel's old drinking friends.

'Of course,' Malebranche said gently.

'What does it matter?' said Locke.

'Felix and I both deal with the human body,' the doctor reminded her.

Their question for her hung in the air: When did *you* know? It was evident in their eyes, but they didn't voice it. Locke ached to reach out to Inez then, to soothe her with his bumbling male hands, but now more than ever he didn't dare. All he could do was say various things to her, keep the chatter going and remember how she looked.

'Everyone here is from elsewhere,' he said.


Concentrated by dehydration, he no longer looks out of place in the female ward. Like all the *typhoids* he is neutered and made smaller by the helplessness of illness. No more arrogant spunky bearing. The ginger sheen and stiffness has gone from his hair. Fever sweats have long since eliminated the last whiff of pomade.

The levelling has taken place much faster than expected.

When his dry voice calls her to him it's a quarter to six and the first glint of dawn is showing at the edge of the canvas curtains. In the yard, magpies burble at the sun. She hears a couple of birds land heavily on the tin roof of the kitchen and their feet bump and skitter down the slope.

'Open the curtains,' whispers the photographer Axel Boehm to the nurse Inez Gosper in his last minutes.

She does so. Then he motions her closer to the bed. Dust motes dance towards his beckoning arm. He is trying to say and do something, and to word it properly.

'The *light*, the *light*,' he says with as much good-natured emphasis and ironic humour as he can muster.

He's smiling at her as he indicates the sunray falling across the bed. His timing and position are commendable. It's the perfect manly, sporting gesture.

Taking the ray in his palms, he offers it to her as his gift.

Cajoled and controlled by eight pumping stations along its route, pumped at differing pressures and speeds, the water left the Mundaring reservoir and coursed steadily uphill along the raw orange scar in the eucalypt forests and banksia scrubland and across the gravelly dips and valleys, crossing creeks and skirting hills, and over the still-rising plateau of the interior.

The seven gangs of men working under William Dance, believing they were keeping just ahead of the advancing stream—swearing they could hear the headwaters surging behind them—laid three-quarters of a mile, then one mile, then one and a half miles of water main a day.

Working, eating and sleeping alongside his work gangs in the gravel beside the pipetrack, Will understood why men coming in from the desert of an evening unselfconsciously hugged the pipeline and pressed their faces against the steel. Listened to its soughs and sighs. He could easily picture the invisible water. It had colour, movement, sound, personality. By now he secretly thought of it as his own: his inheritance from O'Connor. He visualised the water in grey and foaming waves roaring and swelling along the gullet of the aqueduct, billowing through the tunnel, individual slabs of rushing form and power.

It took this water he felt belonged to him eight months to travel on its journey from the reservoir in the coastal ranges to the western edge of the goldfields.

The pipeline itself was also flowing smoothly on *its* journey, snaking further and faster into the desert. (Like formerly quarrelling relatives chastened by a death in the family, the parliament and press, embarrassed, had ceased their snapping and offered the scheme their subdued support.) The reason for the burst of progress in the eight months since the Chief's death was that Will's machine-caulkers had finally hit their stride. Using James Couston's revolutionary caulking machine to join together Mephan Ferguson's radical locking-bar pipes, the work gangs became increasingly proficient the closer they came to their destination.

Despite the early summer heat scorching the pipetrack, the aqueduct took only another four weeks to travel the last thirty miles to the centre of the goldfields. The water wasn't far behind. Will and the Department of Public Works checked the flow at the number eight pumping station.

It was arranged for the water to reach its destination in another twenty-five days. Six days—to be on the safe side—before the official opening ceremony.

The hands were long-fingered, pale and capable, with prominent veins. The nails clipped efficiently short. Felix Locke took a lot of time with the hands.

In the goldfields he had prepared many acquaintances for burial. This was the first friend. *Once was. Used to be.*

The preparations had gone briskly and professionally. Axel's body lay outstretched in the embalming room under a strong light. He had settled the features and washed the hands.

He'd been priding himself on his clinical detachment. The embalming took him two hours. Then the dressing. He took a professional pleasure in the natural fall of Axel's cream tussock silk lapels and the smooth-fronted waistcoat. The jaunty ginger wave in the pomaded hair.

His last gesture. He folded the hands together across the umbilicus, in a position of peaceful repose. An attitude of final ease. Right hand loosely clasped over the left.

The hands were important. He stepped back and studied them. *No.*

He placed the left hand over the right instead. And stood back.

He tried the other way again.

Time was getting on, well into the dangerous heat of midday, but still Felix Locke couldn't make up his mind.

He tried the left hand over the right once more.

When, after ten months out on the pipetrack, Will returned to the Prince of Wales, to his old room with its balcony overlooking the street and the hospital of the Sisters of the People, he found preparations for the celebration of the arrival of water almost complete, and the town in a high state of excitement and expectation.

In the January heat small children were rehearsing dancing around a maypole. Knees pumping high, sprinters and cyclists, horses and camels, in training for various celebratory race meetings, plunged and heaved around the town. Bright new electric trams clanged and clattered up the main street. Carpenters and painters were putting the finishing touches to the new theatre and to the new grandstand at the sportsground. Lacking only its central ingredient to attract custom, the new swimming baths yawned glistening and enticing, a green-tiled, rectangular hole in the ground.

Still the townspeople found it hard to believe that fresh water was already flowing uphill over the ranges and across the plains and into the desert, and would soon reach the town.

He carried his bag upstairs and swung it onto the bed. The bedsprings were new and tight. The room smelled of paint, but it only barely overlaid the remembered aromas of stale tobacco and smouldering sandalwood. On the freshly calcimined walls hung framed sepia photographs of goldfields' scenes, stamped THE AXEL BOEHM STUDIO.

She'd often mentioned the photographer, 'Axel', but hadn't answered the question: 'Are you spoken for?' Whereas he spoke of no one at all but couldn't stop himself from answering.

The disappointment in her eyes. The urgency and heightened emotion his answer gave her actions.

Her orange segments like smiles on a saucer.

As he unpacked he glanced across at the hospital. The familiar view. His mind and body were recalling the way Inez had last entered the room. Without speaking, taking his face in her hands. Pressing almost violently against him.

The familiar voice booming up from the lobby.

This must be the delirium returned. In a daze he found himself out on the landing, and there they were below—how strange yet how inevitable—already heading up the stairs.

In this dream he gripped a bannister while their voices preceded them. Their particularly dulcet tones. Ham and Angelica projecting across the greatest possible space.

A middle-aged, hot and pink-faced woman, a maid of some sort, trailed behind them. Before he backed quickly into his room, the pulse in his throat almost choking him, there came another sound not familiar. *What fever went this far?* The older woman was carrying and endeavouring to soothe a wriggling child.

Only someone living out on the gravel of the pipetrack could have missed the news. The posters were all over town. As a highlight of the celebrations for the arrival of water, Hammond and Angelica Lloyd—father and daughter on stage together!—would be appearing in a new play, *Daughter of Midas,* specially written for the opening of His Majesty's, the goldfields' first theatre. A season in Perth, followed by a tour of the eastern capitals, would follow. Marcus Doyle had every hope of repeating the triumphant tour of *The Princess of the Golden West* three years before.

As the newspaper columns said, now the goldfields were truly featuring on the world stage. What a coup, the West End coming to the heart of the Golden West!

The hotel room door. The strange sense of history repeating itself. He caught a rising whiff of floor wax and old lunchtime gravies. Dust specks danced in the warm beery sunlight of the landing. He stood there breathing deeply. Their crisp voices murmured and declaimed behind the door. Above their words the burbling nonsense of a child.

This time he knocked.


The drama of a hotel room. All the intense emotions it aroused. Intrusion. Escape. Pleasure. Violence.

It was she who opened the door and stood there no more than the length of an embrace from him. He could have stroked her actressy silk robe, its pattern like a stage magician's cloak, all wine-dark stars and blue-black crescent moons shimmering around her body. Her hair was long once more, and pinned up. Beginning at her collarbone, an inverted triangle of skin pointed to her breasts. Her bare feet planted on the floor, crimson toenails on the jarrah boards.

For three years he had fantasised they would embrace at such a meeting. Or that cruel things could happen. But neither of them moved or spoke. Behind her, the room stretched empty to the balcony and beyond to the low gun-metal clouds.

'Will,' she said finally.

'I didn't dream it.'

'No.'

'You have a child.'

'She's bathing now. My happy puppet.'

She went no further. But she showed little surprise to see him standing there. 'I wondered when this would happen.'

'You expected it?' Of course his brain was spinning at her presence, at the idea of the child. He couldn't bring himself to ask the real question. At the same time he felt vaguely offended at not causing more of an upset. 'I only arrived here this afternoon myself.'

'You can't know someone so well and not anticipate things,' she said.

'I suppose that's the advantage of a past life.'

'This life has been hectic enough.'

'Yes,' he said. 'Although I've been here two minutes and not been shot yet.'

She took his hand then, briskly turned it over in her own, frowned at the scar and patted it like an aunt.

'You still could be.' Ham said, strolling into the room with the little girl in his arms. He, too, wore a silk robe. The child was naked. Her hair was wavy and gold. Her white arms and legs were straining back to the doorway from which they had come, and on her angelic face was the widest, most affection-ate smile.

Will could say nothing.

'You've come at bathtime,' Ham said loudly. 'You must excuse us.' His colour was higher, his face oddly rough and peeling; only his pallid bare feet and hairless legs avoided that violent puce sheen. He carried the child from the room again, smiling like a magistrate. 'I must say, dear boy, everywhere one goes these days one hears your praises sung.'

He pulled up a chair and sat without being asked. She was still standing, but he was feeling too shaky. The feeling of delirium, then the trembling—this was like typhoid in reverse. Eventually she sat. They faced each other silently across an open portmanteau. Toys and small clothes spilled out of the bag. Twice the nanny, Edith, came and went from the room without speaking.

All the time, boisterous splashing sounded from the next room. Above the splashing he heard Ham's solicitous murmurs and the child's shrieks and babble. Then there were sudden disappointed wails, followed by the rush and gurgle of water pouring into other water, and then more childish laughter.

Angelica blinked at the rumpus and looked off to the side. 'He loves to bath her,' she said. 'And she lives for it.'

Her hands moved restlessly, her face was animated and her conversation skipped along neutral subjects. Wasn't the bathwater here most peculiar? Either it smelled of rotten eggs or tasted of smoke and salt. The management kept the bathroom locked! You had to purchase your own bath cabinet and have it delivered and pay outrageous money for water, and then it left white, crusty deposits on your body!

'Not for much longer,' he said. 'Why did you come here?' In his confusion his voice sounded harsh and territorial.

'You'll find this strange, but what most appealed to me about the *Daughter of Midas* tour was the notion of the desert.'

'The desert?'

'The dryness, the healthy air. I was led to believe the desert might be helpful for her disorder.'

'Disorder?

Her voice was as thin and light as a husk. 'The absence of water was a factor. She is a *marionette joyeuse.*'


These happy-puppet children, Angelica explained, were marked by common characteristics. Heightened activity, insomnia, limited speech, a lack of coordination and muscle tone. Despite these mental and physical handicaps they were happy children with very lovable dispositions. They laughed all day long.

At three the child still couldn't walk. She was floppy. When she was excited she flapped her arms up and down, her elbows flexed like a marionette.

'The doctors say she will probably walk by the age of five or six,' Angelica said. 'Meanwhile she needs us to pull her strings.'

His head was swimming. 'She's so fair and pretty,' he murmured. The blue-white eyes, milky skin and flyaway gold hair. A picture book angel. Needless to add: and no resemblance to him. Or, for that matter, to her. Both he and Angelica were olive-skinned by comparison.

She couldn't avoid his questioning look. She said,

'*Marionettes joyeuses* resemble each other more than their parents.'

He could see deep into the grey-green depths. No trace of blue in the irises. He saw her floating back in the dark estuary. The thick, sluicing river water. External cold, internal heat.

'I knew the instant of her conception,' she said.

Was she remembering the surroundings, the conception's furnishings and accompanists? Midnight algaes fluttering against her thighs. The cool brush of scales and jelly in the black river. Did she hear African water music that night?

'You were ill,' he said. 'The blackwater fever.'

She was still looking at him, though her face was expressionless. 'Maybe that, too.'

The little girl was named Ada.


Ada has a vocabulary of six words. Four of them are to do with liquid. In her obsession, a bowl of brown Windsor soup equals the Indian Ocean for excitement. She tries to climb into seaside picture books, into illustrations of streams and ponds. Her jaw is determined as she endeavours to submerge herself in flowing inks and colours, to plunge into paper and cardboard.

Diving into books of water, she blinks and smiles and thrusts out her tongue in pleasure. Apparently the tongue-thrusting is another characteristic of the happy-puppet children. She pushes it through a little gap in her front teeth.

To hear her mother talk, Ada is a formidable personality. In Wiltshire, he thinks, such a wispy fairy child would be called a killcrop, a changeling. He wants to buy her books to swim in.

'Please don't come to the room again,' Angelica says suddenly.

'I must.'

'The situation is difficult. I have lots of lines to learn for this play. Rehearsals to attend.'

'I want to see Ada. And you.'

'I am a different person.'

Nevertheless it seems perverse not to touch her. He strokes her cheek as he stands to leave. The briefest brush of his scarred hand.

She rises, too, and stands motionless. 'Goodbye.'

How oddly quiet it is. The splashing in the next room has ceased, the hum of drinkers not yet risen up from the public bar. The walls, the furniture, watching and listening. His pulse drumming in his head. Conscious of his exposed back, but heedless of any gunshot, even inviting it, he walks slowly out the door.

Now his poem is under way, Felix Locke writes as soon as he rises each morning. Coming to his desk straight from sleep, fragments of dreams still clinging to his quieter mind, he allows the process of writing to properly wake him. Before his morning coffee, before he begins work, before he has seen a single body or run the chamois and Fowler's Polish over the rosewood coffins which now arrive twice a day on the Perth train, he sits down and begins to write.

It's a big poem. It tells of unrequited love and of the death of an old drinking companion. It's neither bush ballad nor traditional lyric. Something different? He hardly knows, but he likes its images. He likes the way he has scattered figures in his own personal landscape. (An odd effect of the poem: from the moment he began to write it his imaginary illnesses dropped away.) It tumbles along, encompassing the simplest and grandest topics in his experience. Lust and loneliness, fevers and fortunes, the mysterious disguises of the private self. Romance in a time of gold and typhoid.

He is as avid a *reader* of the poem as he is its *writer.* He's keen to see where it is leading.

His images? Women wearing parrot feathers and cringing from an undertaker's grasp. A body's hands folded for burial. A droll, exhausted nurse flicking hair from her forehead as dawn rises over deaths in the desert.

Life nevertheless prevailing. Time for a joke now and then. A drink. Always the prospect of love. He is an optimistic man (an American, after all) and he has the help of Whitman and Thoreau.

Inez lets herself into the studio. It is dustier, otherwise unchanged. The same theatrical backdrops. The same sky streaming placidly across the skylight. The same familiar smell. Her throat prickles, constricted not only by this odour of Axel—which still clings to the walls and photographic equipment and furniture, still hovers in the cool, monochromic air—but by the shocking idea of his smell outlasting his body.

As executors of Axel's estate, Dr Malebranche and Felix Locke will be coming to inspect his property, all his equipment and belongings. To add everything up. But she has the keys. She was his nurse. *She was . . .*

'Tell me something,' Dr Malebranche had asked her that day at the Prince of Wales Hotel after they admitted Axel to hospital. The doctor was gently matter-of-fact about the revelation, and concerned only for Axel's health. His tone was kind, of course, professional, but—it must be said, as they stood to go, after perhaps one drink too many—also inquisitive. 'His famous cream suits, naturally. But what—*ah*—other form of subterfuge did Axel use?'

She looked at him and looked away. Felix was pink with embarrassment. She could hardly speak, and was prim when she did so. 'I have no idea.'

Now she sits on the sofa *where . . .* She goes into the bedroom *where . . .*

She fights off visions of herself as she pulls open each drawer in the chest of drawers, as she draws out the trunk from under the bed and unlocks it, as the smothering intimacy of his belongings, of his lingering personality, almost floor her.

There she is. She collects the photographs of herself from the trunk. His *other* photographs.

In the chest of drawers she finds three of the padded leather things. What are they called again? Cricket protectors, the cupped leather shields that batsmen and wicket-keepers wear under their trousers to protect their balls from cricket balls. The leather is worn and wrinkled, the edges creased and stained with sweat. There are a lot of straps. She briefly holds one against her pelvis, gives herself a bulge.

How uncomfortable in this climate, she thinks.

She carries the photographs and protectors out to the backyard.

Dr Malebranche had sighed, 'How hard for a . . . *woman* to keep up that masquerade all these years.' All three of them on the hotel balcony flinching at the sharp emotion of the word. *Woman*. It was impossible to imagine changing Axel's pronoun to *she*. They looked intently at her.

'You know he's tall and wiry. His manner is masculine . . . in a foreign sort of way.' She sounded defensive to herself. 'He's an adventurer and a traveller. He feels at home in raw, dry places. Places with new people.' She didn't say he wasn't the only one choosing to escape too-moist-and-emotional Europe. That the unconscious mind of many an outsider needed to dry out in a fiery male domain. Or even that the Western Australian desert in summer wasn't a million miles from hellfire.

She glared at them instead. 'What's the matter with his cream suits? Should he wear bloody sequins?'

The men were mortified. It was an uncomfortable moment.

Axel is dead now, but there is no reason for further

embarrassment. She drops the photographs and the leather groin protectors in the incinerator, douses them with paraffin and sets them alight.

Watching the oily smoke curl up, she feels a thin, sharp emotion, something between guilt and grief, escape her. She lets it pass away, turning from it as she turns her face from the smoke and the stink of burning leather. Surely that hadn't been her, Inez, here?

She takes a last quick look around the studio. Having closed doors on affecting memories before, she has hardly any trouble doing so again.

Why then does she feel compelled to pause by the bust of the *Unknown Woman from the Seine*? To finger a cool eyelid, to pick it up, with some difficulty—it was surprisingly heavy— and take it with her?

When he had walked out of the hotel room Angelica stood for a moment staring at the closed door. A scene already seen. And a scene she knew wouldn't be repeated.

The brush of his hand on her cheek.

The sound of her sob surprised her.

She hurried to the door and opened it. A gust of bluff, yeasty air struck her face as she looked out along the empty corridor. She closed the door and sat heavily on the bed—the bed they had avoided sitting on, the bed they had treated as invisible—while the framed photographs on the wall danced in front of her.

Photographs by THE AXEL BOEHM STUDIO. Sepia mining scenes. Afghans and camels in ceremonial regalia. Two dimpled coquettes in sausage curls and party frocks struggling to hold up a gold nugget. Submerged in the dusty landscape, a filthy moustached dryblower staring at her with burning eyes.

In the adjoining bedroom, still wet-haired and snoring quietly: her naked father and daughter, actor and puppet, sleeping in each other's arms.

A mystery to her was how a photographer could capture such picturesque proof of human existence, its industriousness, optimism and diversity, could even make it decorative, whereas she walked from the sleeping pair to the window, looked out into the stark world and saw nothing at all.

# THE RESERVOIR

TIME WAS SLOW and hot here. Was it only two weeks since the photograph? Since they had dropped down a mine shaft half a mile into the earth? Since his incandescence?

Only their second day in town, and the Chamber of Mines was already urging the 'noted visiting thespians' to go down a mine. To see the workings, view fabulous reefs of gold and, of course, be photographed adventurously doing so. The Chamber's reasoning was clear enough: Hammond and Angelica Lloyd were famous London actors, and the head offices of most of the big mines were in London. (The only goldmine with a postal address not in E.C. was in Glasgow.)

That photographer, Boehm, accompanying them and Mr Winterbottom, the mine manager, was a German judging by his accent. His sighs and hair flicks and odd languid manner making it clear that photographing celebrities in the bowels of the earth was a commonplace assignment. But this time his photographs would have extra newsworthiness. As the enthusiastic Winterbottom kept stressing to them, 'Miss Lloyd is the first woman to go underground!'

Helping her into the cage at the shaft head, Winterbottom set the tone for the peculiar day. The cage jerking a yard upwards before it dropped. Winterbottom's skin trailing sweet varnish-whiffs of alcohol as he offered her his peppermints.

'You might note that our impending descent is the equivalent of climbing to the top of the Eiffel Tower three times. In reverse, of course.'

The image clearest in her own imagination: Aladdin's cave. Expecting to step out into a glowing cavern of gold and riches. Dripping pearly stalactites. Somehow even diamonds, rubies and sapphires weren't beyond possibility.

Instead, stepping from the cage into a rock dining room. Eight hundred feet below the surface of the earth, thirty miners stolidly eating their midday meal. Ore-coloured men sitting primly on stools of rock, their pannikins glistening in the candlelight, munching bread and beef and fruit cake, sipping their tea. Hardly looking up.

Down again, another two thousand feet. A narrow-gauge rail line curving into infinity. Along the rails the ash-faced men pushing small trucks loaded with ore. Above and below and beside them, jackhammers supposedly drilling and dynamite allegedly exploding. *But*, she thought, *you would never know of these whirlblasts within the rock.* The phlegmatic rock giving no hint of its interior turmoil.

Its silence was threatening enough. Its colossal *weight*. She felt enclosed by rock, down too deep, jammed in rock like a fossilised leaf. At the bottom of this hard and pressing sea the dark air was so thick and cloyingly warm that the Annexe for the Less Lunatic sidled into her mind. And around the bend here was black nothingness.

Was it this sickly warmth so affecting the photographer? Making him so pallid and sweaty as he tramped around the rubble in his search for clarity, for a spot to set up his tripod away from the dust of drilling? Positioning them eventually by a cavernous rock wall supposedly bursting with gold. Gold? All she could see by candlelight were distinctive green veins of something—did Winterbottom say vanadium? And the photographer's hands starting to shake.

Of far more news interest than a woman, even a London actress, going underground—to judge by the disbelief, then panic, bright on Winterbottom's face—was the magnesium flare exploding and igniting the head of Hammond Lloyd.

The famous actor was carted on his back in an ore truck, kicking and howling, to the shaft. Pushed into the cage, willed upwards to the blissful stinging glare and sky.

In the clattering, apologetic rush to the cage, to the sick bay and back to the hotel to await a thorough medical examination, she forgot, then recalled, the photographer white and mortified, doubled over his case of plates at the bottom of the mine.

'Accidents do happen. Of course Mr Lloyd was a sport about it.' This was Mr Winterbottom to the local reporters, urgently attempting to sidestep lawsuits on two continents, glowing around his collar at the thought of adverse publicity and the *please explain* telegraph from head office in Bishopsgate.

Ham in fact cursing and tearing furiously at his smoking eyebrows every foot of the half mile to the sunlight. Coming up from the depths, the smell of his hair like burning goose feathers in the cage.

But the attending Dr Malebranche said he had seen the desert sun do far worse damage to the tissues of a face. And just a bland paragraph appeared in the *Miner* and *Express* below the photograph: 'Miss Angelica Lloyd Breaks Convention by Going Underground at the Golden Kingdom Gold Mine'. (A blurry Ham-on-fire cropped from the picture.)

The impresario Marcus Doyle, putting his faith in makeup and professionalism, and the healing passage of a fortnight, said his only concern was for the comfort and wellbeing of Mr Lloyd. (Of course the play would go on.)

The actor's daughter? She had seen him underground crowned in shocking radiance, and she could see him curled up baby-naked now, his arse crossed by a rectangle of sun.

God, he had seemed to implode. The sane air burnt right out of him.

Will's fantasy is to set fire to the theatre on opening night. His Majesty's: a new wooden building, dry heat, combustible materials. *No water supply.* Such a blaze could never be contained. To strike a match against a simulated outback heatwave backdrop—still damp with turpentine—and see the place consumed from stalls to gods.

He wants all the drama of the theatre. He wants to see this exuberant form of death piercing the sky with its arrows. Catch Ham in his dressing room before the audience arrives. (The surrounding stores and banks are vacant after-hours. No need for innocent first-nighter deaths.)

*How tragic and ironic! The water here at last, but not yet piped to town!*

The fire brigade could try fighting that one with their long-handled shovels and natty red sand buckets!

Earlier, sleep had put him and Angelica back in the bath at Bath. In this fantasy his dry hands peeled and blistered with lost opportunities. Of course he tried to stroke her softest flesh. Naturally she pulled away. They walked home along the canal path as tortoises galloped up the banks and children skimmed stones at them across the canal. Stones scudded by, smashing windows, scattering splinters of glass.

He wakes then, thinking instantly of her, and can't sleep again. The theatre conflagration is only the latest of three years' vengeful three-o'clock fantasies. Except in this one her fate is ambivalent and cloudy. She's the merest whiff of turpentine on silk.

Now there is the child.

In realistic noonday life he takes a different decisive action. On his way out of the hotel he leaves an envelope for

Angelica at the front desk. An invitation—for her alone—to the opening ceremony of the water scheme. Then he catches the afternoon train to the coast.

Can he bear the suspense? A week of constant train travel and official celebrations and band music to endure before the opening ceremony.

First the arrival of the Royal Mail Steamer *Britannia* in Fremantle harbour with the official guests from the eastern states: the federal ministers, state premiers, army generals, business leaders—even sportsmen and famous *artistes*. And Forrest of course, now Lord Forrest, Minister for Defence in the first national government. Greeting them at the wharf is a buffeting January heatwave. And then there is the bustle to Perth, the special trains carrying them up into the ranges, into the teeth of the hot easterly, for the opening of the dam, with Lady Forrest officially starting the pumping machinery at the number one pumping station at Mundaring Weir as the Bavarian Band strikes up 'See the Conquering Hero Comes'.

Inside the great white marquee erected on the stony floor of the valley the temperature is rising past 105 degrees. Even with the sides of the tent open to catch the air, the distinguished visitors look dazed, kept awake only by the constant activity of brushing flies from their roast beef and wine glasses and their dripping foreheads and collars. As the after-luncheon speeches run on, Dame Nellie Melba, the operatic soprano, fans herself with her programme and says something *sotto voce* to Mephan Ferguson, the inventor and manufacturer of the revolutionary locking-bar pipe, and he laughs out loud.

In his speech the owner of the *West Australian*, John Winthrop Hackett, feigns surprise at the presence in the marquee of 'some politicians and public men who used to discuss the water scheme with murder in their eyes'. Then Lord Forrest himself bellies up to the lectern to pay tribute to the dead Engineer-in-Chief, regretting that 'the great builder of the work is not among us this day to receive the honour that is due to him'.

Will can't bring himself to look at O'Connor's widow, proud and sorrowful at the main table. Instead he recalls the barrow-men abseiling down the slope, the cool smell of virgin stone, the workmen's ironical whistles. He hears the novel throb of the pump engines and sees only the blue skin of the water in relation to the walls of the dam. The level seems low. High evaporation. In sudden fright he envisions the dam drying up before the opening of the pipeline itself. He sees the grand moment at the other end of the pipetrack culminating in a nightmarish trickle, a sterile puff of dust.

*What would she think?*

Over the hum of speeches and the mingling buzz of crickets in the gum trees drooping over the valley, he hears a sudden break in engine rhythm, a faltering heartbeat, and rushes from the marquee to investigate. Outside, the glare stuns him like a concussion. Sunflashes exploding from the brass of the Bavarian Band. Jackets unbuttoned, drenched vests and braces and hairy stomachs hanging over their pants, the bandsmen slouch by their tubas and flugelhorns drinking beer. Squinting into the glare, he hurries along the path of baking rocks. Bile floods into his mouth. His anxious saliva tastes of horseradish and claret. But at the pumping station the machinery, surprisingly, is turning smoothly and purposefully. Applause patters in the distant marquee. The only arhythmic sound in the whole droning day is the throbbing of his head.

The completed water main rises beside him, and keeps unrolling and inclining east until it disappears in a heat mirage over the raw boulders. A continuous line drawn in the waterless haze of the interior. People existing at the other end of it.

There it is.

The sun hangs over the valley like a bridge.

The buzzing of blowflies and the urgent sweetness of early decomposition sliding under the door from the funeral parlour: when he's writing nothing else registers. Pressed by this conjunction of sound and smell, Felix Locke quickly finishes his poem in mid-morning one hot Wednesday in late January. He calls it simply 'The Hands'. More than 850 words long. He's neither pleased nor disappointed with it. He only knows he feels drained and hollow. But it's finished. In a daze he drops it off at the *Weekly Miner* office before he can change his mind.

But a moment after he submits it he's hot-faced with embarrassment. In the street outside his pulse is racing. His extremities tingle. Ten yards from the newspaper office and he's puffing already. His ears ring. *What terminal illness is this?* In the familiar bright street his vision is so blurred he hardly recognises acquaintances. Those he can make out among the flickering shapes make him feel as self-conscious as an adolescent. Smirking as if they've read the poem already.

He consoles himself: the *Miner* probably wouldn't publish it. At that length, they'd have to bring out a special edition! He's an undertaker, not a poet.

But why shouldn't they publish it? The thought of rejection makes him indignant. It's the best thing he's written—and maybe even read.

But if they did? It isn't too late to withdraw it. At least erase a vital part of it.

He swerves into the public bar of the Prince of Wales seven hours before his usual evening drink. Whatever had possessed him? He'd never live it down.

The dedication under the title.

*For Inez.*

To the strains of a jovial *Schottisch* from the Bavarian Band, a special train steams out of Perth the next day, passing, then heading away from the afternoon sun, carrying the official guests to the goldfields. The real opening of the water scheme can only take place there. Seventeen hours of humid, jolting travel lie ahead.

Will hadn't realised how often the pipeline diverted course from the railway, crossing jauntily from one side of the line to the other, or disappearing under or around some natural obstacle. Now he restlessly roams the corridor, hardly daring to take his eyes off it in case it snakes off and escapes through the scrub. The politicians, generals and businessmen try to pass the time with card games, whisky and sleep (Nellie Melba plays canasta with the Forrests) while the Bavarian Band squeezes up and down the aisle playing waltzes and, after sunset, when the musicians have forced a party mood on the passengers, a little brassy *Nachtmusik*.

They wake in the desert. In the early hours of Saturday the haggard visitors reach the western edge of the goldfields. The yawning bandsmen are first off the train. Flags and bunting flap in the dawn easterly over the railway station and across the wide welcoming streets of the thirsty township.

By eight o'clock all the guests except Will are breakfasted and feted and arranged on seats to view a parade of the Bavarian Band, the district fire brigade and the local Afghan cameleers in their most brilliant silks and gold vests and turbans. Will is at the number eight pumping station anxiously supervising water-pressure adjustments as Lord and Lady Forrest step up into a cart decorated as a ship and are drawn along the street by twenty children dressed in sailor suits.

After these ordeals Forrest declares this preliminary portion of the goldfields' water scheme 'open for the use of the people'. A ceremonial marble fountain has been erected. He turns a guiding wheel and opens a valve. Will holds his breath. The procession and celebrations have stirred up so much dust the pipeline is barely discernible against the red earth.

A clear stream of water spurts into the thick air.

To witness this is as good as any dream he aches to share with her.

And then, following the official luncheon and more speeches, the visitors haul themselves on board once more. The carriages have been standing in the heat for eight hours. The temperature inside is 110 degrees. Thankfully, the final leg of their journey to the hub of the goldfields is only twenty-five miles. Nevertheless they all drop instantly into heavy sleep. Again they wake from their stupor to see the skyline transformed. In the hazy distance now are tall smoke-stacks, high poppet heads like forest-fire watchtowers, and snowy heaps of tailings luminous in the heat. Few of the visitors have seen such an unearthly sight. The moat of mirages and alabaster salt lakes surrounding the town gives a first impression of shimmering watery depth and impenetrable defences, but the train steams across the pipeclay surfaces and arrives at the town.

On this afternoon, Ham suddenly feels bound to copy the child's mannerisms. Pushing out his tongue. Flapping his arms from their flexed elbows. Pretending to be a *marionette joyeuse*. Screaming and splashing in their endless bath.

Of course Ada shrieks at yet another wet and delightful game. Ham's pleased and shrieking, too. Another role carried off to perfection: the three-year-old happy puppet.

Angelica can't believe the cruel mockery. 'Stop that!'

He plops out his tongue and flaps water at her.

She's nauseated by the performance. The smell of rotten eggs. His patchy face and stubbly eyebrows. His nakedness. She is desperate to bathe and dress.

'No more.'

Now he's wearing the dripping wash-flannel on his head, wagging a scolding loofah. Pursing his lips into a cat's arse. Covering his chest and groin like a shy virgin. Mocking her now.

This is Ham being placatory.

*Soothing old King Neptune says he's sorry.*

*'I'm such a bad boy.'*

*Reeds and duckweed hanging from his ears. A big scratchy kiss as she's still gasping for breath. Tongue thrusting into her panting mouth.*

Just now the air has become a solid wall around her. She hears a creaking, as if something is rocking back and forth on the floorboards. The creaking comes up behind her, then stops and a peculiar sensation passes through her. Her muscles feel paralysed, her skin is clammy, and her hair, just as in the bluntest melodramas—*The Spectre Bridegroom!*—seems to stand on end.

Then she forces through the barrier of air and lifts Ada screaming from the bath. Slippery, boneless body arching backwards like a bridge.

Ada is screaming for him, a *marionette furieuse*, limbs flapping angrily for her splashy Hammy.

He's roaring ferociously and rising rampant from the eggy water.

And she's bursting out of the room in tears calling for Edith. 'Take her, for God's sake, take her.'

Passing squirming Ada to the nanny. Slamming doors. *The sudden urgency of attending the ceremony!* Dressing quickly. Making up her face. Endeavouring to compose herself. Prevailing over events. *After all, I am an actress.*

And Ham is standing in the doorway in his silk robe, holding his script, his face arranged in the wise, stern lines of someone playing a famous actor just three hours before opening night. The late afternoon light is complimentary. Calming shadows lengthen across the room. He sniffs at her eau de Cologne and smiles wistfully.

'I do hope you're not running off before we go over our lines?'

The desert is not completely horizontal. There is a hill outside town, rather grandly named Mount Charlotte. On top of it a reservoir has been built to hold and disperse the water from the coast. It's basically a metal tank eighty feet in diameter, fifteen feet deep. Here the Chief's pipeline comes to an end at a big silver, wheel-shaped tap. As 5 p.m., the time of the ceremony, approaches, the people of the goldfields climb the winding path up the steep slope. Despite the still scorching heat, and the mines and shops and offices still being open and working, more than twelve thousand people are trudging up the hill and crowding around the small circular reservoir to await the arrival of water.

The national leaders gather on the dais by the reservoir as the restless crowd cheers and whistles. Some wags recognise famous faces from the newspapers. '*George!*' they shout at a prominent Sydney politician. '*Nellie!*' they cry to Melba. '*You beauty! Sing us a song!*'

Will is confident that by this final stage the procedure is foolproof. The number eight pumping-station generators have proved in perfect order. Everything works. The water can't but flow profusely at the proper moment. And thereafter. All the water has to do is fall, to reclaim the horizontal. Do its job as the transitory element, the essential metamorphosis between fire and earth.

Then why can't he compose himself like the glazed politicians and mining magnates and operatic soprano perspiring beside him? Like O'Connor's serene, proud widow? Let Forrest's biblical self-satisfaction wash over him.

Again his eyes rake the eager brown-faced crowd.

'I promised to bring you from the west coast a river of pure water,' Lord Forrest entones, and pauses for applause, 'and that river has delivered itself in the arid desert, *351½ miles from its source!*'

*Where is she?*

Forrest, the gruff old explorer-turned-politician, is as emotional as anyone in the circle of upturned, cheering faces as he grabs the big tap-wheel, swings it around and turns on the water.

And so is the engineer moved, touched by the gushing scene before him, the round after round of cheers under the low burning sun. A sob lodges in his throat and almost chokes him. Water is truly the most receptive of elements. Gratitude flows after it.

Heads are swinging towards this woman. She is hurrying up the slope, her hair disarranged, all in sweet, hot disorder, smiling and waving.

M en had torn off their clothes and died of thirst with this
hill in their eyes. Now around its base the water celebrations were beginning. Of course the Bavarian Band had
started up, and the children's maypole dancing. Afghans and
their elaborately caparisoned camels were noisily assembling.
Giggling and wise-cracking members of the Dramatic
Society, perhaps thrown out of gear by the threat of serious
competition from the London theatre, flitted through the
crowd dressed, inexplicably, as butterflies. On the ant-bed
track Arthur Postle, alias the Crimson Flash, the footrunning
wizard from the Darling Downs, was limbering up for his 75-
yard race against the world champion, R.B. Day of Ireland.

The sweating crowd scuttling down the slope from the
reservoir was keen to move on to the next event, skittish with
the excitement of the entertainments to come: the banquet to
be held in the electric tramway barn (the only building big
enough), the first night of the first real goldfields play.

Ten minutes after the opening of the water scheme the
people had gone.

'Hello there,' she said. She might have been a girl liaising in
the Pump Room or on the banks of the Avon. She peered
over the lip of the reservoir. 'Are there fish in there?'

'No.'

'I thought tiny fish materialised in desert waters? That some
miracle of nature put them there.'

'Give them time.' He was looking at her face, feeling half-
mad, thinking: *It's the liquidity in our eyes that makes these
fantasies occur.*

'Your reservoir needs something on its surface. Maybe a
swan.'

A swan. He remembered the reckless times they had made love outdoors. In the reeds and willow fronds and frost. He said, 'That was him watching us that night on Batheaston common.'

'Yes.'

He thought of change, of the way events in the desert had gradually become a *becoming*. A change in levels had occurred, from potentiality to a higher level of reality. See, engineering could do it just as well as philosophy. Move against the tide, push water uphill. For a moment you could forget that water always flowed, always fell, always ended in horizontal death.

She touched his face. 'I'm thirsty, strangely enough,' she said.

He laughed. 'That might be difficult.'

It was while searching for some cup or scoop, any container to hold liquid, to dip down into the tap's coursing flow, that they heard the steps sounding on the gravel and the joyous ululations of the child trill across the skin of water.

Ham stood glistening and panting with Ada in his arms on the rim of the reservoir. Two minds slipped free of any other concern but the water and the reflected sunset shining below them.

When he jumped it was surprisingly without drama or any remark that they could understand. They were moving cautiously around the rim towards him. He was half-smiling and still puffing from the climb. It was a ten-foot drop: Ada stayed in his arms when they hit the water, and even after their circle of ripples widened and spread and bounced against the smooth walls of the reservoir.

In his mind he was saying, 'The night that never sleeps awakens the waters of a pond that is always sleeping,' but his shout sounded nothing like that. Both he and Ada were gurgling and splashing, as they loved to do, inhaling and coughing and threshing and—at last—sinking satisfactorily for once, reaping the full benefit of the pure crowding water.

Will's leaping after them was instinctual. The swimming, the diving down, the fighting over the choking child. Of course Ham wasn't going to let her go. He made keening sounds like hers at Will's efforts to release her. He was crying in frustration as he held her under and allowed the water in.

It took all Will's force just to raise her gaping face above the surface now and then, and stay afloat; all Ham's essence to submerge her and himself. Only the ferocious attack from Angelica—the sudden fierce hands around his throat, the relentless pushing down—could break the stalemate in the shadowy pool. As Will prised the little girl away—that pale, strange, half-conscious angel—Angelica was growling astride Ham's head and shoulders and still bearing down.

Festooned, ballooned, in the wet and smothering folds of dress and petticoat, Ham allowed himself to sink—encouraged it—and disappeared.

They were locked in silence, treading water in the dusk, floating and holding each other up. They had told each other they could be patient. They had long since shrugged off their heavy and confining clothes. Off and on, Ada snored across their linked and outstretched arms. In the distance fireworks crackled and showered into the clear air. A sliver of moon and the red fading sun of a hot summer day both streaked the surface of the little reservoir.

Coolness is a characteristic of water.

# AUTHOR'S NOTE

As this romance touches on various elemental fancies it was appropriate to present a stylised Wiltshire and environs, East Africa and Western Australia. And to take liberties with geography, dates and a few historical figures (notably, a childhood hero of mine, C.Y. O'Connor) who did inhabit the time and place I gave them in this fiction.

I wish to acknowledge the generous assistance of: in England, George and Louie Baker, of West Lavington, Devizes, Wiltshire; Lavinia Greenlaw and the London Arts Board; and the Arts Council of England; in Zimbabwe and Zambia, Bill Williams; and in Australia, Charlie Baker, Susie Carleton, Jill Hickson, Dr Allan Meares and Professor Ron Trent.

I appreciated some insightful discussions in London's South Bank Centre with Matthew Sweeney and Thomas Lynch and would like to acknowledge information drawn from Mr Lynch's article 'The Undertaking' in the *London Review of Books* (22 December 1994).

Other informative sources were the excellent *Gold and Typhoid: A Social History of Western Australia 1891–1900*, by Vera Whittington; August Sander's classic book of photographs, *Anlitz der Zeit* (Face of Our Time), whose foreword, *Faces, Images and their Truth*, by Alfred Döblin, I drew on; a quotation by Richard Avedon on studio photography in Susan Sontag's *On Photography*; *Hamlet* and *Richard III* by William Shakespeare; *In Old Kalgoorlie*, by Robert Pascoe and Frances Thomson; *The Chief*, by Merab Tauman; *Daughters of Midas*, by Norma King (a singular version of whose title I borrowed for the play at the novel's end); *Water in England*, by Dorothy Hartley; *Village Notes*, by Pamela Tennant; *Wetland:* Life in the Somerset Levels, by Patrick Sutherland and Adam Nicolson; and, not least, *Water and Dreams*, by Gaston Bachelard, especially the section from which I gleaned part of the funeral oration on pages 79–80. I also thank Murray Bail for the *Guide to Rhodesia for the Use of Tourists and Settlers* (Bulawayo, 1914).

*Marionette joyeuse* is a term coined by French molecular geneticists (F. Halal and J. Chagnon, 1976) for Angelman Syndrome.

R.D.

## OUR SUNSHINE

'Immediacy and freshness, the sense that we are eavesdropping on the birth of a mythology, are the most notable achievements of this fine novel. *Our Sunshine* is a marvellous book ... A remarkable literary feat.'

A.P. RIEMER, *Sydney Morning Herald*

'A tour de force ... A model of style and passion. It could become a classic.'

THOMAS SHAPCOTT, *Age*


## THE BAY OF CONTENTED MEN

'This is writing at the highest level of narrative achievement, a book which deserves international acclaim and respect.'

JIM CRACE, *Times Literary Supplement*

'Robert Drewe is masterly ... one of Australia's most original writers, exploring contemporary culture and identity in ways which keep exposing new angles of our uneasy repose.'

HELEN DANIEL, *Sydney Morning Herald*

*FORTUNE*

'Complex and thoughtful, lyrical and satiric . . . A compelling treasure.'

*Time*

'He is justly seen as one of this country's most distinguished fiction writers, whose work exemplifies the kinship between the best skills of the reporter and those of the novelist.'

*Australian*

*THE BODYSURFERS*

'A remarkably seductive and exuberant collection which manages, in its portrayal of human relationships, to be both mordant in tone and playful in manner.'

*Times Literary Supplement*

'His characters repeatedly hurl themselves at life and love. There is something very powerful and poignant in these stories.'

*Newsweek*

## A CRY IN THE JUNGLE BAR

'Shaped with precision, wit and tenderness. It is impressive both for the sharpness of its comedy and for its control of serious themes. It is the work of an Australian writer who deserves that blessed double-rating: he's Important and Entertaining.'

*Age*

'A milestone in Australian literature.'

*Financial Review*

## THE SAVAGE CROWS

'*The Savage Crows* has the magic of a great book about it. It is your genuine and rare "compelling" story.'

*Vogue*

'I was riveted by it. I more than liked it, I was compelled by it.'

THOMAS KENEALLY